CHIKKAMMA TOURS (PVT.) LTD

Unmana lives in Mumbai with their husband. Their short stories have been nominated for the Best of the Net and the Deodar Prize. *Chikkamma Tours (Pvt.) Ltd* is their first full-length novel.

CHIKKAMMA TOURS (PVT.) LTD

A BIBLIOMYSTERY

UNMANA

Published by Tranquebar, an imprint of Westland Books, a division of Nasadiya Technologies Private Limited, in 2024

No. 269/2B, First Floor, 'Irai Arul', Vimalraj Street, Nethaji Nagar, Alapakkam Main Road, Maduravoyal, Chennai 600095

Westland, the Westland logo, Tranquebar and the Tranquebar logo are the trademarks of Nasadiya Technologies Private Limited, or its affiliates.

ISBN: 9789360453183

10 9 8 7 6 5 4 3 2

This is a work of fiction. Names, characters, organisations, places, events and incidents are either products of the author's imagination or used fictitiously.

Typeset by Jojy Philip

Printed at Thomson Press (India) Ltd

To Nilesh

Contents

PROLOGUE

Evil Outside the Door

It was a sweltering summer night in Bengaluru. Inside Jagdip Book House, all was quiet—no voices, no hum of the AC, not even a footstep.

Jagat Desai sat in his office on the upper floor, sweat pouring down his face despite the fan spinning above. He gripped a glass paperweight as if longing to throw it at someone. Now he spoke softly, letting out a long string of swear words in an impressive mix of four languages—Kannada, Gujarati, Hindi and English.

Eventually, he let go of the paperweight and pushed his chair back. He stepped out of his office, locking the door behind him, and surveyed the shop. Shelf after shelf of books stretched across the large room. But they gave him no thrill of anticipation for stories he hadn't read yet or fondness for old favourites. In fact, he didn't think of the stories at all. The silver and green cover of the latest fantasy book didn't transport him to a fairyland where wicked and good fairies battled for control of the universe: it made him wonder whether the book would sell enough copies or if it was wasting his shelf space. His mind was a calculator converting each book, each shelf, each aisle into cash: inventory worth so many rupees, so much profit to be made.

The numbers were never high enough. He flicked off the light switch. Through the big windows to his right entered the faint light of the city reflected by the red sky.

He walked past the cash counter and through the door. As he stood on the landing, putting his keys back in his pocket after securing the padlock, he heard footsteps coming up the stairs. His heart pounded in alarm.

A face floated into view. 'Oh, it's you,' he said, relieved. 'What are you doing here?'

There was no answer. He opened his mouth to speak again but he felt a sharp pain in his throat. His fingers were wet when they touched his neck.

Blood glimmered on his hand. He saw the blow coming just before the fist landed on his stomach and knocked his breath out. His head hit the iron door with an ominous clang. *That was dangerous,* he thought as he collapsed onto the floor. *I might have seriously hurt my head.*

But he needn't have worried: the stab to his throat would kill him first, he realised. He wanted to laugh but what came out of his mouth was an eerie gurgle.

He turned his eyes towards his attacker. 'Ambulance.' The face did not change. Had he not spoken out loud? He tried again.

'Call an ambulance,' he mouthed.

The pain was intense now, blocking all thought. He kept gazing up at that calm face till everything went blank.

CHAPTER 1

The Body in the Bookshop

Sunlight filtered through two small windows into the unprepossessing premises of Chikkamma Tours (Pvt.) Ltd. Three cheap plywood desks rested against the walls, black swivel chairs pressed up next to them. Desktop computers sat on two of the desks. A filing cabinet languished in one corner. One end of the office had been walled up into two smaller rooms: a toilet and a cabin with a glass door.

Behind this door sat Shwetha Shetty, frowning as she typed away at her laptop. The tube light over her head flickered ominously from the fluctuating voltage. The time on her screen was 9.17. She had at least half an hour to work in peace.

Poorna Radhika, an enterprising twenty-three-year-old who had worked at Chikkamma Tours since it opened last year, always showed up by ten unless she had work outside the office. The only other employee, Nilima Deka, usually sauntered in sometime between ten and eleven, but she had set her alarm for today earlier, skipped her toast-and-jam-and-coffee breakfast (she preferred butter, but it melted in this weather and she didn't have a fridge) and taken a cab. The metro was cheaper but took much longer, and she might have missed her chance to talk to Shwetha alone.

Nilima clambered out of the cab, smoothing the spiky edges of her short hair. Her blue-framed glasses fogged up as soon as she stepped outside the air-conditioned car. She wiped them on her T-shirt. Now that she could see properly again, she thrust her hands into her skirt pockets and marched into a narrow lane between Kamath's Bar, its magenta walls blazing in the sun through liberal coatings of dust and grime, and a decrepit apartment building that looked like it should be demolished for safety but had clothes drying on the balconies and plants in the windows. The building she made for was a dispirited grey—faded from its original white—and was overpowered by a massive blue sign for Jagdip Book House. Below this was a much smaller sign for Chikkamma Tours, and an inexpertly painted arrow.

The iron gate was wide open—it was rarely shut and almost never locked. Instead of going straight as the arrow indicated, Nilima turned right and walked around the building to the car park that made for half of the ground floor. The other half was the Chikkamma office, behind a door to her left.

She skipped down the few steps and pushed the door open. When she saw no one in the main office, she stepped unerringly towards the glass-fronted room. Shwetha looked up, her easy smile already on her face. Her large eyes were, as always, lined in velvety black, and her curls fell down to her shoulders. At thirty-three, Shwetha was only a few years older than Nilima, but seemed infinitely more capable and intimidating.

'Hey, boss, I need to talk to you.'

'Good morning, Nilima.' Shwetha's voice was cool but friendly. Her fingers, the white of each fingernail a perfect crescent moon, still hovered over her laptop.

Nilima launched into the spiel she had been rehearsing in her head through the cab ride. It was such a brilliant idea: it would bring in a new audience, a steady stream of new registrations; it might even become one of their flagship tours. Shwetha would be so impressed ...

'Give me specifics. What places would we cover?'

Shwetha's practical question brought Nilima back to reality with a thud. 'We'll start with the Majestic area,' she said, shifting uncomfortably on the hard metal seat. While Shwetha sat regally on a similar chair as if it were a throne, Nilima was spilling out of hers in all directions. Her head rested against the door behind her, an elbow jutted out at a right angle and her feet knocked against the legs of the desk. She made the room, barely bigger than a cupboard, feel even smaller.

'Why?' asked Shwetha. In deference to the unusually hot weather, she was in a pale green cotton chikankari kurta, the dupatta fluttering slightly in the breeze from the fan whirring noisily overhead.

With an effort, Nilima looked back up at Shwetha's face. 'Zac O'Yeah. His *Mr Majestic* books are set there.'

'Oh, yeah.'

Nilima grimaced at the pun but soldiered on. 'Then Koshy's, for *The Cosmopolitans*—Anjum Hasan's novel.'

Shwetha's eyes flickered up from the email she had been answering. 'Actually, my friend says the coffee shop in *Ghachar Ghochar* is also based on Koshy's.'

'Brilliant. I loved *Ghachar Ghochar.* After that, we'll go to a couple of art galleries in Sadashiva Nagar—you can't find those easily anyway, they never seem to have signs up—and maybe the National Gallery of Modern Art.' Nilima grandly drew out a cigarette from her pack.

'Don't light that. There aren't even any windows in this room.'

Nilima tapped the cigarette on the desk instead. 'And we'll end with a walk through one of the Shivaji Nagar markets.'

'Which market?'

'Doesn't matter, I'll figure it out.'

'All of this running around, we'll need to hire cars. And it sounds like an all-day tour.'

'Yep, that's the idea.'

'What idea?'

Nilima started at the reedy voice, which was fortunate, because her head came off the door just before it was pulled back and Poorna stepped into the room. Nilima was always caught off guard at how much voice was contained in Poorna's small body.

'Nilima is planning a Grand Literary Tour of the city,' Shwetha explained with considerable patience, despite both her employees being in her inner sanctum and intent on talking at her while she had work to finish.

'Like a tour of bookshops? Blossoms? Bookworm? And that other one?' Poorna's petite form, clad in jeans and a floral print shirt that reached halfway down her thighs, practically vibrated with coiled-up energy.

'Which other one?' Nilima demanded, pushing her glasses up her snub nose. The apparent lack of an intimate knowledge of Bengaluru's bookshops—despite her otherwise unbridled enthusiasm for the city—was just one of the reasons Nilima regarded Poorna with suspicion.

'Ah yes, Goobe's!' Poorna remembered triumphantly.

'Nilima's idea is a tour of places featured in novels,' Shwetha dropped into the silence.

'Oh.' Poorna paused before adding, 'I came to say I have an idea too.'

'Today is my lucky day,' said Shwetha wearily.

There wasn't a third chair in the room for Poorna to sit on. She rocked on the balls of her feet as she explained, 'My grandmother's brother is visiting, and he was telling me how Bangalore used to be part of two states. He would go every morning from Malleshwaram, which was in Mysore, over to Madras Presidency where his office was. We could offer a tour of that area—Malleshwaram and other places that were part of Mysore, maybe find a couple of old residents to talk to.'

'That could actually work,' Shwetha said slowly.

'Great, let me work on the details.' Poorna bounced out as abruptly as she had come in.

'What do you mean *that* could actually work?' Nilima thrust her cigarette back into its box with some vehemence.

'Your idea is a tad ... niche. I can think of one person who'd be interested in that tour.'

'One is good. It's a start.'

'It's you.'

'Oh.'

'We need to do more popular tours, Nili amma. We're barely breaking even. We can discuss this again in a couple of months, all right? For now, why don't you focus on getting more people on this week's tours?'

That's the job you were hired for, after all, Nilima heard Shwetha's voice continue in her head, even though her boss was merely smiling benignly. *You're not doing very well at that, are you?*

Nilima shuffled to the outer room. Poorna was already in her chair, her long plait swaying to the Kannada film songs playing on her computer. Nilima's scowl deepened as she got to work. Only one person had registered so far for Poorna's cycling tour on Saturday. She gleefully called out the status to Poorna. The tour would have to be cancelled if there were no more sign-ups. Maybe Nilima wouldn't always be the worst employee.

Poorna seemed unfazed. 'I'll text all my friends,' she promised. 'One of them runs a cycling club: I'll call her. I'm sure a few more people will sign up by Friday.'

Nilima grunted. 'Can you put on headphones or something? I can't work with that noise.'

'Sure.'

The music was cut off, and now every squeak of Poorna's chair sounded loud. Shwetha talked into her phone in the little room, her voice barely muffled by the glass door. Nilima pursed up her mouth and tried to focus on work. She had been at Chikkamma for two months and ten days. The literary tour was the first tour idea she had come up with, and she had stayed up last night feverishly making notes. And it turned out she had got it all wrong, yet again.

At least the office was quiet now—too quiet, Nilima realised. Even Poorna seemed to have stopped fidgeting.

Nilima wheeled her chair around to see Shwetha glaring balefully at her.

‘What’s up, boss?’ Nilima said with forced casualness. Poorna was staring at her computer with intense concentration.

‘I just received a call from Big Sys,’ Shwetha said.

‘I didn’t know you had a sister.’

‘Short for “systems”,’ Shwetha hissed. ‘You took the tour with their visiting executives yesterday.’

‘Oh, right.’

‘Nilima, you can’t call our clients ignorant and imply they are racist.’

‘I didn’t say they’re racist.’

‘You didn’t have to; it was quite obvious what you meant. The HR person who’d booked us called me. Thank God she was more amused than angry.’

Nilima extricated herself from her chair, but since she was nearly a foot shorter than Shwetha, it didn’t make her feel any more powerful. ‘They only wanted to take pictures of slums! And they saw this young woman sitting on the footpath with her child and were so rude about her. Do you know what they said?’

‘I don’t care!’ Shwetha said through gritted teeth.

‘And she tells me my English is good! The nerve of that German who can’t use articles! You can’t expect me to just take that as a compliment!’

‘I can, and I do. We need to make money off these white assholes, not piss them off. Do you realise the sort of trouble we’ll be in if we lose this contract?’

‘But what else should I have done?’

'Played nice? We can't afford high principles.'

Nilima ran a hand through her hair, making her look like a dishevelled porcupine. Shwetha repressed a smile and said more gently, 'You know, this is only the second time you've conducted a tour. Maybe you should shadow Poorna and me for a bit longer.'

Nilima's jaw tightened. She glanced at Poorna, whose eyes were still fixed on her screen even though her keyboard had made no sound in the last few minutes. Being chastised didn't hurt so much as being told, yet again, that she was worse than Poorna.

'I'm going for a smoke.' Nilima stalked out of the office.

She made for the stairs, longing to put some distance between herself and Shwetha, and Poorna, and the office, everything that reminded her that she was useless, that she couldn't get anything right. The stairs were dim, but her feet found their familiar way up to the narrow windowless landing. On her right was a closed shutter under another large blue sign like the one on the outside of the building, proclaiming that this was Jagdip Book House. A feeble wash of daylight from downstairs alleviated the darkness. Nilima switched on the overhead light and walked on up the stairs.

She came to an abrupt stop on the second-floor landing. There was no shutter here, just an iron door to the upper floor of the bookshop.

There was something on the ground: a cloth with a dark pattern. She flicked on the overhead bulb. No, not just a cloth but a shirt, trousers, leather shoes—a body. Her eyes travelled up from the feet to the man's face—the fleshy nose, thick eyebrows, greying hair. It was the owner of Jagdip Book House, his face frozen in an expression of horror and pain.

What she had thought was a pattern on his shirt wasn't a pattern at all: it was blood. On the floor too was a dark patch that began near his shoulder and extended to the door of the bookshop. She stepped back hastily, wondering whether the floor was uneven. If the blood had spread in the other direction, it might have reached the stairs, and she would have stepped in it ...

She turned and hurtled down the stairs.

When she reached the office, Shwetha was still standing by Poorna's desk, discussing the proposed Malleshwaram tour. It felt odd to hear them talking as if nothing had happened. Like she had stepped out of her life into one of the murder mysteries she read regularly, but Shwetha and Poorna hadn't moved.

'What's up, Nili amma?' Shwetha noticed her first.

'There ...' Nilima pointed a finger upwards. Shwetha and Poorna's heads tilted towards the ceiling: greyish white, with a damp patch and peeling paint in one corner.

'Upstairs?' Shwetha guessed.

Nilima stabbed the air with her upright finger. 'Him. De ...'

'Mr Desai?' Shwetha said. 'From Jagdip Book House?'

'Which one?' said Poorna. 'Jag or Dip?'

'Jagat.'

'What happened to him?' asked Shwetha.

'B-b-blood.'

'Eh?' said Shwetha.

'Dead.'

'What?' said Poorna.

Nilima took a deep breath. 'I think. There's a lot of blood.' She staggered back as Shwetha ran past her and sprinted to the stairs.

'Are you okay?' Poorna asked.

'Yes, of course I'm okay,' Nilima said defensively. As she made for the stairs again, she heard Poorna lock the office door behind her.

On the second floor, Shwetha was bending over the body. 'Don't touch him,' Nilima said sharply.

'Just checking for a pulse.' Shwetha gingerly touched his wrist. 'No, nothing.'

Poorna was standing a few steps down the stairwell, her hands over her mouth. Nilima felt an odd relief at seeing her own shock echoed on Poorna's face.

Shwetha's poise did not waver. She dialled 100 and explained the situation, patiently answering questions and providing the address.

After Shwetha removed the phone from her ear, Poorna asked, 'Shouldn't we tell someone? The family?'

'Why is no one here yet?' Nilima glanced at her phone. 'It's nearly eleven. Oh, it's Monday.'

'Yeah, they're closed Mondays,' Shwetha said, thumbing her own phone. A loud ringtone made Nilima jump. The dead man's shirt pocket was glowing.

'Is that you?' Nilima asked, just as Shwetha pressed a button and silenced Jagat's phone.

'I was hoping he might have left his phone at home or something,' Shwetha explained. 'We had exchanged numbers back when I'd first set up here, in case we needed to talk about anything related to the building.'

The dead man's right arm was curled up towards his shoulder, as if he had tried to reach the phone in his pocket but hadn't quite managed it.

'I have Sampath's number.'

'Whose?'

Nilima felt their surprise. Not only was she new to the building, she was also the least friendly of the three Chikkamma women, less ready to exchange pleasantries with her colleagues, let alone near-strangers. 'He's one of the employees. The bald, short guy? He had given me his number once when he'd offered to find out about a book I wanted.'

'Could you call him then?'

Nilima couldn't think of a reason to refuse. 'I'll do it from the terrace. I still want that smoke.'

She stepped carefully around the body. The light from the landing didn't reach all the way up the stairs, but she didn't think to turn on her phone's flashlight, just kept pushing her feet on till she reached the heavier darkness that was the terrace door. She felt for the latch with her fingers and stumbled out.

The bright sunlight made her blink. She walked to the edge and leaned on the low wall, deeply breathing in the fresh air that didn't smell of blood. Without an audience, her bravado melted away. She sank onto her knees, her fingers holding on to the rough brick of the wall. It took her several tries to light a cigarette.

Heart still thumping, she called Sampath. His voice boomed in her ear, and she swallowed before speaking.

'What? Madam, what did you say?'

'We found Mr Desai—Mr Jagat Desai. He's passed away. I'm so sorry. We've called the police.' To her relief, he seemed to take the news more readily the second time. He didn't ask any questions, just said he would inform 'Dipen sir' right away.

Nilima sat on the filthy terrace floor till she heard the siren, till she saw the police cars turn into the lane. Then she got up and walked inside, latching the terrace door behind her.

CHAPTER 2

Partners in Solving Crime

The police came and took charge. Nilima, Shwetha and Poorna were asked to wait on the lower floor of the bookshop. Nilima kept watch by the glass door to the landing while Shwetha and Poorna sat on stools and gazed at their phones—Shwetha working and Poorna texting friends. A man in a pale blue shirt and jeans walked past the door and up the stairs. Nilima remembered seeing him at the bookshop, and guessed he was Dipen Desai. He looked much younger than his brother, whose body—she shivered—was softer and hair greyer. Had they looked similar once? Nilima opened Facebook and searched for Dipen. An array of photos confronted her: Dipen slouching against a wall, Dipen seated on a motorcycle, Dipen framed in front of a sunset. She zoomed in on a beautiful face: a straight nose between sharp cheekbones and a full mouth.

A constable wandered down the stairs, holding a sheet of paper and making calls. Nilima pushed the door ajar to overhear. He was talking to the shop employees, telling them to show up at the police station in the afternoon.

Nilima darted aside as another police officer herded Dipen down the stairs and through the door. They walked past Nilima to the back of the shop, where they held a murmured conference. Nilima crept as close as she dared but couldn't make out what they were saying. Dipen's voice was steady, its low bass lending it a gravitas she had never heard in Jagat's loud baritone. The police officer beckoned to the constable outside, who promptly stepped into the shop and stood at attention, gazing unwaveringly at Dipen.

Now the officer walked up to where Shwetha and Poorna were sitting, and Nilima stepped closer. The silver tag on the policewoman's chest read 'Sharmila Lamani'. She was all angles, her jawline as sharp as the creases on her uniform. Her hair, pulled back in a rigid bun, was mostly hidden by her official cap. For a moment, she loomed terrifyingly over them. Then Shwetha stood up, taller than the other woman, and offered her a gracious nod.

The policewoman responded, asking, 'It was you who called the police, madam?'

'Yes, Inspector. My colleague Nilima here found the body. She immediately came and told us, and Poorna and I came up with her to double-check. After that, I called 100.'

'You didn't call an ambulance?'

Shwetha was unruffled. 'I couldn't find a pulse and his arm was stiff. I knew there was no point.'

Before the inspector could say anything, she added, 'I only touched his wrist, none of us touched anything else.'

That earned her an approving nod. 'You work in the office downstairs, madam? All of you? Will you go down there and wait for us? I'll come and take your statements in some time.'

Nilima let out the breath she had been holding. They walked down the stairs in single file, not saying a word. A few reporters and curious neighbours were hanging around the building—retreating a few steps when a constable half-heartedly pushed them towards the gate and coming back in as soon as her back was turned. Nilima and her colleagues slipped past them, attracting no more than a curious glance or two.

It was over an hour before Inspector Lamani and a policeman came down to their office. With Shwetha's reluctant permission, they searched it methodically, opening every desk drawer and shaking out the files and loose papers in the cupboard. The inspector scrutinised the pinboard with photos of groups of smiling tourists standing next to Shwetha or Poorna and colourful flyers with alliterative titles in bold letters, like 'Witness Weavers at Work' and 'A Personal Peek at Pete'. She searched Shwetha and Poorna's bags, and asked Nilima to turn out her voluminous pockets. The other officer surveyed the bathroom and the inner office: neither had shelves or cupboards, so he soon came out again, looking a bit disappointed. He opened the lid of the electric kettle and peered in. Shwetha sweetly asked if he wanted tea; he grunted his refusal and bent down to inspect the glasses and cups on the shelf beneath, lifting a few and then putting them back. He even squinted into the narrow gap behind the water purifier, shining his phone flashlight into it.

The police questioned all three of them together, and they obligingly described the events of the morning. But when asked for her fingerprints, Nilima baulked. She should have expected this, she realised, but felt reluctant to hand over something so personal.

'It's within our rights to refuse,' Shwetha said coolly. 'If you insist, I'll call my lawyer.'

Inspector Lamani smiled. 'It will help us with the case, madam. How else will we eliminate your prints from the murderer's?'

Shwetha raised her eyebrows at Nilima, and in response Nilima held out her hands. The policeman carefully took fingerprint samples from all three of them.

Eventually, the officers left after telling them to be available for further questions later. Nilima peered out of the window and reported that Inspector Lamani was driving off in a car while her colleague returned to the bookshop.

By unspoken accord, Shwetha and Poorna went back to work. Nilima had anticipated more discussion of the murder, and felt relieved. Work seemed a welcome distraction from the dread produced by finding a murder victim and being questioned by the police.

But they kept getting interrupted by phone calls from relatives, friends and business associates who had seen the news on any of the local TV channels that had aired it already. After a frantic call from her grandmother, Poorna looked sheepishly at Shwetha. 'It's okay,' Shwetha said. 'Go home. She's worried about you.'

'I wish everyone didn't know where our office was,' Shwetha muttered after Poorna had left and Shwetha had fielded yet another call from a relative. 'If only Jagdip's wasn't so famous.'

'There,' said Nilima, spinning around in her chair, 'that's the Facebook messages taken care of. I've also sent emails asking for feedback for last week's tours.'

'Thanks, Nilima. You've been a rock today.'

A warm fuzzy feeling spread through Nilima, making her feel less like a rock and more like a gulab jamun suddenly dropped in hot sugar syrup.

'No big deal,' she said gruffly. 'There were only a few messages.'

'I didn't mean that. I know it's been a hard day.'

Had Shwetha noticed how shaken she had been after finding the body? Nilima squirmed in embarrassment. Her eyes caught on Shwetha's feet framed in cognac brown leather thongs, one toe covered by a silver filigree ring.

'I hope we don't lose any business because of this. We were just beginning to take off as it is.'

Nilima hadn't thought of this, but gamely said, 'We'll be okay.'

'If they catch the murderer soon. Otherwise, the police will keep disrupting our lives.'

'I don't have much faith in their competence.' Nilima lifted her legs onto her desk and lit a cigarette, hoping Shwetha wouldn't ask her to go outside. She even had an excuse ready—she didn't want to risk running into a reporter. But Shwetha's reprimands were always selective, and she wasn't going to chastise an employee who had dealt ably with the unexpected emergency that this day had been.

'That Inspector Lamani seems all right,' said Shwetha.

'She came to search our office after letting us come back here,' Nilima pointed out. 'We could have destroyed evidence in the whole hour we had before they came ... if we'd had any to destroy. Besides, they're asking all these questions, but do you think anyone will tell the police the truth?'

'Why not?'

'You don't normally tell the police things.'

Shwetha looked at her quizzically, so Nilima added, 'I mean, Jagat was a jerk. I've seen him yell at his employees for trivial things.'

'Who did he yell at?'

'This one time I was in the store, I had asked Sampath about a book and he was looking it up for me on the computer. They didn't seem to have it, and he was trying to find out if they could get it. Suddenly, Jagat stormed in and demanded to know what Sampath was doing. Sampath explained but Jagat just kept yelling, calling him names and saying he didn't know how to do his job after thirty years. Thirty years this man has been there, can you imagine, and he gets yelled at like that. He told Sampath to go to the back and dust books, and he took over the computer. And then he turns to me, all smiles, and says, 'How can I help you, madam?'

'No!'

'Yes, can you believe it? I stammered out that I wanted a book by Ankush Saikia ...'

'And?' Shwetha prompted, even though she knew this was going to be another of Nilima's obscure literature jokes.

'And he said all the books by that author were on the mythology shelf. He pointed too, and said I should look there. I was surprised, because that's the wrong genre, of course.'

'Of course.'

'I didn't want to stand and talk to him, even though he was being all smiley now, and I thought maybe they'd placed it in the wrong section. So, I went to the shelves and looked and looked.'

'No book?'

'Nothing by Ankush Saikia. Then I figured it out. He'd thought I was asking for Amish Tripathi.'

Shwetha *had* heard of Amish Tripathi. 'No!'

'Yes! I tell you, the man knows nothing. I don't know why he owns a bookstore.'

'I know why. It was handed to him by his father to run. Or rather, he took over when his father died.'

'Oh. But he could have sold it off and done something else, couldn't he?'

'Actually, I heard he tried. There was gossip about him, years ago. He wanted to go into the movies.'

'What, become an actor?' Nilima asked.

'No, produce or direct or something. He did a bunch of other things too—I believe he owned a café at some point. Nothing worked out, so he reconciled himself to managing the bookstore.'

'Ah, how sad.'

'Yeah, well, we can't always get what we want.'

'I meant for the bookstore. To be managed by someone who isn't interested in books. Such a waste. And that explains why the store is in such shape.'

'Is it that bad? It's quite well-known, but. Everyone who's been in the city for some years knows it.'

'I wouldn't know about that. It just doesn't seem well run. Books aren't categorised properly, there isn't enough of a selection, the staff never know where anything is—even Sampath, who tries to help ... And there are rarely many people there. Who would come here instead of going to Blossom?'

'You go quite a bit, it seems.'

'Only because it's right upstairs. Even so, I rarely buy anything, and then only out of guilt. I'd much rather go to Goobe's or Bookworm, and not just because they're cheaper.'

'No?' Shwetha turned back to her laptop.

'I mean, that's most of the reason, obviously. I can even get second-hand books there. Besides, there are so many more books in Church Street. I wish I could go there more often.'

'Very sad for you.'

'You see what I mean, though? Sampath is not going to tell the police how Jagat treated him.'

'If only because that might make him a suspect.'

'Have you been thinking that too? That maybe one of the employees did him in?'

'It's the obvious place to look, isn't it?'

'The store is closed on Mondays,' Nilima said slowly. 'No one was likely to go up those stairs between last evening and tomorrow.'

'And Jagat is usually the last one to lock up and leave.'

'You're sure of that?'

'Yeah, I often saw him leave while I was locking up myself. Of course, I don't usually stay as late as that.'

'Only a few times a week,' Nilima said mockingly.

'So,' Shwetha continued, 'one of the employees could have stayed back and killed him after everyone else left.'

'Exactly. But they have a security guard, shouldn't he have been around?'

'Maybe they let him go at his regular time, if Jagat and this employee were staying back for some reason? Or it's possible that Jagat stayed late alone and this employee knew about it and came back and killed him?'

'The security guard is going to be in trouble, isn't he?'

'Yeah, I suppose the police are questioning him. Poor Maniram.'

'Wait, you know him?'

'I gave him a lift once,' Shwetha explained. 'I saw him leaving as I was driving out and offered to drop him at the bus stop. Then I found out he lives only a kilometre or so out of my way, so I dropped him home.'

'So you know where he lives?'

'Yeah. And you know what? He's from Assam too. His Hindi is patchy, and he doesn't speak much English.'

'Oh cool, I had no idea! I should talk to him—maybe we can talk in Assamese.' Nilima leaned forward in excitement. 'Do you understand what this means, boss? You know where he is and the police don't.'

'Yeah, Lamani got a call while she was here, no? She was yelling at the constable they'd sent to find him. Turns out he doesn't live at that address anymore.'

'Yes, and earlier, when the other constable was trying to call him, apparently he couldn't get an answer. Do you think Maniram is the murderer, and that's why he's fled?'

'Let's not jump to conclusions about a nice young man. He probably just switches off his phone when he's not at work.'

'I wish I could,' Nilima muttered and then bit her lip. 'I mean ... can we go see him? Maybe he knows something!'

'Shouldn't I just give the inspector his address ... But then, they might scare him. It might be better for us to talk to him first.'

'Exactly! We need to get to him before the police does. Let's go!'

Shwetha's car was an old dark blue sedan that only had a few scratches. The inside was squeaky clean and smelling of incense, even though the grey pleather was moulting. Inside BTM Layout, Shwetha stopped at the mouth of a lane. 'Better park here, I could barely get out of that lane last time.' She got out and brushed off her clothes out of habit, while Nilima scratched at her arms to get off the bits of the seat that had stuck to her skin.

Shwetha stopped at a four-storeyed building and led Nilima into a dim lobby. Two nondescript white doors presumably led to flats, and on the right, narrow concrete stairs veered upwards.

'Do you know which flat is his?' Nilima asked hopefully.

Shwetha shook her head. 'Should I ring this doorbell and ask?'

'Hold on,' said Nilima.

Now Shwetha too heard the footsteps coming down. The young man who appeared on the stairs had a friendly face, and his grey trousers and white shirt were threadbare but well-pressed. Curls fell luxuriously over his forehead and his ears.

'We're looking for Maniram,' Shwetha said in Kannada, and then in Hindi when he looked puzzled.

'Maniram!' He nodded eagerly. 'Wait!' He held up a hand to reinforce his message and disappeared back up the stairs.

Nilima and Shwetha stepped outside the gloomy building to wait in the fading sunlight. A flock of children rode merrily on their bikes. An autorickshaw sped into the lane, honking and scattering the children.

The curly haired man came out of the building, now smiling triumphantly. Behind him was the bookshop's security guard. Slim and clean-shaven, in a black T-shirt and pale blue jeans instead of the dull blue uniform Nilima had always seen him in, he could pass for a teenager, though he was in his early twenties. He greeted Shwetha by name and stood awkwardly, while his neighbour slapped him on the back and waved at the two women as he hurried away. Nilima wondered, with a twinge of guilt, if they had made him late for his bus, or for work. But Shwetha was introducing her to Maniram now, and she needed to talk to him, to find out what he knew.

Maniram hadn't heard of Jagat's death, and shock at the news rendered him quiet. He responded in monosyllables to Shwetha's prodding, but perked up when Nilima spoke to him in Assamese, soon chattering away like they were old friends.

He ushered them to a small eatery in the next lane, and Nilima eagerly ordered biryani. She hadn't eaten all day: she had not wanted to walk out of the office for her usual afternoon dosa or sandwich, with reporters and police swarming the building. Shwetha and Poorna had offered to share their packed lunches, but Nilima had refused with the excuse that her stomach was too queasy to eat—though really she had been reluctant to accept a favour she could not return. Shwetha had a cook, and Poorna's mother cooked lunch for the entire family every morning; Nilima only had herself and an induction cooktop on her table-cum-desk, and rarely managed to make herself a sandwich in the morning to take for lunch.

Shwetha picked at her food for a few minutes before stepping out of the eatery to make some calls. Nilima scarfed down her first plateful so quickly she barely tasted it. Then she and Maniram made their way through their second helpings. This time she registered that the food was too dry, too spicy; still, she kept eating till her plate was empty again.

Meanwhile, Maniram appreciated the food out loud, talking about how difficult it was to share a kitchen with seven other men. Nilima revealed her own lack of a proper kitchen. He grinned in sympathy and asked where she had grown up.

'I lived in Guwahati till I was twenty,' she said shortly, and quickly turned the conversation around on him. He didn't seem to mind; with only a little encouragement he talked about his childhood and his family home near Bongaigaon. He spoke with affection of his sisters and his cousins and his parents, and about fishing in the beel near his village.

'Don't you miss home?' he asked suddenly.

'No.' Surprise flared on his face before he politely masked it, and Nilima offered an inadequate explanation: 'I've been away for a long time now—eight years, a little more. I've got used to being away.'

Outside the window, dusk had deepened into evening, and the yellow sodium vapour streetlights had turned on. Amid pedestrians and vehicles jostling for space, Shwetha was leaning against a lamp post and looking at her phone. The eatery had been empty; now two middle-aged men walked in and claimed a table in the corner. The dinner rush was still an hour or two away. Under cover of the table, Nilima turned on an audio recording app before placing the phone on her lap.

'How long have you worked at the bookstore?' Nilima asked.

'It's only been a few months, baideu. The earlier guy went home for Diwali, so they put me there on a temporary basis. When he didn't come back, I stayed on. I got lucky; my last job was at an office, and I had to stand for ten hours every day. Here I only have to stand up when customers enter or leave and open the door for them. There aren't that many customers, so sometimes I can sit for a whole hour at a time.'

'Was everyone in the store yesterday?'

'Yes, they were all there. Mr Sampath was in first as usual; he was unlocking the shop when I got in.'

'He has keys then?'

'Yes, he opens the shop in the morning. Mr Jagat usually locks up at night, unless Mr Sampath's staying late.'

'And both the brothers were there all day? Jagat and Dipen Desai?'

'Mr Jagat, yes, he came in the morning, around eleven. Mr Dipen doesn't usually come early. He came around four, I think. The evening is our busiest time, even on Sundays, so Mr Dipen is usually around then.'

'And you said all the staff was in?'

'Everyone as in, there's only Sampath and Mehnaz madam.'

'Mehnaz is the tall one with pink hair?'

'That's right. She came at ten, soon after me.'

'You got there at ten?'

'It must have been a few minutes before ten. I am supposed to get there at 9.45. Mr Sampath usually beats me to it.'

'So, Mehnaz got there around store opening time.'

'That's right. And she worked till seven.'

'Oh, she left early?'

'That's her regular shift, ten to seven. Sometimes she'll stay later if she has to. She doesn't like it.' He grinned.

'There's another woman who works there sometimes, isn't there? I've seen her once or twice.'

'No, that's all the staff. There was one more till last week—Pallav. He lost his job.'

'He was fired? Why?'

'They'd hardly tell me, Nilima baideu. Mr Jagat called me in and said—right in front of Pallav too—that I was not to let him in the shop anymore. It was awkward for me. Pallav was nice; he had bought me lunch once, when we had both gone to that darshini nearby.'

'That can't have been easy. How did Pallav take it?'

'He just smiled and said it was fine, he'd leave. And he did; he just went to pick up his bag from behind the counter and left. He didn't even say anything to Sampath sir, who was asking him what happened, where was he going so early ...'

'But I swear I've seen this lady. Long wavy hair, very prettily dressed in salwar kameez ...'

'Oh, that's Ronita madam. Mr Dipen's wife. He just got married last year, soon after I started working there. She comes in and helps out sometimes. Yesterday, she came in around five and left at nine, with Mr Dipen. We close up at 9.30.'

'Sampath stays so late even though he comes in early?'

'Only when it's busy or they're short-staffed. Now because Pallav isn't here anymore, Sampath stays late on Saturday and Sunday. Otherwise, he leaves at seven.'

'What about Jagat? He was still inside when Sampath locked up?'

'Yes, on the second floor. He often leaves directly from there. We keep that door locked so customers can't use it, and of course it's not a nice big glass door and shutter like we have on the first floor. They don't want to pay for a second security guard to stand up there. There's a staircase inside the shop that customers and staff use.'

Nilima nodded; she was familiar with the layout.

'Mr Jagat and Mr Dipen mostly use that door to get in and out easily from their office on the second floor.'

'And you don't think there's any reason Jagat would have come back to the store this morning?'

'Najanu, baideu. Mondays are my day off, so I'm never there. All I know is he was there when I left last night.'

'You left at 9.30?'

'I think it was 9.40 when Sampath locked up. The two of us walked out of the gate together. At the end of the lane, Mr Sampath hailed an auto and I walked to the bus stop.'

Shwetha came back as he was speaking, though all she understood was 'auto', 'Sampath' and 'bus stop'.

'You took the bus home?' Shwetha asked in Hindi. 'Last night? Sampath saw you?'

Maniram obligingly switched to Hindi too. 'He didn't see me get on the bus. I walked on to the bus stop while he was talking to the autorickshaw driver. I turned the corner so he couldn't have seen me anymore.'

'There are no security cameras, right? No way to make out if anyone came to the shop after you left?'

'No, madam. Jagat sir kept saying he wanted to get a security camera installed, but that never happened.' He understood the implications of her questions. 'Should I be worried, madam? I've never been in trouble with the police.'

Shwetha drew out her business card. 'Just go and tell them the truth, Maniram. We'll come with you to the police station. And if you feel like you're in trouble, give me a call. I have a lawyer friend who can help.'

Maniram agreed that going to the police station with them now, instead of waiting for the police to come and find him at home, was a good idea. They got in the car. Nilima pulled up Google Maps on her phone and offered to navigate, but Shwetha knew the way. The roads were teeming with office-goers making their way home. Loud honks bloomed all around them.

It was past eight when they finally got to the police station, a low building painted cream with red trim. They entered a spacious room that had a few large desks of solid wood surrounded by wooden chairs with mesh seats. Policemen—and one woman—sat behind the desks, and a few more walked around purposefully. A few civilians sat desultorily on the benches lined against the walls, as if resigned to a long wait.

Shwetha gave their names to a constable and asked to speak to Inspector Lamani. He frowned but obligingly turned into the corridor that led inside. He came back almost immediately and ushered them into the inspector's room. Sharmila nodded from behind her desk, wearily shutting the file in front of her. Maybe it was the lighting or she was tired; the lines on her face were more visible. The constable parked himself next to her desk and stood as stolid and unmoving as a pillar.

Shwetha launched into a few easy lies. 'We were going home, and as we passed Maniram's place, I realised that he probably didn't know what'd happened. So we decided to drop in and tell him, and he insisted on coming right away and meeting you, in case you were looking for him.'

'We were,' the inspector said shortly. Her steady gaze moved from Shwetha to Maniram and Nilima and back again. Nilima wished she was standing next to Shwetha and could clutch her arm for support. She lowered her eyes to the large walnut brown desk that was polished to a shine.

'This is very helpful of you.' The inspector's tone belied her words, and she did not ask them to sit down.

'And you, madam?'

Nilima looked up in horror at those sharp eyes focused on her. 'Were you also going home with Shwetha madam?' Inspector Lamani asked.

'I ...' Nilima stammered unhelpfully. She remembered the inspector standing by while her colleague had taken down their names and addresses this afternoon. *She knows I don't live anywhere near Shwetha.*

'Yes,' said Shwetha. 'I'd invited her home for dinner. We've had such a difficult day.'

Sharmila's steely eyes did not soften. 'I'm sorry our investigation has come in the way of your meal.'

'Not at all, Inspector. We ate before we came here. Had biryani, all three of us. Nilima was in shock and hadn't eaten since morning, you see.'

'Where did you eat?'

Nilima's fists clenched in panic at the questioning, even as Shwetha answered smoothly, 'Rafiq's Biryani House, near Maniram's apartment. Do you want to see the bill?'

'That won't be necessary.' Sharmila stared at Shwetha, then added abruptly, 'We'll talk to Maniram now. You both can go.'

'Thank you so much, Inspector,' said Shwetha, still smiling sweetly. She turned to Maniram. 'Remember, if you need anything, give me a call. And I have your number, so I will check up on you later.'

Inspector Lamani recognised this for the warning it was. Shwetha sashayed out, unconcerned by her glare, and Nilima hurried after her.

✍

Shwetha insisted on driving Nilima home, over her protests: 'It's almost ten kilometres out of your way.'

'It's fine, Deka. There's not much traffic now. Also, I want to know what Maniram told you. I'll drive, you talk.'

By the time Shwetha pulled up on the lane outside Nilima's apartment building, she was all caught up. Nilima reached for the car door, but then turned to Shwetha. 'Do you think he'd just died, when we found him?'

'Huh?'

'Jagat. When we found him, did it look like he'd just been killed?'

'I don't know, how could we tell? Oh, he was stiff when I touched him. So maybe he hadn't *just* died.'

'And he ... his body, I mean ... had stopped bleeding. The blood was ... it had dried.'

Shwetha switched the engine off. 'He was probably killed last night, not this morning.'

'If I hadn't gone up for a smoke, the body wouldn't have been found till tomorrow morning, and it would be harder to say when he was killed.'

'Do you think the murderer intended that?'

'That would mean it was premeditated. It's not a brawl gone wrong or something, it's an actual murder.'

'That's scarier,' Shwetha said slowly. 'That level of malice and planning ... that's evil.'

'What do you want to do about it?'

'What do you mean? What can I do?'

'I mean,' Nilima said, avoiding Shwetha's eyes, 'we shouldn't have an evil murderer running loose in the building. Poorna's grandmother is worried enough.'

'Yeah, but it's not exactly our job to catch a murderer. Isn't it up to the police?'

'Meh, police. I bet you and I could find out more than they could.'

'Nilima ...'

'You know you want to. Admit it, you're curious.'

Shwetha fiddled with the car key. 'Actually, I may have already started investigating.'

'I knew it! Go on, Shetty, spill it.'

'When you were talking to Maniram, I didn't want to hang around and get in the way—he was talking so easily to you. So I went out and made some calls.'

'I knew you were up to something.'

'I called, to be accurate, most of the gossips I know in Bangalore. Relatives, old friends and neighbours, anyone who could tell me anything about the Desais. They were happy to tell me what they knew because I told them about us finding the body.'

Nilima winced at the idea of the news spreading through the city, passed on by the nodes in Shwetha's network. But they must have heard about the murder already, and it didn't hurt to pass on the correct version, instead of the rumours that would otherwise be flying around.

So she said, 'I'm impressed you have so many acquaintances in the city even after spending five years away.'

'I grew up here, Deka. And I spent the last year trying to get my old life back.'

'Did you?' asked Nilima, distracted from the murder.

'Yeah, it's like I was never away. Actually, not quite. I lost a few friends, and one or two have moved away, but I'm making new ones, and most of my relatives seem happy to have me back, even though some were a bit catty about it.'

'About what?' Nilima asked indignantly.

'The usual things people say when you get divorced. Did he cheat, does he drink, is she barren ... Nothing I can't handle. Do you want to talk about the case or what?'

'Of course, boss. What did you find out?'

'Nothing too shocking, really. Jagat wasn't a pleasant man; he was something of a social climber. Not like his father, who was universally liked, the aunties say. The father's story is something of a legend: he worked in an insurance company after college and was always interested in literature without being a writer or a critic. He saved enough money to set up a small bookstore, and grew it over the years. Then he died and left behind two sons who weren't interested in books—or in the business.'

'Hah. Who else is in the family?'

'Jagat has a wife and two daughters. Dipen got married recently—six months or so?'

'Yes, I've seen his wife—at least Maniram said that was his wife. She's very pretty.'

'Hmm.'

'What?'

'There's some gossip that the marriage isn't very happy.'

'Oh, any idea why?'

Shwetha unhooked her seat belt and shrugged gracefully. 'She's in her thirties and had never lived away from her parents. She's finding it difficult to adjust, is what I heard.'

'What about Jagat? His domestic life is okay?'

'There was no gossip about that—and if there was anything bad, someone would know. He wasn't a very polite or charming man, but apparently he was a good husband and father.'

'Is their mother still alive?'

'Jagat and Dipen's? No, she died a few years after the father, of a heart attack.'

'I don't blame her. If her husband was all that, imagine having to live through the disappointment of two sons like Jag-Dip.'

When Shwetha didn't answer, Nilima asked, 'Did you know him? Jagat I mean?'

Shwetha thought of Jagat Desai's dead body, how his skin had felt under her fingers ... 'Can't say I know him well. I've spoken to him a few times. The usual hi, hello when I saw him by chance, and once or twice when we met to discuss building maintenance stuff.'

'What did you think of him?'

'He was polite enough. A bit full of himself.'

'I'm not surprised.'

'You know what I'm wondering?' Shwetha said. 'Why no one came to check on him last night.'

'You mean from his family?'

'Yeah. Guy doesn't come home, his family doesn't bother to find out where he is?'

'Do you think Sampath knows anything?'

'Why don't you call him?'

'Now?'

'Why wait? It's only 9.20.'

Sampath answered on the second ring. 'Nilima madam,' he said warmly, and went on before she had a chance to say more than hello. 'I'm sorry I couldn't come to the shop and meet you. The police kept me at the station for a long time.'

'No, Mr Sampath, *I'm* sorry. It's a difficult time for you.'

'Yes, madam. I don't know what Desai sir would have said. The police in his shop! These are bad times.'

After a startled second, Nilima realised that he was referring to Desai senior, Jagat's father. 'Yes, indeed,' she said meaninglessly, pressing the speaker button so Shwetha could overhear the conversation.

'Thank you for letting me know when you found him. It must have been such a shock for you young girls.'

'No, we're fine. I mean, Poorna's grandmother seems a bit worried but we're okay, really. I was just concerned for you.'

'Yes-yes, the police everywhere, Jagat sir killed that way ...'

'Do the police have any idea what happened?'

'No-no, I don't know what they're doing. They haven't told us anything.'

'Will the store be open tomorrow?' Nilima realised as soon as the words left her mouth that the answer was obvious.

'The police won't let us open it. Dipen sir will of course be busy, but I would have opened the shop. But no, the police say we can't open it till they finish their search. Though what they are looking for, God only knows. Moving books and papers, making a mess ... I just came home from the shop, I'd gone directly from the police station, but they wouldn't even let me inside the door.'

Nilima made a sympathetic noise, then asked, 'Do you think we could come and meet you tomorrow? Maybe we could go visit the family? Shwetha and I would like to pay our respects.'

'That's very nice of you, madam. Yes-yes, please come, please come. I also haven't gone yet. Desai madam and the children only reached home this evening.'

'Oh, were they away?' Nilima's eyes met Shwetha's over the phone.

'Yes, they were in Gujarat, visiting her parents. Her uncle had died of cancer. Death upon death. Very sad. Should I meet you there?'

'I think it might be better if we met you first, if you don't mind?'

'Of course, madam. Will you come home? My wife will make us breakfast. Maybe ten in the morning?'

'That's perfect, Sampath. Thank you.'

'I'll send you the address, madam.'

After Nilima ended the call, Shwetha said, 'The wife and kids were away. That's why no one checked on him. That's very lucky for the murderer.'

'I don't believe in luck,' Nilima said ominously.

'Go rest,' Shwetha said, patting her shoulder. 'I'll pick you up at 9.30.'

'Do you ...'

'Yeah?'

'Do you want to come up? Have a drink? I have whiskey.' *Only McDowell's No. 1,* Nilima reminded herself nervously, *and no ice.*

'It's been a long day. And I can't spend my morning lazing at home, as I'd planned, now that we have to go detecting tomorrow.'

Nilima felt emboldened by Shwetha's smile. 'You could stay over?'

'That's sweet, but I want to go home, water my plants. Goodnight, Nilima.'

Nilima walked inside, mentally cursing the landlord's stinginess—he switched off all the lights at ten. She turned on her phone's flashlight and trudged up to the third floor, wondering if she'd ever enter an unlit stairwell again without thinking of Jagat Desai.

Her one-room-plus-bathroom flat was less dark. The curtain was drawn aside at the window over the bed, and there was some light from the buildings nearby. Nilima stubbed her toe on a box of books as she moved to and fro, changing into a T-shirt and shorts and going to the bathroom. Finally, she was on her bed, and she got on her knees to pull the curtain and push the light out.

CHAPTER 3

After the Cremation

Sampath was a short, bald man of sixty odd years. He ushered them into his flat over a sari shop, letting out an uninterrupted string of welcoming phrases.

'Namaskara, good morning! Banni, madam, welcome, madam. Please sit, please sit.'

The living room was crowded with furniture: a single bed covered in bright cushions, a three-piece sofa set upholstered in somewhat faded blue floral fabric, a long coffee table, a small, round dining table with four chairs huddled around it and a glass-fronted cabinet filled with knick-knacks and books (mostly in Kannada and a few in English, including a few self-help books that Nilima guessed belonged to their host's son). A doorway led to a narrow corridor, across which was a small, neat bedroom and a shut door to the bathroom. Through the window wafted in genial shouts from the flower market Nilima and Shwetha had walked through after they had parked the car.

Sampath's wife, as short as her husband and smiling as widely, brought in avalakki and filter coffee but refused to sit with them. 'She has kitchen duties,' Sampath solemnly informed them. The son, a shy young man of around Poorna's age, nodded at them as he walked out on his way to work. Nilima gobbled down the delicious food—last evening's biryani was already a distant memory, and she was ravenous after spending an hour in the morning doing her weekly cleaning of the apartment, scrubbing the floors and every surface. Shwetha ate more daintily, chattering pleasantly to put the older man at ease. Once the plates were empty and they had all settled back with their coffee, Shwetha brought the conversation around to the murder.

'It was a terrible thing that happened.'

Sampath shook his head in agreement. 'Yes, terrible, terrible. And right there in the shop. I'm glad Mr Desai isn't around to see this. It would have broken his heart.'

'You knew him well?'

'I've worked in the shop since it first opened, thirty-five or thirty-six years ago. Desai sir, he gave me a chance. I was working as a peon in the insurance company then, where he worked as well. My wife and I had just had a baby—our eldest daughter. Times were hard. When Desai sir left to start his shop, he asked if I wanted to join him. Those first few years, things were very difficult. The shop was making losses. But he never failed to pay me on time, even if that meant he didn't have any income.'

'That's nice of him,' Shwetha said politely. Nilima guessed she wasn't impressed because she would have done the same.

'It's a big thing, madam. He himself was struggling. His sons were small, he had put all his savings into the shop, taken a loan ... He had to sell all his wife's jewellery. He couldn't afford to hire any other employee for a long time. Day and night we worked, and his wife came and helped sometimes too.'

'You were more a business partner than an employee, it seems,' Shwetha flattered him.

'Yes-yes, madam.' He threw a glance at the doorway to the corridor and lowered his voice. 'My wife wasn't very happy at first. She wanted me to get another job because the shop might go under. But I couldn't abandon Desai sir. And then the shop started to do well. In ten years, we had moved into this building, first one floor, then the second a few years later. He built up the business.

'And people loved him, you know. He used to remember the names of our regulars, the kind of books they liked. We would give them a call when there was a new book they might be interested in. This was before the internet and all that, and Desai sir's recommendations carried a lot of weight. He used to read a lot of the books himself. He was very knowledgeable about literature. Publishers used to try to influence him, but if he didn't like a book he refused to recommend it.'

'He died in 2006?' Nilima asked. She had spent a couple of sleepless hours last night looking up everything she could find online about the bookshop.

'Around ten years ago—no-no, you're right, madam, it was 2006. It's hard to believe it's been so long, close to thirteen years. He was still quite young, not yet sixty. Cancer—it got him quite quickly. His wife followed him a few years after—her heart was always weak. Poor sir, he had tried to train his sons in the business. Neither of them was interested, no-no. They thought it was old-fashioned.'

'What did they want to do?'

'Jagat wanted to produce movies. He kept trying to get his father to give him money, but Desai sir didn't have much to spare. Even in our better days, we never managed to make enough to buy the entire building; any profit Desai sir made, he put into expanding the business and buying the two floors of the shop. It took years and years—decades—to pay that off, and then the two flats that his sons now live in—the smaller one that is now Dipen's, and the bigger one that sir bought not long before he died and which Jagat then renovated. I assume he found his father's taste in furniture as old-fashioned as his father's taste in business. But he had it done up tip-top, I must say. You will see today.'

'Was Jagat upset when his father wouldn't give him money?' Shwetha said.

'Desai sir gave what he could, but it was never enough, and Jagat ... Well, he said his father should sell the shop.'

'Oh, no.' Shwetha sounded suitably horrified.

'Yes, imagine that. Of course, Desai sir wouldn't agree. Jagat was very upset, yes; he said his father should retire and give the money to him so he could start his own business. Retire! At fifty! Give up the business he had built with so much love!'

'So they quarrelled?' Nilima asked.

'Yes-yes, I remember there were some loud arguments in the shop also. Then Jagat borrowed some money and started an internet café. That was all the craze back then. But it didn't work—he didn't make any money and his father had to help him pay off the loan. Then he started a restaurant. That didn't last long either, maybe a year. Dipen was still young then, and he was busy with his music—he was always practising with his band.'

'Dipen?' Nilima was surprised. 'What kind of music?'

'It was a rock band. He used to play the guitar, you know. Not to my taste, that music.'

Nilima thought of Dipen, with his conservative shirts, his close-cropped hair and his grim expression—well, that last one might've worked. 'But Jagat didn't sell off the store after his father died,' she said out loud.

'Yes-yes, Jagat finally accepted that the shop was working better than anything he could do, so he started spending time there. He kept trying other things—real estate was a new fancy—but it never worked out. He never had his father's way of understanding people, no-no. That's all that matters in business, Desai sir always said.'

'What about Dipen?' Nilima asked. 'Didn't he get a stake in the store too?'

'Yes-yes, they both became owners. Desai sir divided everything up between them. He didn't even leave much to his wife. Almost as if he knew she wouldn't last long, the poor lady.'

Shwetha framed her question delicately. 'The brothers inherited everything?'

'There wasn't all that much, just the flats and the shop, like I said. There was very little cash. That's why Dipen wanted to sell the shop, but Jagat knew by now that it would be a bad decision. So, at last Jagat gave him some money and took over the shop on his own.'

'Wait, so Dipen doesn't have any stake in the business?' Nilima leaned forward. 'It's all Jagat's?'

'Yes-yes. Jagat had some money from his wife, so he paid Dipen, and Dipen signed over his share. I think Jagat wanted to be like his father—run the shop on his own, be respected. But he is not his father.'

'What about Dipen?' Nilima asked. 'When did he start working there?'

'Now, that Dipen, since he was a child, he never liked coming to the shop. But four or five years ago he started coming in regularly, helping us out. Jagat paid him a salary. He must have needed the money.'

Nilima opened her mouth but Sampath added, 'I don't know where all the money went. He doesn't tell me anything, of course. I just think that if he came back to work at the shop, he must have run out of money.'

Shwetha laughed, then said hurriedly, 'You know the family quite well, it seems.'

'You learn a lot about people by working with them. I'm sure you know that, madam.'

'Yes, indeed,' Nilima piped up. 'How someone is as a boss says a lot about how they are as a person.' She winked at Shwetha. 'Was Jagat a good boss?'

'He was ... you know how it is,' Sampath said evasively.

'I thought he was a bit rude,' Nilima said. 'I've heard him yell at employees.' She tactfully refrained from mentioning that Sampath was the employee she had heard Jagat yell at.

'Yes-yes, he had a temper. He could be very nice sometimes, but if he was in a bad mood he could be very insulting too. But Dipen is worse.'

'Really?'

'He would come in drunk sometimes, no. I shouldn't be saying this, but it was shameful, shameful. His father never drank. He had a kind word for everyone. He treated his employees like friends, he knew our children's birthdays, he sent books for them. When my Manika got her BSc, Desai sir came home to congratulate her and gave her a cheque. Mrs Desai wasn't well then—she was recovering from one of her heart attacks and she was quite weak—still, they both came.'

'Jagat and Dipen aren't like their father?' Nilima asked.

'Dipen only talks to us when he gives us orders. Jagat—he talked about his children and how well they're doing at school, but he never asked after my wife and daughters and son. He knew them since childhood, but he never asked. But what to do now.'

'It must have been such a shock, him being murdered?' Nilima's throat tightened as she pictured Jagat's body, his face pale and grotesque in the dim light. 'Did you know he was going to stay back at the shop that night?'

'I only knew he had a meeting. He told us to lock up downstairs and leave. He said he would leave by the door on the top floor.'

'You didn't know who he was meeting?'

'He didn't say. And he's not the kind of person you could ask. He'd have thought it impudent. He used that word to me sometimes: impudent.'

'Did he have such meetings often?' Nilima wasn't sure if Shwetha was tactfully changing the subject or going after the most promising angle.

'Only during the day. He would meet the accountant or sometimes a publisher. I thought maybe he was meeting the accountant Sunday night. He was complaining about paying too much tax earlier that day, so he could have wanted to consult Mohan. But I don't think Mohan would come so late.'

'Mohan is the accountant?'

'Yes. He's worked with us for a few years. I don't know him well. Jagat sir dealt with him.'

'Dipen was also in that day?' Nilima asked.

'Yes, and Ronita madam, his wife. They left together sometime before the shop closed.'

'And Jagat's wife? What's she like?'

Nilima was afraid she had been too blunt, but Sampath smiled. 'She is a very nice, refined lady. Always says good afternoon, asks how we are. She only comes to the shop occasionally. I don't think she has come in the last week.'

'Mehnaz was also in yesterday, wasn't she?' Shwetha prompted him.

'Yes, Mehnaz left at seven as usual. I stayed till closing time.'

'And Maniram,' Nilima said. Shwetha immediately shot her a warning look—why tell Sampath they had talked to Maniram?

'I mean, did Maniram stay back?' Nilima quickly covered up. 'Doesn't he usually stay till everyone has left?'

'No-no, it was the end of his shift too, and Jagat sir said he could go. When I was done serving the last customer, I went to tell Jagat sir—he was upstairs in his office. That's when he told me to lock up and tell Maniram to go. We walked out together.'

'How do you get home on nights when you work late?' Shwetha asked with a casual air, pretending she was making conversation and not questioning him. 'You don't have a scooter?'

'No-no. I take the bus, and when I'm tired, I take an auto. That time of the night, it takes just twenty minutes to get to Shivaji Nagar. I took an auto that night.'

'Isn't there another boy who works there?'

'Oh, you mean Pallav? He was fired last week.'

'Jagat fired him?'

'Yes-yes, I don't know why. Jagat was shouting at him in the office—something about not knowing his place and looking through his private things.'

'Pallav was digging into Jagat's private stuff?' Nilima asked.

'Something like that. The office door was shut, I wasn't trying to listen, it's just that Jagat was shouting and I couldn't help hearing a few words. Then they both came out. Pallav didn't look at me, didn't talk, he just walked straight out of the shop. Jagat told us later that he wouldn't be back.'

Mrs Sampath came out with fresh orange flowers in her hair matching the print on her sari. She offered them more filter coffee.

'No, thank you,' said Shwetha. 'And thank you for a lovely breakfast. We should go to Mr Desai's house now ... Will you come with us?'

'Yes, to pay my respects,' she told Shwetha in Kannada. 'I've known him since he was a little boy. I'd gone to the opening of the shop, all those years ago. Even now I remember, he was running around in yellow shorts that day. It's so sad.'

Nilima sat on the edge of a sofa in the living room of Veena Desai's second-storey flat in Koramangala, pinned between Shwetha on one side and Mrs Sampath on the other. Shwetha was talking—in Tamil, as far as Nilima could make out—to Ms Subbalakshmi, one of the Desais' neighbours. Mrs Sampath was talking to a middle-aged Mr Rao, Sampath joining in from his corner. Nilima smiled tentatively at Veena's father, but he was stretched out on the rocking chair and gazing at his phone. There had been more people in the room—Veena Desai, her mother, a friend of Veena's whose name Nilima hadn't caught, Mr Rao's wife, the domestic worker who had opened the door—but they had drifted inside, leaving the others to make conversation among themselves.

Nilima gazed at the chandelier, many shards of glass arranged seemingly haphazardly in a big sphere, and wondered what it looked like lit. A sharp glance from Shwetha alerted her that her leg was shaking rhythmically. She stilled it.

She got up, muttering that she was going to the bathroom. No one paid any attention to her.

The very first door she encountered led to a bathroom, but she surreptitiously shut it and walked past. The next door was ajar, displaying a room that had the tidy characterless appearance of a guest bedroom. Two people stood by the window, deep in conversation: Veena's friend and Mrs Rao, the wife of the neighbour in the living room. They didn't look around, and Nilima moved forward. In another room, several children were piled up on twin beds, and a boy sat drawing at the desk—Jagat and Veena had two daughters, so presumably the other children belonged to the Raos and to Veena's friend in the guest bedroom. The door opposite was shut. Nilima stood as close as she dared, listening to murmured voices. It had to be Veena and her mother, but she couldn't make out what they were saying.

A movement made Nilima look up. The Desais' domestic worker was watching her warily from the kitchen. Nilima smiled ruefully and walked in.

'Can I help you with anything?' she asked in halting Bengali. 'I feel so useless. I wish there was something I could do.'

Lotika smiled, any suspicions apparently allayed. She gestured at the kitchen table, but Nilima perched on the marble countertop instead. Behind her were windows covering the width of the wall, looking out on a neighbour's terrace garden. Sunlight flooded into the kitchen, warming Nilima's back and making the white cupboards, all metallic and modern, dazzle brilliantly. The dining table and chairs were of pale wood, lightly scuffed by time and use.

Lotika moved briskly between counter and table. She was thin and a little taller than Nilima. Her thick hair, streaked with grey, was gathered in an elaborate coil at the nape of her neck, and her dainty, calloused hands made no unnecessary movement as she poured tea into half a dozen cups. Nilima helped by portioning out chips and biscuits onto small plates.

They carried out trays to the living room. When Veena didn't reappear even after tea was over, Shwetha, Nilima and the Sampaths said their goodbyes to her father.

After they dropped the Sampaths back home—'no need, madam,' Sampath kept saying all the way to the car, and then 'so nice, so nice of you'—and refused offers of lunch by saying they had a meeting, they went to a Malayali restaurant. Nilima eagerly tore pieces off her appam and used them to spoon up beef fry and chicken stew, while Shwetha languidly speared the smallest piece of beef with her fork and nibbled on it.

'We didn't get much at the Desais' home,' said Shwetha.

'Well, we couldn't really have questioned anyone. It was odd enough for us to be there as it was. At least we know most of the principal cast of characters now. And one character whose absence was conspicuous—Dipen.'

'It's natural enough that he wasn't there. They said he and his wife had gone on directly from the crematorium to make arrangements for the rituals.'

'I'd like to talk to him. Even if he didn't do it, he could be a crucial witness. His wife too. Is it odd the other employees weren't there?'

'Maybe they'll go later, or they are being interrogated at the police station.'

A grey-moustached waiter in a uniform that was fading from red to pink came by with more appam, and Nilima asked for a Coke. 'Do you want one?' she said to Shwetha, who winced delicately and ordered tea without sugar.

'You didn't think Veena Desai was pale or anything, did you?' Nilima continued. 'Before her mother took her in to lie down?'

'I couldn't tell; she was carefully made up.'

'That's what I thought. It's a lovely bathroom though. Bathtub and everything.'

Shwetha had got used to Nilima's non sequiturs and didn't blink. 'Yeah, I'd expect that, looking at the rest of the flat.

Brocade sofa, big chandelier ... Jagat's taste in interior decor was rather opulent.'

'Does that mean business is booming?' Nilima frowned at her memory of empty aisles at the bookshop and a quiet only leavened with soft music.

'It's not a new flat. You heard Sampath—he inherited it from his parents and decorated it soon after. All we can tell for sure is they're not doing badly enough to sell it.'

'What're you scribbling?' Shwetha asked when Nilima pulled out a tattered little notebook and started writing vigorously.

'Just noting down who was there. Might be useful later.'

'I can't believe you carry a notebook in your pocket instead of using your phone like the rest of us in the Year of Their Lord twenty-nineteen.' Then, 'Did you get anything out of the woman who works there? You were talking to her inside, weren't you? Was she at home while Mrs Desai was away?'

'Lotika? She doesn't stay there at night. She works all day and goes home after cooking dinner. She seems devoted to Mrs Desai. Didn't think much of Jagat.'

'Did she actually say that?'

'Not in so many words, but it was obvious. Apparently, Veena is a kind employer and is putting Lotika's daughter through private school—without Jagat Desai's knowledge. He doesn't—didn't—spend a lot of time at home, and he seemed to have treated Lotika with some contempt. She says she stayed for Veena madam, not for him.'

'Jagat doesn't seem like a nice man, does he?'

Nilima pushed her plate away, leaned back and lit a cigarette with a flourish. 'Let me tell you something, boss. Nice men don't get murdered.'

Shwetha suppressed a smile at this impression of a noir detective and peered at Nilima's notebook. 'What else did we find out today?'

Nilima tapped her pen against the notebook for emphasis. 'That the post-mortem was done last night or early this morning.'

'How do we know that?' Shwetha thought for a second and answered her own question. 'I know. He was cremated this morning. They'd just got back from the crematorium when we got there.'

'That's right. The police released his body this morning—that's what Veena's dad said. They must have done a post-mortem, right?'

'Let me check the news.' Shwetha pulled up news reports on her phone while Nilima asked for the bill. 'There was a post-mortem but there's hardly any info. Just that he was stabbed in the neck, which we already know. We should talk to Inspector Lamani.'

'I don't think I want to face her again.'

'Fine. You go home and see what you can dig up online about Jagat. I'll go talk to Sharmila, see if I can get anything out of her.'

'What are you going to say? You'll need an excuse to meet her.'

'I'll just thank her for going easy on my friend Maniram.' Shwetha opened her eyes wide and used her sweetest voice. 'I called him this morning; he said they let him go after a few hours of questioning. And I'll talk about how shocked we all are and that it'll affect business and can we expect results from the enquiry soon?'

Nilima gaped in admiration. 'You've got balls.'

'Oh no, darling. I've got something much better.' Shwetha adjusted her gauzy white dupatta over her chest as she got up.

✍

Instead of going home, Nilima went to the office to use the computer. As she unlocked the door, she felt a little thrill at having been entrusted with a key, and at using it on a day off when neither Shwetha nor Poorna had come in.

She conscientiously did her Chikkamma work first, making up for the lost hours yesterday. She reviewed and updated ads, responded to messages, wrote out the newsletter she had started, in which she highlighted one cool place to visit in the city every month, and sent it to Shwetha to review.

She opened another file, typing up her notes from the morning. Her mind kept drifting to Shwetha, who had looked a vision today in her white clothes, a white bra edged with pink flowers visible through the thin cotton whenever her dupatta slipped. Nilima had stopped herself from staring with some difficulty.

She blinked and moved on to looking up everyone connected with the case, glancing at her phone every few minutes until it pinged with texts from Shwetha.

No luck with Sharmila

Waited 3 hrs and she got rid of me in 5 mins

> Turned up late for my Church Street tour ugh
>
> I should not have let that agent talk me into doing a tour on a Tuesday I'm so tired
>
> Otoh it was packed—fourteen people!
>
> Omw home will write up tour notes and email tonight

Nilima typed out a response and then opened Instagram. Something on the screen made her eyes widen in surprise, and she zoomed in on a photo. She opened WhatsApp again and typed furiously.

By the time she had emailed her report of the case to Shwetha and locked the office door behind her, it was nearly ten. Around this time two nights ago, Jagat had been alone in the bookshop, waiting as death walked inexorably closer. A faint light emanated from the stairwell. The shop was closed; why was a light on? She kept her phone in her hand, thumb near the icon to dial Shwetha, and walked up. The light on the first-floor landing was off, the shutter down, the padlock secured. She crept further up, softly, almost reluctantly. A figure was haloed in the overhead light on the second floor, and her heart skipped a beat. Then she realised it was a constable on duty, stretching his arms desultorily. He saw her and instantly assumed a more attentive position.

'I'm Nilima,' she said quickly. 'I work downstairs in the tour agency. I'm so glad you're here, Hawaldar, sir.' She squinted at his name tag.

'Constable Reddy,' he introduced himself. She hadn't seen him before.

'I was working alone today and was a bit scared. It's such a relief to know that you are here, Constable. What if the murderer comes back?'

'He won't come back, madam,' Reddy said with conviction. 'And I'm here for your protection.'

'Thank you, sir, that makes me feel much safer. Do you know who killed him?' The policeman looked suspicious, so she added, 'I found the body yesterday morning. It was such a shock.'

'Oh. That's very shocking, madam. No, we have not found him yet, but rest assured, the criminal will be apprehended.'

'I have full confidence in you, Reddy sir.' Nilima tried to imitate Shwetha's wide-eyed flattery. 'We're very worried; what if the murderer comes to our office next? With the bookstore closed, we are the only people in the building. Have you found the knife he stabbed the victim with, or does the murderer still have it?'

'We didn't find a knife,' he admitted. 'No murder weapon in evidence.'

'So the murderer took it with him? Was Desai meeting someone, do you know?'

'Can't say, madam,' he said firmly.

'You don't know,' Nilima said sympathetically.

'No, madam,' he agreed. 'Everyone says he was meeting someone. No one knows who. It's a mystery.'

His phone rang, and he answered at once with a sharp 'Yes, Inspector madam!' Nilima's chest constricted: Sharmila finding out that Nilima was interrogating one of her constables would not help. She waved at Reddy and beat a hasty retreat.

CHAPTER 4

A Sharp Instrument

It was a few minutes to ten when Nilima arrived at the café in Kalyan Nagar for her meeting with Mehnaz. The café was empty except for a petite young worker in a ponytail and a yellow checked apron. Metal chairs painted in cheerful reds and yellows sat around tables covered in yellow checked tablecloths, and white bookshelves lined one wall. Nilima was selecting a book to read while she waited when she heard the door open behind her. Mehnaz stood on the threshold in a purple midi dress that highlighted the hot pink streaks in her hair. Several silver earrings glinted against her angular face. On her left arm, a tattoo of a vine wound from her elbow down to her wrist.

'Hello,' Nilima said. 'Thanks for meeting me.'

'Happy to have an excuse to get out of the house.' Mehnaz said, her voice deep and musical.

Nilima guided her to a table by the window. In their Facebook conversation last night, Mehnaz had seemed wary, and Nilima was nervous.

The server walked over, and they ordered coffee and breakfast—scrambled eggs with bacon for Nilima, a grilled cheese sandwich for Mehnaz. As Mehnaz was placing her order, Nilima pulled her phone out under the table and pressed the red button on the audio recording app.

'I'm sorry about Jagat Desai,' Nilima said after the server had walked away.

Mehnaz pursed her mouth. 'It's so surreal, you know?'

Before Nilima could ask a question, Mehnaz spoke again. 'I heard you found the body?'

'Yes.' To Nilima's relief, the server came just then to place knives and forks on the table. Nilima knew she should play up her discovery of the body, cater to Mehnaz's obvious curiosity. But she couldn't. She didn't want to picture the bloody scene again; she had just about managed to get the image out of her mind after obsessing over it all night.

'The police must have questioned you,' Nilima said instead when they were alone again.

'The police,' Mehnaz snorted. 'Yeah, they acted as if Sampath sir or I had stabbed Desai in the neck. How absurd!'

'They interrogated my cousin Maniram too.' Nilima had called Maniram last night and got his blessing on their new kinship. 'I'm so afraid the police might pin it on him. Like I told you, I'm trying to find out anything that might help him.'

Mehnaz did not question this story. 'I don't know anything,' she said regretfully. 'I can't imagine who would have done this to Jagat.'

'What was he like to work with?'

'Ugh,' she said, placing her elbows on the table and her head on her palms. 'Bosses, you know?'

Nilima nodded in sympathy and thought, with a twinge, of Shwetha.

'He used to yell at the others if they made mistakes—Sampath sir got it a lot, and Pallav too. Pallav's the other guy who used to work there. Jagat fired him over some silly thing—I don't know what, I was downstairs when it happened, Sampath sir told me later.'

'Can you think of anyone who'd want Jagat dead?'

'Naah. I mean, if you went around knocking off bad bosses, there'd be a lot more murders.'

'Or who he might have met that late at night?'

'No idea. I was at a party in Indiranagar. One of my friends was getting engaged. I was there till two in the morning.'

'Oh wow, how did you get home?'

'Uber, what else? As usual, the first few cabs cancelled, then finally this one came. Good thing too, because I was able to show the police on the app that I wasn't anywhere near the office.'

'What's it like to work there? It seems nice and quiet.'

'Yeah, I love that. I can study. I'm working on my library degree, and I have a book open on my lap when there aren't many customers. I've seen you though. You come often.'

'Every couple of days,' Nilima admitted. 'Sometimes if I've been talking to a difficult client or something, I'll go up and spend half an hour reading a book I can't afford.'

'That's what libraries are for,' Mehnaz said. 'We need more of them.'

Nilima agreed fervently, and the two of them spent a few minutes exchanging memories of their favourite libraries. The food arrived. Nilima's eggs were rubbery and the bacon chewy, but Mehnaz closed her eyes in pleasure as she chewed on her sandwich.

After a sip of black coffee, Nilima asked, 'So there was nothing different about Jagdip lately? Nothing difficult or surprising or unusual?'

'No, except the missing things. But that's not new.'

'What missing things?'

'Didn't Maniram tell you? Things go missing from the store.'

'Missing? You mean stolen?'

'No idea. We would usually find out while doing inventory. Small things. Parker pens. An Uno deck. Books. Money, Jagat thought. Just a little here and there. Some days the cash total didn't add up.'

'What did Jagat say to that?'

'He yelled sometimes,' Mehnaz shrugged, 'and sometimes he just laughed, like, "Oh, Sampath has kept it in the wrong drawer again."'

'Did Sampath do that?'

'I don't think so. He is very careful. It was only a couple of hundred every two or three weeks, so Jagat didn't seem bothered.'

'How long has this been going on?'

'No idea. It was happening all the time I was there—I only joined in January.'

'Oh, you've only worked there four months?'

'Yeah. This girl Saima—she was leaving because she got a better-paying job. She's the one who recommended me to Jagat. I've known her since childhood—her mother and mine are friends. She also trained me for a week before she left. I wish she'd stayed—gosh, she was so much nicer to work with than Pallav. If only Jagat had fired Pallav earlier.'

'Did Saima like working at the shop?'

'Yeah, except that she wanted more money. Also, there was a thing with Dipen.'

'What kind of thing?'

Mehnaz finished her sandwich and wiped her mouth delicately on a napkin. 'It seems he flirted with her? Saima thought it was harmless at first and even flirted back, but then he started asking her to have lunch with him and offering to drop her home at night.'

'Is that why she quit?'

'She told me it was because of the money, but who knows? Dipen's never tried anything like that with me. He was always a gentleman.'

'And the others, they were all nice to you? No one gave you grief for ...' Nilima hesitated.

'For being trans?' Mehnaz sat up. 'I don't think any of them clocked me—except Sampath sir.'

'How do you know he knew?'

'I told him,' Mehnaz chuckled. 'I didn't mean to, I was just so angry that day. Something a neighbour had said to me that morning.'

Nilima nodded and waited for Mehnaz to say more.

'Sampath sir could tell something was wrong, so when no one was around he talked to me. I ended up telling him everything.'

'How did he react?'

She smiled wryly. 'He patted my head, told me people will talk and it doesn't matter what they think. That I am a good girl and should just focus on my job and my studies. It wasn't helpful, exactly, but ...'

'It was kind.'

'Yeah. And he didn't treat me any differently after, you know? If anything, he was nicer to me.'

They were quiet as the server came back to clear the table, and Nilima asked for the bill. As soon as they were alone again, Mehnaz asked, 'How did you know? About me?'

'I noticed that your social media presence is only a year old, even though you've been very active since. I looked through your friends' old photos, and I found someone who looked like you but the caption mentioned a different name. So I wondered. And now, after meeting you properly, I was almost sure. You see, my best friend, Preeti, she's trans too.'

'Whoa, that's a lot of work! Proper detective, you are. That's what you're doing, right? You want to try being a detective and solve the murder? Don't lie, I know you go straight to the crime section in the bookshop.'

'You're right,' Nilima said, her face screwed up in a mixture of pride and embarrassment.

'Promise you'll tell me as soon as you find out who the murderer is. I bet you'll find them before the police does. I should be able to guess who did it, right? But I have no idea.

I've been thinking, but I can't really imagine anyone at the shop doing it, even Pallav—he's annoying, not violent. I wish I had gone to work somewhere else; all this is so stressful. But it's not like I had a lot of options. My parents paid for my treatment and all, and my college fees, but they don't have much money, so when Zarina Aunty said her daughter was quitting her job ... And I'd already started my librarian course, so the interview was pretty easy.'

'What about your paperwork, though? Didn't Jagat ask for documents?'

'Naah, all he asked for was my PAN card. You don't need a college degree to work at a shop now, do you?'

Nilima grinned and thanked Mehnaz, and refused her offer to pay her share of the bill. 'You've been so helpful already.'

'Eh, I was bored at home. All my friends are at work during the day, and they don't get it—they're concerned for me, but they don't know what it's like to have your boss murdered and then to have to go to the police station and be questioned by the police. But you understand. You found the body, the police talked to you too ... It's nice to be able to talk about it.'

Nilima said bye and walked out, and Mehnaz pulled a big textbook from her sequinned pink backpack and settled more comfortably into her chair.

CHAPTER 5

Madam, Will You Leave?

It was past noon when Nilima entered the office, so she was taken aback when Shwetha smiled warmly at her. Shwetha was dressed appropriately for the peak of summer in a short cream-coloured dress with intricate embroidery on the bodice. Her hair was piled on top of her head in a messy bun.

'Thanks for the murder report,' Shwetha said. 'You've captured everything really well.'

Nilima's cheeks burned. Luckily, Shwetha was looking at her laptop again.

'I want to talk about this list of suspects,' Shwetha said. 'Mrs Desai, she inherits his property, and she may have other more personal reasons for wanting to get rid of her husband—but wasn't she in Gujarat when it happened?'

'I thought it was possible she had someone else do it?'

'Ooh, you mean she ordered a hit? Like hired a supari killer? Or maybe she was having an affair and her lover killed him?'

'I did consider both of those possibilities,' Nilima admitted. 'They're a bit melodramatic, though.'

'Nonsense. We keep her in, then. What about the kids?'

'What about them?'

'Shouldn't we have the kids in the list too? They might have hated their father and wanted him out of the way.'

'Shwetha, they are eleven and eight.'

'So what? Do you remember being that age? I'd have tried to off my dad if I'd thought of it.'

'But you didn't think of it, did you?'

'We didn't have the internet back then! You don't know what kids these days get up to. There was that Blue Whale challenge that was all the rage a few years ago.'

It took Nilima a second to realise what Shwetha was referring to. 'I think cyberbullying and self-harm are a little different from outright bloody murder. Pun intended.'

'Fine, we won't put the kids in the list for now. But you've got to keep an open mind about this!'

Nilima giggled and sat down. Shwetha flashed a smile—absent-mindedly, as if she didn't see the joke—and turned back to her screen. 'I see you've noted we need to find out if Jagat left a will.'

'Yes, I'm wondering how much he was worth. And did he leave it all to his wife or does Dipen get anything?'

'Hmm. And if Dipen has a financial motive, his wife would too.'

'Exactly,' Nilima said.

'And you've got Sampath.'

'I know he seems like a good man, but we don't know him that well. What if he has violent tendencies? Jagat treated him like shit—maybe he snapped.'

'And that goes for the others as well—Maniram and Pallav. Mehnaz isn't on your list?'

'I spoke to her this morning, but I found nothing suspicious. She left early; it's unlikely Jagat would have told Sampath to leave if he had a meeting with her. I mean, she might have known he'd be there alone and come back and laid in wait for him and killed him when he stepped out of the door, but that's a bit far-fetched.'

Nilima trailed off and stared into space.

'What's up, Nilima?'

'The door.'

'What?'

'It was locked, right? Do you remember? The padlock was on?'

'Yeah, it was locked. Why?'

'I was just wondering. If Jagat was killed by the person he had a meeting with, why was he killed outside the door? If the body was inside ...'

'You wouldn't have found it.'

'It would have stayed undiscovered longer, maybe even by a whole day, since his family wasn't home and may not have raised the alarm.'

'Who'd have been suspected, but?'

'Whoever Jagat had a meeting with,' said Nilima thoughtfully. 'Or the store employees. Someone who had a key.'

'So, either he was killed by the person he was meeting or by one of the store employees who wanted to make it seem like it was a stranger, or he was actually killed by someone not connected with the store. That doesn't help us at all—we can't rule out anyone.'

'Welcome to detective work, Shetty.'

'Don't be a smartass, Deka, I'm still your boss. Let's see, who else? J. Mohan is the accountant?'

'Yes, I've got his address. You're to go interview him.'

'Did you hear what I just said about being the boss?'

'You're better at it, boss. You're more charming.'

'Fine, I'll do it.' Shwetha moved on to the next item on the list and said, in her best Poirot impression, 'And we have an X, for person or persons unknown.'

'Whoever Jagat was meeting, if it isn't Mohan.'

'You'd said you were going to look up everyone online?'

'I did. I went through all their social media profiles. Everyone seems pretty normal—or good at hiding their shit. Sampath comments on pictures of his grandchildren on Facebook, Mehnaz puts up makeup videos on Instagram, that kind of thing.'

'But you found something. You look like you've got a secret stash of chocolate.'

'I always have a stash of chocolate. It's in my drawer; you're welcome to help yourself to it. But you're right. I found Pallav. Through Mehnaz's Facebook. She's friended everyone—Sampath, Jagat, Dipen.'

'You're sure it's the right Pallav?'

'He's got photos up. I've seen him at the bookstore: it's the same guy. I messaged him and asked if we could talk.'

'And?'

'I'm meeting him at Toit later today.'

'Fancy.'

'I'd suggested Pecos, but he only drinks craft beer.'

'Sounds like a wanker.'

'I think he's hoping to get a few free drinks. But we need him, so I agreed.'

'You don't have an expense account, remember?'

Nilima stuck her tongue out at her boss.

'Be careful. And call if you need me.' Shwetha briefly touched Nilima's arm. 'By the way, did Mehnaz say anything useful?'

Nilima summarised the conversation, leaving out the revelation at the end. The details of Mehnaz's gender seemed irrelevant to the murder. 'Looks like Dipen is a bit of a sleaze,' she ended.

'I don't think we can say that based on what Mehnaz said. Seems very sketchy.'

'That's why I want to talk to Saima and find out what really happened.'

'Let me. I can talk to her.'

'You were just objecting to my asking you to talk to Mohan,' Nilima pointed out.

'Well, yeah, Mohan sounds boring. Let me talk to Saima too. I need to make up for my absolute failure with Inspector Sharmila yesterday. She gave me that piercing glare and said nothing.'

'She didn't succumb to *your* charm?'

Shwetha pouted, and Nilima felt a pinprick of disappointment that had nothing to do with the murder. 'No. I tried my best Vidya Balan impression too.'

'You're adorable.'

'This is serious! It'll be hard to do this if Sharmila doesn't talk to us.'

Nilima had been waiting for this opening. 'Don't worry, she'll talk to me.'

'What? Are you joking?'

'Not at all. In fact, I talked to her first thing this morning, and she agreed to answer our questions if we tell her everything we find out.'

'Why would she do that?'

'Because someone important asked her.'

'Who? Her boss? I was wondering if we could get to her that way. The father of one of my college friends is an Assistant Superintendent of Police; I was saving him for when we really need help. Who did you ask, the DSP?'

'Nope. Her girlfriend.'

'Sharmila has a girlfriend? But why would her girlfriend ask her to help us?'

Nilima looked sheepish. 'Because she's my friend.'

'Yeah? I'm sensing there's more to the story here.'

'She's also my ex.'

'You used to date the inspector's girlfriend? Wow.'

'Why are you so surprised?'

'That you're such good friends with your ex that she'll do this for you? That's pretty cool.'

'I'm a good girlfriend,' Nilima said smugly.

'I don't doubt it.'

Shwetha's warm smile made something flutter in Nilima's stomach. She wanted to say something that would extend this line of conversation, something that would further demonstrate her desirability as a romantic partner. What came out was, 'When I was doing all that research last night, I opened my Instagram after a long time. That's when I saw my ex had a photo up of Sharmila and her.'

'I thought you'd only moved to Bangalore last year.'

'That's right. Hafeeza and I met over a decade ago, in Guwahati. She's a few years older. We went to the same college, and then we were roommates. We broke up because she was moving to Bangalore for her postgrad studies.'

'And you followed her here?'

Nilima laughed. 'No, I'm not a stalker, Shetty. That was a coincidence. We've remained in touch over the years, and we've met only once since I moved here. I knew she was involved with someone, but she didn't tell me much about her. When I saw the Instagram post, I texted Hafeeza to ask how she knew the inspector, and she told me they've been living together for a year.'

'You kept this really close to your chest, didn't you?'

'I just found out last night. Boss, don't tell anyone, okay? Feeza said I could tell you, all *her* friends know, but Sharmila is not out at work.'

'Of course, Nili. Can I ask ... are you? Out in general, I mean?'

Nilima grinned. 'I've been out for a decade, Shetty. I would hate to be mistaken for straight. So go ahead, tell all of Bangalore and save me the trouble.'

'All right. Tell me more, what happened? What else did Hafeeza say?'

'Oh, I asked her for help, and she said she'd make sure Sharmila called me in the morning, and she did; she called me at fucking eight.'

'What did she say? Have they found the murder weapon?'

'No, they're baffled. It's a very thin stab wound—straight in some big vein or something. He bled out and died. But there was no weapon anywhere in the building.'

'Ah, that's what they were looking for when they searched our office.'

'Exactly. She also said he died sometime between nine and one that night. That's what the doctor said.'

'That aligns with what we thought. Anything else?'

'Well, it looks like he didn't see it coming. He didn't have any other wounds—nothing to indicate he fought back.'

'That means it wasn't someone he thought of as an enemy.'

'I mean, I don't know if I have enemies, but even if I did, I don't think I'd expect one of them to stab me in the throat. I would probably freeze and go down without a fight.'

'I wouldn't. Anyone who tries to stab me is not getting away without a few scratches. Did Sharmila want to know why we're interested?'

'Feeza told her I'm really into mysteries. When we were dating, I used to spend hours in bookstores reading Agatha Christies and Patricia Highsmiths.'

'And Sharmila wasn't annoyed at us for interfering?'

'She was her regular unbending self at first. I reminded her about our friendships with Maniram and Sampath, and that we're right here on the premises, and she agreed it couldn't hurt for us to work together on the case.'

'Awesome!' Shwetha actually clapped her hands together. 'Good work, Deka!'

Nilima was still smiling when she went to her desk. The smile stayed on through much of the workday, especially as Poorna didn't make an appearance; she was out conducting a full-day tour. Nilima did her work, made notes on her conversations with Mehnaz and Sharmila and listened with half an ear to Shwetha charming prospective clients on the phone.

Her smile faded when she met Pallav that afternoon. He was in his late twenties, well-built, clean-shaven, with hair falling over his forehead in a careful wave. His voice was a little too loud, his smile a little too eager. His hands—large, smooth and manicured—not like Nilima's with bitten nails—flitted about the table and often got too close to her, once touching her arm and once her palm. She pulled her hand back with distaste.

Nilima disapproved of how fast he drank, especially since she was paying the bill; his large mug of beer was over before she'd had half her whiskey sour, and he waved at the waiter for a refill. She downed a glass of water and continued to sip slowly from her drink, even though she suspected she could have tolerated Pallav's presence better if she had gulped it down. She picked up another handful of fries. She hadn't eaten anything since her breakfast with Mehnaz, and she tried not to sniff in the aroma of a burger from the next table. Even at three in the afternoon, it was full of people, men in pale shirts mostly talking loudly in groups, though there were one or two typing away industriously at their laptops between sips of beer.

She tugged at her Florence and the Machine T-shirt and focused on what Pallav was saying. He had worked at Jagdip for eight months: 'a long time for anyone to work there,' he smirked, 'except for that old turtle Sampath.'

'You don't like him?'

'He's so slow. He looks like a turtle too, right? With his round body and his big head, always poking into other people's business.'

'Did he poke into yours?'

'He was always asking questions. About work, even though he wasn't my boss—what time did I leave last night, did I remember to put in bookmarks in each bag, did I order more stock ... Also, he asked personal questions. Who did I call on my lunch break, why did I leave my last job, what was I going to do on my day off? He is too meddlesome.'

'You don't think he was just being polite?' Against her will, Nilima felt a twinge of sympathy with Pallav.

'Naah, the old man had to know everything,' Pallav chuckled. 'And yet, he never knew anything important that was happening.'

'What do you mean?'

'He kept talking about the old times, right? About his old boss Samudra Desai, who was this brilliant guy? The two Sams, I once called them in front of Sampath. He didn't appreciate it. And he was practically dripping with contempt for Jagat Desai, for not being his father. But hey, Jagat was the boss, right? How do you think he felt about Sampath's lack of loyalty?'

'I suppose he resented it,' Nilima said, while thinking Sampath would probably feel his loyalty belonged to the long-dead boss he had idolised.

'You bet. If you ask me, Jagat only kept Sampath on because he was willing to work for little money. The old man hadn't got a raise in five years. And where would he go for another job anyway, at his age?'

'What about you? Did Jagat like you? Value you as an employee?'

'Oh, yeah.' Pallav's smile did not flicker. 'When I told him I was leaving, he offered me a raise, tried to get me to stay. But I had made up my mind.'

'Why did you decide to leave?'

'I was bored. Why sit around those musty old books all day? We have Netflix now, no one reads. It's a dying industry.'

'You mean Jagdip Book House wasn't doing well financially? Did Jagat say that?'

'No, no one told me; it was obvious. We weren't selling enough. Jagat was always looking worried. He tried to blame us for it, said we weren't nice enough to customers. Bullshit! We didn't have enough footfalls. When people did come, we either didn't have the right books or we weren't offering enough discounts. You know what most customers do, right? They come in and look at a book and then take out their phone and buy it on Amazon. We can't compete with those kinds of discounts—we weren't even trying. I gave Jagat some ideas based on what I'm learning at business school—I am doing my BBA part-time—but does he listen?'

'No?' Nilima guessed obligingly.

'No. Why, there were things stolen all the time, and we didn't know how it happened.'

'What was stolen?'

'Nothing important. A few books, a little money, things like pens or keychains sometimes ... maybe college kids shoplifting. We didn't have a modern security system, just that one untrained guard at the door. That's what I told Jagat when he ...'

'When he what?'

'Nothing. When we were discussing the thefts, I meant.'

'Did he suspect you?'

'Did Sampath tell you that?'

'He didn't. But is it true?'

Pallav deflated. He said sullenly, 'Jagat called me into his office. He said he would forgive me if I returned the money. The other stuff was minor, he said, but this was getting too much.'

'How much money?'

'Some six hundred rupees was missing one day. No one even knew for sure it was stolen, really, one of us might have made a mistake in billing. It happened often enough.'

'Jagat accused you?'

'I didn't do it. I wouldn't take a few hundred rupees!'

'Why did he suspect you?'

'Because he saw me coming out of the office. The cash was in his drawer. Every evening he or Sampath, or sometimes Dipen, would count the cash and lock it up there, and every couple of days one of them would take it to the bank. Except for what was needed for expenses. Oh, and Dipen.'

'What about him?'

'He also took money sometimes. Just took it out of the drawer. I heard Jagat yell at him about it once.'

'But this time he suspected you.'

'Dipen hadn't been in the office that day, so it couldn't have been him. And Dipen doesn't steal. He takes the money openly. He thinks it's his money too, so he helps himself whenever he wants.'

'Doesn't he get a salary?'

'Of course he does. Why else would he work there? But he is the owner's brother—the store carries his name. I wonder if he owns the business now—do you know?'

'No, I wish I did,' Nilima said. 'Why had you gone into Jagat's office?'

Pallav looked like he was going to refuse to say more, but then he kept talking. 'I wanted to know more about Jagat's other business. The property business, right? I figured that was more lucrative, and I wanted to get in on that. Maybe work for him. I wanted to get out of the books business anyway.'

'Did you tell him that?'

'I tried to. He kept yelling at me and didn't listen. So I left.'

'That must have been frustrating.'

'It made me very angry. I yelled back at him and walked out of the office. And then I realised that I was free. I didn't have to come back to work the next day; I never have to touch a book again.' Like a light switched on, his face again exuded delight in himself.

'And you don't need a job?'

'I've already got another job—I start tomorrow. It's a home fabrics store in a mall, just off Whitefield, much closer to my place. Classy store, expensive curtains and so on.'

'I'm happy for you,' Nilima said evenly. 'Tell me more about Jagat. He was a good boss, then?'

'Yeah. He worked as hard as any of us. In spite of his other business, he was at the store every day.'

'What do you know about this other business?'

'Not much. That's why I was trying to find out. Sometimes people came and sat in his office with him. That's about all I know.'

'How often was that?'

'I don't know, once or twice a month?'

'Who were these people?'

'I don't know for sure, but I assumed they were business associates.'

Nilima didn't bother trying to keep the scepticism off her face. Instead of annoying Pallav, it made him want to convince her. He leaned forward. 'I've been to his house, and he can't have bought that just by selling books, right?'

'When did you go Jagat's flat?'

'He took us all, on New Year's. We were all working on 31 December; he didn't let any of us take the day off. That night, we closed up early and went to his place for dinner.'

'Who's "we", apart from you and Sampath?'

'There was another guy, Vivek, who was working part-time. He left soon after, and then Saima left, so they hired Mehnaz. Saima didn't come with us though, she went home. Dipen was there—he too had worked all day with us. He'd been married for just a few weeks then. His wife came to the party too.'

'What was Dipen like to work with?'

'He was cool. Friendly. I've visited his place a few times.' A twinge of pride showed in his habitual smirk.

'He invited you home?'

'Yeah, me and Vivek. Not Sampath; Sampath always went straight home to his wife after work, if he wasn't drinking at Kamath's—the bar nearby, you know it?'

Nilima nodded.

'I used to joke that Kamath is Sampath's brother, that's why he felt so much at home there—they have similar names, right?' Nilima's face was stony, and he continued, 'On nights when we worked late setting up fresh stock or something, Dipen sometimes invited us home for dinner. It was usually Sunday nights, because we could stay up late and not worry about getting up for work the next morning. This was before he was married, you understand, or when his wife was away.'

'Of course.'

'There was always booze at his house, and we'd all drink and eat pizza and play darts or watch a movie or something.'

'Very fraternal.' She had a sudden thought. 'How did you get there—did he drive you?'

'Naah, he lives in Jayanagar only. Walking distance from the store. It's called Aquamarine Haven—lovely light blue building. And inside as well—it's smaller than Jagat's but more modern. But you didn't say why you are so interested in all of this.'

Nilima gave him the same cover story she had offered Mehnaz. 'Maniram—the security guard at the store—he's my cousin. My aunt is very worried about him after what happened to Jagat. So I said I'll find out what's going on, just make sure it's not a shady place. I've always looked out for Maniram.'

'Ah, you're his big sister. I get it. No, it wasn't a bad place. What happened to Jagat sir, I don't think it had anything to do with the store. It was a real estate rival who killed him, believe me.'

'Why do you think so?'

'I told you, right, the store isn't making much money. Where's the motive? Now, real estate, that's big stakes. Just last year, I heard about this old lady who owned a house in Marathahalli, one of those big old bungalows. She wouldn't sell it, even though all the other houses on the street were brought down and big buildings went up. Then, one day, she was run over by a car. Instant death. Soon after, her daughter came back from America and sold it, and now they're razing it and building a commercial complex there.'

'Did Jagat have land he was refusing to sell?'

'Not that I know of ... But he was involved in real estate, right? Someone could have wanted him out of the way.'

'It's a good idea,' Nilima said maliciously. 'You must be sure to tell it to the police.' She enjoyed the discomfort on Pallav's face.

Nilima stopped her autorickshaw and bought cigarettes at the stall next to Kamath's Bar, its red neon sign already lit—except the bulb in the 'T', which had long blown its fuse. Snatches of a Kannada film song wafted out through the bar's open windows, mixed with stray masculine laughs and shouts.

She walked on. The fading russet light veiled the office building and made its dinginess charming. Nilima added up everything she had spent today at her two interviews and on autorickshaw rides, and came to a total of three thousand and one hundred rupees. Remembering Shwetha's jibe this morning about not having an expense account, she glared at her boss's car (twenty years old and difficult to maintain, yet to Nilima an unattainable luxury) standing alone in the car park. Her envy expanded to include Shwetha's nice big flat (or so Nilima imagined—she hadn't seen it) and to her parents who had the deep pockets and the large hearts to support their daughter's change in career.

'Hi!' Shwetha shut her laptop. 'How did it go with Pallav?'

'He's awful,' groaned Nilima. 'He said a few interesting things, though. I just don't know how much we can trust his version of events.' She recapped the conversation.

'This real estate thing may be worth looking into,' she added at the end. 'Did you find out anything from Mohan?'

'No, he was quite cagey. Which isn't surprising—why the hell should he tell me about his client's business?'

'Did you tell him why you wanted to know?'

'Of course. I told him I just started my business last year, and I need an accountant, and Jagat had recommended him before he, umm, got killed. He asked about Chikkamma and what kind of accounting help we need. I kept bringing the subject around to Jagat. Nothing doing, but. He just gave vague answers. He even refused to answer when I asked if it was true he'd met Jagat the night he died. Just looked at me strangely and asked why I was saying that. Seemed a little threatening even. Like that's going to scare me off.'

'What did you say?'

'I said I'd heard someone mention it. Then I asked him about his fees and said I'd get back to him and left.'

'I don't know, Shwetha, I think Inspector Lamani is going to have to figure out this bit. It's above our pay grade.'

'Yeah, why don't you give her a call? Maybe the police have found out something we haven't.'

'In the morning.' Nilima had already talked to Sharmila once today; she didn't want to wear out her welcome. Instead, she made notes of her meeting with Pallav. It was only a little past seven and Shwetha was working, so she stifled her yawns and tried to look alert. She replied to work emails and Facebook messages with a polite and enthusiastic tone that only came naturally when she was typing. Her conscience assuaged, she looked online for any news about the murder. Engrossed in her computer screen, she didn't notice her surroundings get quieter as the shop overhead and the lane outside emptied of people.

A knock on the door made Nilima jump. At the other end of the room, Shwetha had gone pale. The clock on Nilima's computer said 21.53. Who could it be this late? She thought again of Jagat, murdered around this time, just two floors above their heads.

Shwetha held up a finger to her lips and stepped softly towards the door. Nilima brought up Inspector Lamani's number on her phone.

Shwetha pulled the door open, her body sagging in relief. Nilima heard his voice before Shwetha moved aside to reveal Sampath: 'Hello, madam, you are still here? Oh, Nilima madam is also here. Is everything all right?'

'Of course,' said Shwetha. 'Why wouldn't it be?'

Sampath had already walked in, but Shwetha continued to stand by the door. Sampath twisted his body with the grace of a dancer to alternately look at both of them. 'It's so late. You girls should be at home. Why are you here?'

'We're working,' said Shwetha, and Nilima recognised the measured tone that meant she was angry.

Sampath obliviously carried on, 'It's so late, you should go home. Work isn't so important. And you're young girls. There's a murderer on the loose!'

'No young girls have been murdered,' Nilima pointed out, and was rewarded by a spark of amusement in Shwetha's eyes.

'Yes-yes, but why risk it? What if he's about?'

'Do you think he comes back every night to see who he can murder?' Nilima asked mildly.

'Who knows? Anything is possible. These are bad times.'

'They are indeed,' Nilima said solemnly.

'Kalyug,' put in Shwetha, getting into the spirit of things.

'Yes-yes, madam, yes. How can I help? Can I drop you girls home?'

'In what?' Shwetha asked bluntly.

'I can get an autorickshaw,' Sampath said without taking offence, 'or call an Ola. I have the app on my phone, though I haven't used it—my son installed it for me. Maybe one of you ladies could help?'

'Thank you, Sampath sir,' Nilima hastened to respond first. 'We'll be okay. We'll finish our work in a few minutes and leave together.'

'You should go home,' Shwetha added. 'You have a long way to go. Your wife might worry.'

'Yes-yes, she worries too much, but what about you—'

'We'll be careful,' Nilima cut him short.

'All right, all right, you're smart-smart girls,' Sampath said, shuffling to the door. 'Please go home soon. Everyone else has left. Dipen sir just locked up and walked home. I had left too and then I saw through the window that your light was on and thought I'd come back in and check.'

'We appreciate your concern; goodnight!' Shwetha shut the door on him.

CHAPTER 6

Three-actor Comedy

Loud banging woke Nilima up. Light flooded in through the thin curtain firmly drawn across the window by her bed. The banging resolved itself into drums from the temple down the lane. Her phone flashed 7.34. She pulled the pillow over her head, but now the music was joined by loud singing on the microphone.

She groaned and sat up, deciding that she might as well go to the office. Shwetha would be surprised at her showing up early. 'As long as she doesn't get used to it,' Nilima muttered to herself.

On her kilometre-long walk to the metro station, she hopefully asked every autorickshaw driver without a passenger, 'Halasuru Metro?' They all shook their heads.

It was early enough that the metro wasn't crowded; Nilima could stand against a pole and not be pressed in by bodies. The sun was still mild, and the walk from Jayanagar Station was pleasant. The pretty bungalows, elegant apartment buildings and green neighbourhood parks all looked like they'd got a fresh coat of paint, every leaf polished to a shine. But the footpaths were narrow and often taken over by trees or open gates or vehicles. *I didn't sign up for a fucking obstacle course,* she thought as she stepped off the footpath yet again to skirt past a parked car.

Her phone rang. She bit her lip nervously as she dug it out of her pocket; sure enough, it was Inspector Lamani. She answered the call while looking around for a place to sit and talk. If the inspector had just waited a few minutes longer, Nilima would have been in the office.

'Hello. Inspector Sharmila Lamani speaking.'

'Yes, ma'am,' Nilima said as sunnily as she could manage. 'I was just about to call you.' She momentarily put the phone on speaker as she pressed the record button. A young man hanging clothes in his balcony stared curiously at her. She placed the phone to her ear again as she hurried past and turned in at the next gate.

In the meantime, the inspector was saying pointedly, 'I am calling you. Have you people found out anything?'

The small rectangle of a park Nilima had entered was empty except for one person walking briskly at the far end. She sat on a bench and collected her thoughts. In response to Sharmila's impatient 'Hello? Madam?' she talked about meeting Mehnaz and Pallav and about the hints of real estate dealings. She didn't want to mention the thefts or Saima, not until she and Shwetha had investigated a little further. Instead, she mentioned what Pallav had said about the bookshop not doing well. 'I guess you're already looking into that. We thought you'd be able to check their files.'

'We are looking into it,' the inspector echoed.

'I'm sure you knew most of this already.'

'Hmm.'

'What about fingerprints? Did you find that anyone else had been in there?'

'It's a bookshop, madam.'

Nilima pictured the shop—customers walking in and about, touching books, shelves, banisters, counters and door handles. Even though it wasn't the busiest bookshop, it would be impossible to sort through the prints and find out who they belonged to.

'Not even in the office room?' she asked.

'Too many prints in there also. We are looking into any that don't belong to the employees or the owners. There are a few partial prints we haven't identified yet—but they are smudged and might be old. Even if we identify them, they might not help us.'

'What about the light switch in the landing, and the one on the first floor? Someone must have turned those off—it's got to be the murderer.'

There was a small pause. 'Good thinking, Miss Deka. Unfortunately, we didn't get a clear print, except for one of your index finger.'

Nilima determinedly broke the brief silence that followed. 'Did Jagat Desai leave a will?'

'He left everything to his wife and daughters.'

'Everything?'

'Hmm. It appears he had made his will at her parents' urging, soon after his father died. Since all he had was inherited' (*Hah*,

Nilima almost said aloud), 'his wife's parents wanted to make sure she and the children were protected. Both of the daughters get a little money when they're eighteen, and—'

'How much?' Nilima interrupted.

'It's close to ten lakh now, for each of the girls. By the time they get the money it will be much more because of the interest.'

'Of course,' Nilima said out loud, raising her eyebrows at the idea of ten lakh rupees being 'a little money'.

'Mrs Veena gets everything else, including the life insurance. All in all, about sixty lakh. And the flat, and the two cars.'

'Nothing for Dipen?'

'No.'

'And the store? It belongs to Veena now?'

'Hmm.'

'Dipen doesn't have any share in it? Then it's true he'd sold out to Jagat years ago?'

'That's correct.'

Despite the brief answers, Nilima decided to plunge in. 'You wouldn't ... you wouldn't know how Dipen took this?'

To her surprise, Sharmila responded politely. 'I understand he wasn't surprised. Jagat had informed him when he had made the will, he said. And Mrs Veena was very nice. She said she wanted him to continue managing the shop.'

'Then he wasn't upset? You've talked to him?'

'He doesn't seem to be.'

Nilima pushed her luck. 'Did you find out who Jagat was supposed to meet that night?'

'His accountant came a little after ten. He said he talked to Jagat for half an hour.'

'Mohan?'

'Correct. He thinks Jagat met someone else after him.'

'What?'

'Yes, he said Jagat seemed impatient for him to leave.'

'But he didn't actually hear Jagat say he was meeting someone else.'

'No.'

'And he didn't offer any names.'

'No.'

'So he might have said that to divert suspicion from himself.'

'Correct.'

'Or he might have misunderstood and Jagat just wanted to get home.'

'Hmm.'

'What about the alibis, Inspector?'

'What about them?'

'Umm ... did you get any?'

'We have everyone's statements. We are still verifying them.'

Nilima accepted that the squirt of information had dried up. 'Okay, Inspector. Thanks for calling me.'

'Thank you also, for informing me. I will talk to Pallav.'

'That might be a good idea. Just don't mention me, please?'

'Of course not, Miss Nilima. We wouldn't want him to know we are working together.'

The call ended, leaving Nilima staring at the fallen karnikara flowers on the ground and wondering whether she should feel insulted by that last sentence.

She fished out her earphones from her pocket, put them on and placed a call. The phone rang for so long she got up and started walking again, but then a voice answered, thick with sleep.

'Mnhghh? Nilima, did someone else die?'

'What? No!'

'Then why are you calling me so early? I thought one of your colleagues got murdered this time—maybe your sexy boss.'

'Not funny, Preeti.'

'You're losing your sense of humour. Or you're in love.'

'Don't you have to go to work?'

'Go all the way to Gurgaon in 44 degree heat? No, I've been working in bed with the AC on, thank you very much. If you were here, I could have stayed over at your place.'

Nilima stifled the urge to apologise. It was ridiculous to feel that she had abandoned her best friend; Preeti had plenty of friends in Delhi.

'Give me all the juicy deets,' Preeti said. 'Is everything okay? The police aren't harassing you, are they?'

'Not at all. In fact, I was just talking to Sharmila and ...'

'Sharmila? You're on first-name terms now?'

Briefly, and with some pride, Nilima brought Preeti up to date on recent events. But she didn't get the reaction she had hoped for.

'God, Nilu, what are you getting yourself into? Why are you like this? You know how dangerous this can be?'

'I don't ...'

'I know, you don't care.' Preeti sighed. 'I do, though. I worry about you. How much do you even know about that boss of yours?'

'Shwetha?'

'Yes, Shwetha! How do you know she had nothing to do with all this? May I remind you that you only met her two months ago?'

'She's okay. I trust her.'

'Why? *How* do you trust her?'

'Come on, P, you know she's a friend of Nikhil's.'

'She went to college with Nikhil's brother. That's not the same thing. Nikhil's lived in Delhi all his life, he barely knows her.'

'But I know her.'

'I know you think you do, but be careful, please. Don't just rush headlong into things.'

'Like I always do, you mean.'

'I didn't mean that. I'm just ...'

'Looking out for me, I know. I'll call you later, okay? I'm almost at the office now.'

Nilima's surroundings had grown seedier as she walked. No carefully tended roses in little gardens here, no Audis parked on footpaths. In fact, much of the footpath was broken, and the road was riddled with potholes, ready to trap water when the rains started.

A few puddles had already appeared in the cul-de-sac—mysteriously, given the clear skies. She was carefully stepping around a particularly large puddle when a car honked and she jumped aside. Dirty water splashed over her. She spat some out and bent to wipe her face with her T-shirt. Her pale grey skirt now had unsightly blotches.

There were more puddles on the driveway that led to the back of the office building, so she headed down the front steps and took a right before the flight of stairs straight ahead.

As she entered the empty office, Nilima eased the frown off her forehead. It didn't matter what Preeti thought; she didn't know Shwetha. And Shwetha had been so nice yesterday—maybe her approval would last, and she would continue to beam at Nilima and speak in that soft husky voice she only used when she was happy.

Nilima had just turned on her computer when she heard footsteps outside. She rushed to open the door.

Before her wasn't Shwetha but the office cleaner. Even shorter than Nilima, clad in a maroon sari and with her glossy black hair gathered into a fat bun, she looked sweet and unassuming, but Nilima retreated to her desk before her brisk volubility. She continued to talk in Kannada as she swept and mopped the floor. Nilima nodded occasionally so as to not appear rude, and thought ruefully of the *Learn Kannada in One Month!* book that had been on the shelf by her bed for the last three months.

She had just finished typing a summary of the call with the inspector when Poorna and Shwetha came in together. Nilima remembered they had had an early morning tour with a large group of tourists, and Shwetha had asked Poorna for help managing them. Nilima's mind showed her a picture of Shwetha and Poorna huddling intimately over breakfast at a café afterwards, and sharing confidences on their drive to the office. She felt like she was back in school, excluded from a group she wasn't even sure she wanted to be a part of.

The cleaner finished up in the bathroom and greeted Shwetha and Poorna warmly on her way out. Nilima walked over to Shwetha, who had dumped her handbag on her desk and was fishing her laptop out of it. 'We should talk to her,' Nilima whispered, pointing at the door.

'Anjali?' Shwetha strode to the AC and turned it off. 'What is this, Deka? Why is the AC on and the window shut?'

'It was warm. There was no breeze.'

'It's not hot enough for the AC. I cannot afford to pay to freeze your arse. You will not turn the AC on except between eleven and three on really hot days, which means only if it's over 35 degrees outside.'

'Bangalore has great weather, they said,' Nilima muttered, going back to her computer. 'It rains all the time and it's cool and breezy, they said.'

'It's May,' Poorna pointed out. 'And it rained this morning.'

'What? No, it didn't!'

'It woke me up. Around five.'

'That's not morning, that's like the middle of the night. And is that why there are puddles outside?'

'No, that's a burst pipe,' Shwetha said wearily. 'The landlord informed me this morning. He said he's talking to the water board about getting it fixed so the Desais don't have to deal with it.'

'How long will we have puddles in our yard then?'

'They're supposed to fix it in a few hours. Why were you asking about Anjali?'

Nilima didn't want to explain in front of Poorna, but Shwetha looked impatient, so she said, 'She might have noticed something. We should interview her.'

'I did. Yesterday morning, before you got in. But she didn't know anything, so I forgot to tell you I'd spoken to her.'

'Oh. She does work in the bookstore also, then? I thought she might.'

'Yeah. She comes here at 9.30 and goes there at ten, soon as the store opens. She's worked here for years, much before we moved in—I think she's always cleaned this office, regardless of who the current tenants were. She cleans the stairs and the terrace and the car park too; Jagdip pays for all that. But she doesn't work on Mondays.'

'At the bookstore, you mean?'

'No, here as well. Monday is her day off. How do you not know that?'

'She's rarely in this early,' Poorna commented without looking away from her computer screen. Nilima darted her a poisonous look.

'Did the police talk to her?'

'Questioned her for hours, she said, even though she doesn't know anything about what happened.'

'She doesn't have a key to the bookstore?'

'No, she only goes in after the store's already open. I also tried to get info out of our landlord. I pretended I was shaken by the murder and considering moving. So, of course, he wanted to talk me out of it. He told me everything he knows about Jagat and the store, to persuade me that there's nothing fishy about them and I don't have to worry.'

'And his opinions are completely unbiased,' said Nilima, and Poorna sniggered.

Nilima saw the look on Shwetha's face and added hastily, 'Did he say anything important?'

'Not really. The bookstore has been here since the building was new. The business was doing quite well till a decade ago; Amazon and Flipkart haven't been kind to it, and things haven't been the same since Papa Desai died. He said Jagat was mostly a good neighbour, but kind of stingy—didn't like to chip in for his share of any repairs. That's our landlord's excuse for not getting proper repairs done, because he doesn't want to pay for everything himself.'

'That's why our wall leaks when it rains,' Poorna said sagely.

'Not just the wall,' Shwetha sighed. 'There's a drip from the ceiling too because there's something wrong with the plumbing, and there's more pressure when it rains.'

'And if it rains too much water comes into the office from under the door,' Poorna informed Nilima. 'Last year, we came into the office one morning to two inches of water. It took hours to clean up.'

'If it's that bad,' Nilima asked, 'how do they manage upstairs? Like, how do they keep the books dry?'

'I asked Jagat once and he said they've been spending on water-proofing their roof and walls every year,' said Shwetha. 'I keep asking our landlord to do ours and he keeps putting it off. I wish we could move to a better office, but this was the cheapest place I could find in the area. If we move, we'll lose time commuting—most of our tours are within half an hour's drive from here, at least when there's less traffic.'

They shared a moment of silence over the state of their office premises, and then Poorna broke it with: 'Is our rent low, then?'

'Well, for Jayanagar. My father knows the landlord, so we got a better deal. I mean, it's a dingy little office that shares the ground floor with a car park—not many people would want this.'

'Really?' said Nilima exaggeratedly, looking around at the flaking paint and damp patches, and the old AC that whirred loudly when it was turned on. 'I'm shocked.'

Shwetha continued, 'In fact, our landlord would love to sell off this place to a developer who'd raze the building and build something else. Jagat's been resisting.'

'Jagat was attached to his father's store?' Nilima found that hard to believe.

'He thought he could get much more in a few years, it seems. The market's in a slump right now, even though rents are still up.'

'Funny how that works,' said Poorna thoughtfully.

'Did Jagat tell you that he'd be willing to sell in a few years?' Nilima asked. 'Or did that come from our landlord?'

'I hadn't spoken to Jagat about this. Our landlord said so.'

'So he may be lying. Looks to me he's got a motive for Jagat's death, if he wanted to sell and Jagat didn't.'

'Damn. I hadn't thought of that.'

'Ask your dad if he can find out about the landlord's finances. Does he need money?'

'Will do.'

Nilima hesitated, but Poorna was already in now, so she filled them in on her conversation with Sharmila.

'Interesting,' Shwetha said. 'Dipen doesn't have a motive then.'

'A financial motive, at least.' Nilima paused before asking, 'What time did you guys go home that night? Sunday, I mean? You were both here when I left.'

'Are you suspecting us of murdering Jagat?' Shwetha asked coolly.

'No.' Nilima rolled her eyes. 'I'm asking if you saw or heard anything.'

'I didn't,' Poorna said. 'I left around eight—I remember because I made it home before the family sat down to dinner, so my grandma didn't yell at me for once. And the police already asked us this, remember? I went straight home; you left a little before me and went home and were alone all night; it was the same with Shwetha.'

'I know, but I didn't note down the times,' Nilima said, grabbing her notebook. 'Humour me and tell me when you went home, boss?'

'I left soon after you guys did,' Shwetha answered, 'definitely before nine. And I didn't see any suspicious people lurking around, else I'd have mentioned it earlier.'

'What about cars?' Nilima asked. 'You drove home, right?'

'Yeah, in my Escort.'

'You went home with an escort?' Poorna asked.

'Not *with* an escort. My car is an old Ford Escort—which you've both ridden in, by the way. My parents had it since I was in school. I learned to drive in it.'

'I have ridden your Escort,' Nilima said, and Poorna snickered.

Shwetha scowled and turned to her desk.

'No, hold on, sorry! Do you remember what vehicles were in the parking area when you left?'

Shwetha's eyebrows creased in thought. 'Jagat's car was there, of course.'

'You recognise his car?'

'Of course,' she repeated impatiently. 'It's a bright red Amaze.'

'A mez?' Nilima said. 'Isn't that a table?'

Shwetha never rolled her eyes, so she just glared at Nilima and said, her voice carefully even, 'No, the English "amaze".'

'You mean like the kind of game where you have to find your way out?' Poorna joined in.

'No! Not a maze! Just one word—amaze. You guys are—'

'Amazing?' Poorna grinned.

'"Amazing" would have been better,' Nilima said seriously. 'Or "Amazeballs". What kind of a name is "Amaze"? It's a verb!'

'You're right!' said Poorna. 'How ridiculous to say, "I bought an Amaze." It's like, "I bought a Shock."'

'But that can be a noun,' Nilima protested. 'Not that it's a good car name either. No, it's more like saying, "I bought an Astound."'

'I bought an Appear,' said Shwetha, entering into the spirit of things.

'I bought a Go,' said Poorna.

'That's a kind of Uber ride,' said Nilima.

'Actually, it's also the name of a car,' said Shwetha. 'There's even a Go Plus.'

'The existence of a Go Plus implies the existence of a Go Minus,' said Nilima.

'Yep,' said Poorna. 'It would only have one gear—reverse.'

She and Nilima burst into laughter. Shwetha opened her laptop with a quiet smile. These two finally seemed to be getting along. *Maybe*, Shwetha thought wistfully, *there would be fewer barbs and less sulking in the office, and she would be able to do her work in peace.*

'Wait,' said Nilima, and Shwetha looked up over her laptop. 'What about Dipen's car? Do you know it? Was it there?'

'He doesn't have one, as far as I know. I've seen him ride a Bullet.' She paused but Nilima only smirked and didn't make another pun. 'I'm pretty sure it wasn't there that night.'

'So Dipen usually walks home?'

'That's right, he lives over in 7th Block, across the street that way.' Shwetha pointed with her thumb. 'There were a couple of other cars; I suppose they belonged to customers. I think one was an SUV, I'm not sure.'

'I'll tell the inspector,' Nilima said. 'They're more likely to be able to trace cars. Do you think ... could Jagat have been having an affair? Maybe he was waiting for a lover?'

'In the office?' Poorna scoffed. 'He'd take her to a hotel, no?'

'Ah, our experienced Poorna, who knows how middle-aged men conduct affairs.'

'Plus, Shwetha would have found out,' Poorna argued. 'Someone would have spotted it and gossiped.'

Shwetha's mouth twisted into a wry smile. 'Yeah, not many secrets in this town. There's never been a hint of infidelity about Jagat.'

Nilima waited till Shwetha and Poorna were absorbed in their work—Shwetha had shut herself up in her little room again, and Poorna was talking on her phone, earphones in, so that her hands were free to gesticulate emphatically—and went up to the bookshop. Ever since she had started at Chikkamma, she had been going up nearly every day. But earlier, Jagdip had been a refuge she turned to when her life (usually, just her job) had seemed difficult. Now it had merged into the rest of her life (and her job).

For one, Maniram, who'd always ignored her when she walked past, now got to his feet, saluted smartly and greeted her in Assamese. She nodded brusquely and walked on, feeling miserable. *He'll think I don't want to acknowledge him in public,* she thought. *I just don't want to draw attention to myself!*

There were more customers than usual, and Dipen was at the downstairs cash counter charming a few of them with his bright smile and easy banter. Nilima stopped at the romance aisle a little way inside, where she could listen without being in Dipen's line of sight. He thanked the customer he had just billed, then Nilima heard another express her regrets at Jagat's death.

There was a pause before Dipen said, in a more sombre voice, 'Thank you. We'll all miss my brother very much.'

The customer talked on; she had been coming to the shop since Samudra Desai had first opened it. What an institution it was for this part of the city! She hoped Dipen wasn't thinking of closing up.

'No, of course not. This bookstore is my home. I will honour my father and my brother's legacy.'

Nilima retreated a few steps, thinking about what she had just heard. Dipen, by all accounts, had never been concerned about the shop or his father's legacy. Was he just mouthing words that he thought would make him look good? Or did he feel responsible for the shop now that his brother was gone? The shop didn't belong to him: it belonged to his sister-in-law, who apparently rarely visited. Did that rankle?

Dipen commented on the next customer's purchases and offered a recommendation. The man demurred. Dipen insisted. 'It's a beautiful new series of notebooks; have a look, you'll love it. We just got them, we haven't even had a chance to put them up yet.' He yelled across the shop: 'Sampath sir! Get a set of those new notebooks that just came in.'

Nilima had never seen Dipen so interested in serving customers, and none of the shop's current employees had indicated he was (though Pallav had hinted he was good at his work—maybe she shouldn't have been so quick to dismiss Pallav's judgement). Had Dipen avoided getting involved for so many years simply because he didn't have control?

She ducked into an aisle to avoid Sampath, who was hurrying across with a bunch of notebooks (in different sizes, all with bright, hard covers) in his arms. She had landed in the non-fiction section; there were signs up for memoir, business, finance, philosophy, self-help. She shuddered in distaste. Towards the front of the store were the aisles for mythology, romance, fantasy and Indian writing. And stationery and toys were right up front near the counter. She hadn't spent much time on this floor, except in the comics and graphic novels section at the back, behind the stairs leading to the second floor.

She went up the stairs. The literary fiction section took up most of this floor, and was divided into classics and contemporary fiction. Beyond it was her favourite haunt, the thriller aisle.

Mehnaz was holding court at the cash counter, a cluster of customers around her. Nilima hid behind a shelf. A customer asked about a book he was looking for.

'Try the classics section,' Mehnaz told him. 'At the back, near the modern classics. Or else try downstairs, in the Indian writing section.'

The man wandered off. The other customers in the queue seemed more interested in chatting than paying. They were asking about the murder. Mehnaz replied shortly in a bored voice, and Nilima grinned. *They won't get much gossip out of her.*

Nilima walked towards the back of the shop. The customer whom Mehnaz had just directed found his Volga exactly where she had said it would be. Nilima felt a thrill of happiness at the thought that this bookshop could become the kind of place she'd love to come to, day after day and week after week and maybe year after year, if she worked at Chikkamma for that long.

Then she remembered; what underlay this change was the grim fact of Jagat's murder. When Jagat had been around, both Mehnaz and Dipen had been quiet and sullen.

No one was in the cave of shelves Nilima had just entered, right across the door to the office. She pulled down the first book her hand landed on and dropped onto a stool. But instead of sinking into the book on her lap, she listened. The speakers were emitting, at a volume so low she hadn't heard it earlier, old Bruce Springsteen songs her father used to love—maybe he still did. It must be Dipen's playlist: her extensive social media stalking had revealed that Mehnaz was partial to hip-hop and sufi, and Sampath had already expressed his disdain for rock.

A car honked in the lane outside, and voices drifted up from the first floor. A few voices grew louder, closer. They sounded young; there were three of them—no, four. They were talking more softly now, but on this quiet floor Nilima could hear every word.

'Is this where it happened?'

'Yes, on this floor!'

'I wonder where the body was.'

'Didn't the article say it was outside the door?'

'That's not possible. The door is downstairs!'

'Maybe it was this door.'

They were outside Jagat's office. A gap between the shelves let Nilima glimpse four pairs of feet. The door behind them was firmly shut.

'Let's go in and look.'

Peals of laughter, followed by shushing. 'No! What if someone comes?'

'We'll just say we were looking for the bathroom.'

More laughter. Nilima deliberately scraped her stool back and glared over the shelf. The miscreants were very young, no more than seventeen or eighteen. Two of them sported downcast eyes and sheepish smiles; the other two stared defiantly back at Nilima.

'May I help you?' Neither Nilima nor the teenagers had heard Mehnaz approach. Behind her, the counter was empty, the queue of customers having vanished into nothing.

'No, thanks,' said one of the teenagers with as much sass as he could muster. They shuffled down the stairs in step like a giant spider, giggling again. Mehnaz sneered at their receding heads and turned to Nilima, wordlessly indicating, *See what I have to deal with?*

Nilima smiled in sympathy.

'Can I help you?' Mehnaz asked aloud, as if she guessed Nilima didn't want to acknowledge yesterday's meeting. Or maybe she didn't want to say anything that Dipen or Sampath could overhear.

'No, thank you,' Nilima involuntarily echoed the teenager. 'I'm just looking.' She felt embarrassed and guilty. After all, she was as much of a curiosity seeker as those teenagers—and far more intrusive.

Mehnaz nodded and settled herself behind the counter again. Nilima went back to her stool. The cover of the book she was still holding said *A Necklace of Skulls.* Something about the morbidity of the title had subliminally appealed to her. She didn't read much poetry, but now she opened a page. She barely noticed flipping the page, and then another.

'Nilima madam, good afternoon!'

She jumped up. It was Sampath, of course. And behind him, unlocking the door of the office and now looking around curiously at her, was Dipen.

Her distant response did nothing to dampen Sampath's effusiveness. 'How are you, madam? How is Shwetha madam? What are you doing here?'

'I ... just came to get this book. I'll get it billed, I should get back to work. Nice seeing you, Sampath.' She backed away as she was talking, and bumped into someone. She turned around, apologising, and looked up into Dipen's face.

'Are you okay, ma'am?'

She had never seen Dipen up close before. *He's only a few inches taller than me,* Nilima thought inconsequentially. His hair had no grey; only a few lines around his eyes and mouth bore evidence of his thirty-eight years. His body was lean and lightly muscled—*like he works out every day*.

'Nilima madam, all okay?'

Nilima took a step back. 'Sorry, Sampath.' He was still looking at her anxiously, so she added, 'I'm perfectly okay.'

She turned back to Dipen. 'So sorry I crashed into you.'

'No problem at all. I assume you come to our store often? I see you know Mr Sampath already; I'm Dipen. Dipen Desai.'

'Ni-Ni-Nilima.' She shook his outstretched hand. 'I just ... yes, I came up to buy this book.'

'Aha, very nice poetry,' Dipen said, to Nilima's surprise. 'We have a new book from a local poet, I think you'll like it.'

How do you know what I'll like, Nilima thought perversely. She made an effort to say, 'Thank you. I'll come back once I've read this.'

'Of course. I hope you enjoy it.'

'I work downstairs,' Nilima blurted out. If she didn't tell him and he found out later, he might find that strange, and she did not want to arouse his suspicions. 'At Chikkamma Tours.'

'Ah, I was sure I'd seen you before—I just assumed you were one of our regulars. We're neighbours then.'

Nilima couldn't think of anything to say and just gaped foolishly back at him.

'Thank you,' she said finally, edging towards the counter. Sampath was tinkering with some books in the next aisle.

'See you soon, Nilima,' Dipen said warmly.

Nilima dropped the book on the counter, relieved to have escaped from Dipen. She wished she had a fraction of Shwetha's charm; she would probably have converted an unceremonious collision with Dipen into a long interview without him realising what she was doing. Oh well, she could try to talk to him later, once she had a little more information.

Mehnaz winked as she held out the change. Nilima refused a bag and walked down, clutching the book. She hadn't budgeted for it, but it was important, she felt, to spend at the businesses she really wanted to survive, even though her little money wouldn't make a material difference to them. It was like a wish, a prayer. Such were the rituals of atheists.

There was someone at the first-floor cash counter. Long wavy hair, big eyes highlighted by blue eye shadow, a diamond on her nose. Dipen's wife.

CHAPTER 7

The Unexpected Host

'Tell me something, boss,' Nilima said a couple of hours later, when Shwetha was getting herself her third cup of tea for the day and Poorna was preparing for the next day's Malleshwaram tour.

'Stop calling me that,' Shwetha said exasperatedly.

'Sorry, boss. What's the gossip about Jagat's death? What's the vibe?'

'What do you mean? Everyone's shocked, of course.'

'Okay, why?'

'Why? This is a peaceful neighbourhood. People are horrified.'

'Yeah,' Poorna chimed in, 'my grandmother has taken to calling if I'm not home by eight. My mom is usually cool, but even she's been saying I shouldn't stay out late.'

Shwetha offered a grimace of sympathy. 'My parents are begging me to move the office.'

'Are you going to?' asked Nilima, distracted by this line of thought.

'Of course not. Do you know how much trouble that would be? I'm not moving till our lease ends.' She had another thought and added, 'Or our building collapses, which isn't completely unlikely.'

'In that case, I demand health insurance. I have no money to get treated for a building falling on me.'

'We're too small to afford that. You'll both have to buy your own.'

'*I'm* too small to afford that,' Poorna piped up unexpectedly.

After Nilima stopped laughing, she said, 'Back to the gossip, boss. Are people shocked by the fact of the murder itself or by Jagat being the victim?'

'That too. So many of us knew him. It hits close to home, I suppose.'

'I don't think that's what Nilima means,' said Poorna shrewdly, still looking at her computer.

'I'm not saying this well,' Nilima admitted. 'I mean, are they sad or just shocked? Are they grieving?'

'Oh. I see what you mean. No, actually. I haven't heard much evidence of grief. Everyone's sorry for the wife and kids, of course, but my aunts who knew Jagat's father don't seem all that upset. But then, it's not like they were close to Jagat. I'll find out more; I asked my mum for the number of this old friend of hers—a Mrs Jadhav who lives in the building next to Veena's. She's going to get it from another friend and then I will try calling her.'

Nilima continued her musing. 'Even at his house that day, his wife may have been devastated—we only saw her for a minute—but I didn't see anyone else visibly sad. Of course, that's not something you can always tell ...'

'No, you can't,' Poorna said pointedly.

'It's just,' explained Nilima, 'when I was in the store earlier, it struck me how much nicer everything was. The store seems better for his absence. It made me wonder if Jagat's anger and his meanness had coloured the atmosphere there. And now that it's gone, it's a happier place.'

Nilima's phone rang. She glanced at it before picking it up hastily, as if afraid the others would see who was calling. Poorna and Shwetha exchanged a look as she said 'hello', her voice so much smaller and more hesitant than it had been just a few seconds ago.

Nilima got up and walked away as she listened, though there wasn't much room to walk in. Instead of seeking privacy in the car park, she stopped by the shut door, expecting the call to be over soon. She said a few words in Assamese, and Shwetha realised she had been hoping to eavesdrop. Now Shwetha turned her attention to Poorna, who had a question about tomorrow's tour, and they were still discussing it when Nilima ended the call and came back to her desk.

Shwetha called out to Nilima's back, 'What's up, Deka?'

'Nothing,' Nilima said without turning around. 'It was my mother.'

'Not bad news, I hope?'

'No.' And then, 'It's good news, to be honest. My sister's having a baby.'

Poorna's face lit up. 'Ooh, congratulations!'

'Is it her first?' Shwetha asked.

'Yes.'

'You'll be an aunty, Deka! That's awesome!'

'Thanks,' Nilima mumbled, looking around at Poorna to make it clear she was included too.

'Is your sister older than you?' Poorna asked, eager to encourage this hint of friendliness.

'Younger. By nearly four years.'

Shwetha whistled, and then explained, 'I didn't even know you had a sister. Where does she live?'

'In Guwahati.'

'Oh, with your parents?'

'No.' Realising that the others were waiting for more, she added, 'Nearby, though. She and her husband live only twenty minutes away from my parents.'

'That must be nice for them. Do you visit often?'

'Not really.'

'Why, when did you last go home?'

'I haven't been to Guwahati in two years.'

'She's not close to her family,' Poorna said before Shwetha could push further. 'I haven't heard her answer a call from family before today.'

'I thought she just doesn't take calls at work. Or doesn't talk on the phone much. You know how she is.'

'She's answered calls from friends though.'

Nilima whirled around in her chair, her face red with anger. 'I am right here! If you have to discuss my personal life, maybe wait till I'm not?'

'Sorry,' said Poorna.

'We care about you,' said Shwetha. 'Don't share if you don't want to, but if you do, we're here to listen.'

'And gossip about me to your friends? I don't want all of Bangalore knowing my personal business, thanks.'

'I wouldn't do that!' Shwetha said.

'You know she wouldn't,' added Poorna. 'That's unfair.'

'I know,' Nilima said. 'I'm sorry. I'm sensitive about this.'

'It's fine,' Shwetha said softly. She turned to her laptop and started responding to her emails. Poorna went back to her research. The silence was broken by Nilima's voice. 'I left home when I was eighteen. I didn't talk to my parents for nine years. We started talking again a couple of years ago.'

'What happened?' Poorna asked hesitatingly.

'I told them I was gay.'

When no one said anything, Nilima turned her chair around. She scrutinised her colleagues' faces and seemed to approve of what she saw, because she resumed speaking.

'I waited till I was completely sure. I waited till I felt I *had* to tell my family something so important. They wouldn't like it, I knew, but surely they'd still love me?' She chuckled humourlessly. 'I had no idea.'

'They didn't take it well?' Shwetha asked softly.

'They were more attached to the idea they had of their elder daughter than they were to me. They threatened to throw me out if I didn't stop ... stop being gay, though they never used that word. So I left.'

Almost as one, Shwetha and Poorna walked over, each putting an arm around Nilima's shoulders from either side. Shwetha knelt and placed her other hand on Nilima's.

Of course, there was more to the story. The hours-long quarrels inevitably followed—or punctuated—by her mother's loud wails and sometimes her father's sobs. The time her sister had begged her to be 'normal' so that they could be a happy family again. Not being allowed to leave the house except to go to college. Her parents monitoring her timetable and yelling at her if she wasn't home an hour after class ended. Her cell phone, a treasured gift from her parents on her last birthday, the first phone she'd ever had, had been confiscated, the SMSs scrutinised for any 'improper' friendships. A professor—a friend of her mother's—had called her into her office and spent half an hour berating her for making her parents unhappy.

It had all been about her parents' unhappiness. Like she owed it to them to erase herself, to become somebody else.

I would have if I could, Nilima thought bitterly. By then, she had already tried for several years and given up. Over that long vacation after the school board exams, she had spent many hours on the family computer, reading up about queerness, carefully deleting her internet history each time. She had found more concrete support once she started college—a few queer students who had adopted her into their group—and had found the courage to tell her parents, hoping it wouldn't be as bad as she feared. *Her* parents wouldn't throw her out. They were far too educated and broad-minded. Her mother was a professor of anthropology, after all, and her father was a doctor.

She hadn't realised that they were too respectable to have a lesbian daughter. Once the storm broke, she lived with it for a few months, hoping things would get better. Where could she have gone anyway? She had no income. She hadn't wanted to drop out of college.

Things didn't get better. She had gone home every evening to a house that was filled either with silent resentment that stifled her or sharp words that stung. She had taken to staying back in college most afternoons, finding an empty classroom where she could sit by herself, postponing going home, even if every half hour's delay invited another barrage of interrogation and remonstrance.

Eventually, she had moved into a private hostel. She had saved up some pocket money over the years, and she sold some of her books to a second-hand bookseller. (She wouldn't be able to carry everything anyway, she consoled herself.) It had barely been enough for a month's rent, which she had had to pay in advance. The hostel authorities had been suspicious because she lived in the same city and Nilima had had to think up an excuse. Her home was too far to commute to college every day, she had said. After some questioning, they had finally relented and let her in. She had forged her father's signature.

Without her friends, she wouldn't have survived. She wouldn't even have got into the hostel if her friend Evelyn hadn't vouched for her. Evelyn had lent her bedclothes too. But what Nilima remembered most fondly was that she had tried to cheer her up, introduce her to other girls at the hostel and make sure she wasn't spending much time lying on her bed pretending to be asleep.

Another friend had accompanied her to a jewellery shop where she could sell her gold earrings—the thin hoops she had worn since her mother had got her ears pierced at the age of two, and which were the only precious items she had on her. 'So clichéd, the heroine selling her jewellery,' one of her dates had said with a laugh, years later. That was before Nilima had started closing up, refusing to trust anyone with pieces of her past until she got to know them well.

She had left home with one duffel bag, which she had packed with her mother alternately sobbing and scolding next to her, while her sister was at school and her father at work. Never again did she get attached to things; never again did she stay in one home for more than a year or two. She wasn't sure if she was still running away from home or trying to find it.

The money from the earrings had been for the next month's rent, but something happened before she could pay it. Her parents showed up at the hostel and told the warden she was staying there without their permission. When Nilima came back from class, she was told to go to the warden's home next door. Her parents were in the living room, smiling and chatting with the warden over cups of tea. It was a beautiful room—hand-embroidered cushions and tablecloths on the wicker furniture, a magnificent old wooden cupboard full of books and the sun pouring in through the open windows with lace curtains fluttering in the breeze.

'Come home, Nilima,' her mother had said, still smiling, when she saw her in the doorway. 'Enough foolishness.'

Nilima had stuttered in anger and fear. 'N-n-no. I don't w-w-want—I won't live with you.'

'Stop behaving childishly,' her father had said sharply. But it was the warden's words that had chilled her to the heart. All these years later, that refined voice still rang in her head, each word a clear peal.

'You can't stay here without your parents' permission, young lady. This is a respectable hostel, not a place for girls who run away.'

Nilima hadn't, then, heard the unspoken words—bad girl, disgusting, pervert, dirty. She had filled them in later, after hearing others use them on her.

She had wanted to shout, to shatter the genteel politeness in that living room. It had come out as a plaintive whisper. 'I'm an adult,' she pleaded. 'I can do what I want.'

The warden had shaken her head in disappointment, her long earrings sparkling as they moved. 'I'm not going to allow you to stay here anymore. You're a rowdy, disobedient child. Go, pack up immediately.'

Her parents had looked shamefacedly at the warden as if apologising for their wayward daughter. Her mother had dabbed her eyes.

Back in her room, Nilima had quickly packed the few things she had. She was relieved her roommates weren't back yet; she wanted to slink away before anyone saw her. She could talk to Evelyn in college tomorrow.

A hostel worker had come to tell her to go back to the warden's living room, her parents were waiting.

'I just need a few more minutes,' Nilima had said desperately, pretending to continue packing.

The woman had nodded kindly and left. Nilima folded her bed clothes and placed them on the bed for Evelyn to find. Then she picked up her bag and quickly walked out towards the street, glad the lane wasn't visible from the warden's living room windows. She had hopped on a bus that was pulling away from the bus stop, not even stopping to ask where it was going.

She had been friendly with a group of young women who lived together. They were her seniors in college; in fact, she eventually started dating one of them—Hafeeza, who was now Inspector Lamani's girlfriend. Before that evening, she had only visited them once. Yet when she could think of nowhere else to go, Nilima had showed up at their flat and asked for sanctuary.

They had immediately taken her in; some of them had escaped from difficult parents themselves. They had let her stay rent-free, hiding her presence from the landlady for months until she had started earning enough to pay her share of the rent; they had fed her and taught her how to cook, and they had helped her find tutoring jobs and other part-time work. Those months—sleeping on a mattress on the floor between two beds, in a room so small the mattress had to be rolled up every morning so that her roommates could step on the floor when they got up, eating whatever food her flatmates shared with her, cleaning the house (and being gently mocked for not knowing how to do it well) as the only way she could show her gratitude—had been the happiest time of her life so far. At least on the days she could forget her guilt at having hurt her family and her anger that they had abandoned her.

For months, she expected her parents to show up and threaten her and her flatmates, but they had washed their hands off her. Mixed with the relief had been disappointment at having been erased so easily.

Her sister, however, did not erase her. They had always been too different to be close, but for Nilima, Protima would always be the toddler who used to follow her around, the little girl whose hand she clutched while crossing the street. They did not talk at all for a few years; Nilima had imagined elaborate scenarios for what she would say to her sister if she ran into her and how Protima would react. But it didn't happen. Later, when Nilima was living in Delhi, Protima had added her on Facebook and sent her a message. There were apologies on both sides (though Nilima had never been quite sure what she was apologising for) and a careful revival of the relationship. Protima had even repaired her relationship with their parents to the point that Nilima now received phone calls a few times a year and had been invited to visit. Nilima called her parents on their birthdays. She had never gone back to that house, her old home, where her parents still lived. She had never agreed to meet them again. She wasn't good at forgiveness.

✍

Poorna spoke into her phone, her voice high and slightly breathless as usual. 'Hello? May I speak to Mrs Veena Desai?'

Poorna switched to Kannada. Nilima understood a few words, especially the ones in English: 'When ... I'm Vaishnavi ... bank ... unusual activity ... account.' After a pause, Poorna added some more words: 'mobile phone ... not reachable.'

Nilima's nails were digging into her palms as Poorna stopped to listen again and then ended the call with, 'No, it's fine. I'll call her back.'

Nilima forced herself to unclench her fist.

'You have at least two hours,' Poorna told her. 'She told me to call back after six.'

'*Thank* you,' Nilima said fervently; at the same time Shwetha let out a triumphant, 'Aha!'

'No, it was fun,' Poorna said to Nilima. 'Thanks for coaching me.'

'And they say working at a call centre isn't useful experience,' Nilima said deadpan.

'Listen, you're sure you don't want me to come too?' Poorna asked wistfully.

'She's met me before,' Nilima explained. 'I think she might talk to me if I go alone.'

'And then one of you could do the work that pays all our bills,' Shwetha said drily.

✍

Nilima showed up at Jagat Desai's flat, safe in the knowledge that his wife wasn't home. Lotika, the domestic worker she had met on her previous visit, recognised her at once. Nilima said she happened to be in the neighbourhood, and Lotika welcomed her in with a smile. She brought out a glass of water and offered to make tea.

'Won't Mrs Desai mind? I don't really know her; I just came to see you.'

'Our madam is very nice. She won't mind. Please sit; I'll be back soon.'

'Can I come with you to the kitchen so we can chat while you make tea?' Nilima asked hopefully.

Lotika agreed readily, flattered by the attention. Just as she had on her last visit to this kitchen, Nilima perched on one end of the long counter like a life-sized Buddha.

'How's it going?' Nilima asked awkwardly in broken Bengali. 'Are things well here? How is Mrs Desai holding up?'

Lotika didn't answer as she set out cups and saucers, tins of biscuits and little plates at the kitchen table. Nilima held her breath—had she blown it? Was her cover too transparent? Would Lotika tell her off for being nosy?

It was only after Lotika turned back to the saucepan on the stove and spooned some tea leaves in that she muttered, 'Everything has changed. Nothing is good anymore.'

'I'm sorry to hear that,' Nilima said sincerely.

'Boudi is so sad. She tries to hide it, but she is always weeping. She's talking about taking the children and moving to her parents' house.'

'What, all the way to Gujarat?'

'Yes, Surat. The children are upset. They don't want to go.'

'Of course they don't, they must have friends here. Mrs Desai wants to move back permanently?'

'Yes.' Lotika poured the tea. After they both sat at the table, she went on, 'She doesn't want to live here alone. She feels they will be safer with her parents. After what happened to Dada, she's scared.'

'You mean she thinks someone might attack her?'

'Ki jani? She's not eating or sleeping. She even asked if I would go with her. How can I? I have a daughter in high school, an old mother-in-law ... I can't just move to a different state.'

'When is she planning to move?' *Why hasn't Shwetha's grapevine got hold of this news,* Nilima wondered.

'I don't know, Nilima di. I don't know if she'll really go—she's just so frightened. I told her, I said it's only been a few days, you'll feel better as time passes. Go stay with your parents for a few weeks and then come back. But who knows what she is thinking ...'

'What about the shop? What will she do with it?'

'Ki jani? Dipen babu can keep managing it, I suppose. Who cares about the shop when her husband is dead?'

'You said she's frightened. Is she afraid of someone in particular?'

'I don't think so,' Lotika said thoughtfully. 'No, she seems scared of everything. Even shadows. She doesn't even turn the lights off at night anymore. She sleeps in the kids' bedroom, in Sunny's bed. If only her parents hadn't had to go back so soon, but Papa's brother, his shraddho is tomorrow, and now they are saying, "Forget everything, you come here, we'll do Jagat's shraddho here only—"' Lotika stopped mid-sentence.

Nilima saw the look on her face and slowly turned around. Veena was standing in the doorway, hard and beautiful, like a Greek goddess. Her hair was still in its chic asymmetrical bob, but now looked limp and dull. Her face was pale, and the shadows under her eyes highlighted their stormy beauty. Her blue silk tunic fell in undulating waves over white pants.

She spoke in upper-class-accented English, with just a smidgen of contempt: 'And who are you?'

Nilima froze. Lotika intervened, speaking in a jumbled rush of Hindi and Kannada that Nilima could not untangle, though her tone was clearly placatory.

Finally, Nilima found her voice, though her legs still felt like jelly. 'You don't remember me, Mrs Desai. I work in the office below Jagdip Book House. I had come here on Tuesday.'

Recognition dawned and Veena Desai's body unwound a little. 'You knew my husband.'

'I work in the same building,' Nilima said truthfully, if guiltily. 'I'm sorry to intrude on you like this. I'd made friends with Lotika when I'd last visited and she was kind enough to offer me tea.'

'I see.' Veena shot Lotika a look that didn't bode well for her.

Nilima managed to push herself to her feet. 'I had come to meet Mrs Jadhav in the next building. I thought I'd look in on Lotika, since I was here anyway.'

Veena didn't reciprocate Nilima's nervous smile. *Thank fuck for Shwetha's network,* Nilima thought. *Mrs. Jadhav is real, in case Veena makes enquiries.*

'Well, I should go now,' she said aloud. 'Thanks very much for the tea, Lotika. Sorry again for intruding, Mrs Desai.'

'Not at all,' said Veena, her voice cold and hard.

Nilima walked to the main road and flagged down an autorickshaw, her heart still thudding from being in Veena's angry presence. She didn't want to go back to the office with two other people crowding her in; she needed space to think. She told the auto driver to make for Lalbagh.

Nilima tried to shake off thoughts of the murder. As usual, one set of worries immediately replaced another. *Next salary, should I spring for a Kindle or get a fridge?* she wondered, not for the first time, as she paid the autorickshaw driver, nodding at the old man's litany of complaints about the summer heat. *I really should just save up for the future,* she told herself half-heartedly. *I don't have health insurance.* But life had been so harsh the last year; she wanted to indulge herself with something nice.

'Ticket?' the woman guarding the gate said harshly.

'Sorry,' Nilima mumbled and turned to the ticket counter tucked into a corner on the left. The man in front of her, who had two children with him, seemed to take an inordinately long time sorting out his change. By the time she made her way back to the gate, she felt calmer. This time, the security guard grinned cheerfully and didn't bother looking at the ticket she was waving.

Beyond the open gates, a wide pavement stretched out before her. Bright pink and red flowers lay in regimented rectangular beds. The grass felt soft through her sneakers. This might be her last good time to visit the gardens, she realised, before rain made the ground squelch beneath her feet. She looked up at the tall old trees and breathed in. The only birds she could hear were crows and mynahs; the honks from the street were still audible. She moved on.

Even on a weekday, families were spread out on the lawns, making it look festive. Nilima rolled her eyes at the screaming children and the melding couples as she strolled past.

She stopped at a wire mesh fence that marked off the rose garden. This was where she had first met Shwetha. In early March, the roses had been in full bloom—reds and pinks and oranges and creams, some striped in two colours, and a bush bursting with greenish white blossoms with swollen, kissable petals.

A loud low laugh had sounded behind her, and then a remark about the white roses Nilima had been staring at. Without moving, she had listened intently as the voice had talked about the provenance of some of the roses. It was only when the throaty laugh had come again—in response to a remark she hadn't caught—that Nilima realised what she had been listening for.

A surreptitious glance had revealed the owner of the voice—long curly hair, short green kurta with white embroidery, jeans, silver sneakers. Nilima had caught a dimple on a smooth cheek before the stranger turned her head towards her. Nilima had immediately spun around to face the roses again.

Nilima didn't know how long she would have stood there listening to that voice—Shwetha's voice. But then she had noticed the group breaking up; Shwetha was encouraging them to wander on their own for fifteen minutes before meeting at the same spot.

'Hello there.' The words had erupted next to Nilima's ear, and she had grabbed the fence in surprise. 'I charge for my tours, actually.'

The wire had dug into her palms as Nilima turned to see Shwetha standing close, eyes crinkling with amusement. Nilima hadn't been able to look away.

Shwetha had suddenly looked flustered. 'I didn't mean ... I was only joking. You seemed to be listening.'

'I was,' Nilima had admitted. 'You're Shwetha, right? Ankit said I should meet you here?'

'Ah, you're Ankit's friend Nilima! Thanks for agreeing to this unconventional interview; I thought it might be good for you to start by getting a sense of what we do. If you're going to handle our marketing, you'll have to understand the business.'

'It seems very interesting,' said Nilima, immediately wanting to kick herself for the banal statement.

But it hadn't seemed to matter. Shwetha cleverly elicited details about her past jobs and interests without the conversation feeling like an interview, and Nilima's panic and desperation melted away. Unlike the last few interviews she had been on, she found herself talking easily. By the time the rest of the group had come back, Nilima had the promise of a job—provided her documents and references checked out. Presumably, they had: in her relief at getting the job, she had never asked Shwetha.

Nilima had moved to Bengaluru last year to work with a promising young start-up, which soon failed to pay her for several months before she quit, deciding that not working for no pay was better than working for no pay. After meeting Shwetha, she had spent several sleepless nights trying to make her decision: should she take a job at a two-person business that was less than a year old?

Ultimately, she had decided to give it a try. *What do I have to lose? I can always walk out if I don't like it,* she had thought.

'You could get involved in something illegal and be in too deep before you find out,' Preeti had said ominously when Nilima had got her on the phone.

'Like what?'

'Maybe she's involved in drugs. You said she was with a group of Russian tourists when you met her. Maybe they smuggle in drugs for her.'

'I'd think she'd find easier ways to get drugs from them than leading them on a long tour of a large garden.'

'Who does tours anyway? We have Google Maps now.'

'Well, some people like a personalised touch, and a guide who knows the city intimately.' Nilima had realised she'd quoted from the Chikkamma Facebook page. *I need to improve that description first thing,* she had thought, looking forward to reporting to work, to working beside Shwetha all day ...

'Are you sure you are not taking the job just because you think she's hot?'

'Of course not! I think it'd be fun. I'm tired of working in digital marketing agencies.'

'So you do think she's hot?'

'Let me know if you feel like taking this seriously,' Nilima had said, and Preeti had apologised perfunctorily and moved on to talking about her last date.

Today, there were no white roses, only a few feeble pink and red ones. Nilima pushed away from the fence and set off on a brisk walk towards the lake.

CHAPTER 8

To Confront a Thief

When Shwetha stepped into the office the next morning, Nilima was yelling into her phone before vehemently pressing the disconnect button.

'Don't worry,' she said to Shwetha's raised eyebrows. 'It wasn't a customer, it was just another reporter. Or one of the same ones again, I'm not sure. This one's named Mahadeva.'

'How did he get your number?'

'I gave it to him when he messaged on Facebook. I thought he was a customer. Anyway, what happened with Saima?'

Shwetha pulled the seragu of her sheer blue mul saree more firmly over her black tank top. 'Nothing interesting. I started with more general questions: what it was like to work there, etcetera. She said it was fine. Then I asked her about Dipen. She seemed annoyed that Mehnaz had talked about it. Saima said it was nothing, he was just being friendly. He messaged her on Facebook and liked some of her updates.'

'He was stalking her online?'

'I don't think we can call it stalking. It's not like he made sexually explicit comments—or did anything even mildly inappropriate. She didn't want to talk to him outside of work, so she changed her settings; that way he wouldn't see her posts.'

'And that was it? He didn't try to contact her outside of work after that?'

'No, not at all. She thought the whole thing wasn't a big deal.'

'And he backed off at work as well?'

'Yeah. Actually ...'

'What?'

'She said he offered her a lift home once or twice.'

'Doesn't he live nearby?'

'He brings his bike to work sometimes. Anyway, she said no, and he stopped.'

'And so she found another job?'

'It doesn't seem to be related. She said she'd been looking for a bit. The bookstore was far for her and she spent an hour in the bus each way. This new job is a much easier commute, and she says it's a better career move. She is a receptionist now, and training to be a hair stylist.'

'Did she ask why you wanted to know all this?'

'I told her before we started. I said one of our friends is under suspicion, and we want to prove he didn't do it.'

'Did you record the interview?'

'No, my phone battery was low. I can write a report for you. Should I?'

'Yes, please.'

'Will do. And can I have your office key, Deka? I lost mine again. I'll get a duplicate made.'

Nilima pulled a key off her bunch. 'Why don't you keep all your keys together, boss?'

'Because then I'll lose the entire bunch instead. I keep losing them—it's not like I have a hole in my purse or anything. Last month I lost my flat key, thankfully I'd already given a neighbour one, so I could get in. Thanks for this, Nili, I'll give it back this evening.'

'No problem, boss.'

'Speaking of losing things ... I feel something is off.' Shwetha pointed upwards. 'In the bookstore.'

'Umm, yes,' said Nilima. 'There was a murder. That *is* weird.'

'I don't think it's related. I just felt it's odd. Both Pallav and Mehnaz mentioned it ...'

'You mean the thefts? Yes, I've been thinking about that too. It's too minor to have a bearing on the murder, I think. I have a guess about who did it.'

'So do I,' said Shwetha promptly, taking away Nilima's triumph. 'Sampath!'

'Who didn't tell us about it, even though we talked about the bookstore at such length.'

'Who's the only person who's been there throughout, apart from Jagat and Dipen. And why would they steal from their own store?'

'Jagat's store,' Nilima pointed out.

'Why would Dipen need a little cash—or a few books?'

'I wonder which books were stolen.'

'Mehnaz might know.'

'I'll text her.' Nilima picked up her phone while Shwetha turned on her laptop.

A minute after Nilima put her phone down, it flashed a text. She read Mehnaz's answer aloud. 'These are the ones I can remember: Dan Brown's *Origin,* a Malcolm Gladwell and Sachin Tendulkar's autobiography.'

'The Malcolm Gladwell, was it *David and Goliath*?' Nilima said aloud as she typed back to Mehnaz.

The answer came immediately.

Yes

Nilima smirked. 'I knew it!'

'What was that about?'

'It might be a coincidence, but Sampath's bookshelves had every one of those books. They looked new too.'

'You remember what books you saw in his home?'

'Of course. That's the first thing I notice about a room. Does it have books? What books? Would I want to read any of them?'

'Would you?'

'From Sampath's library? No. But that's suspicious, isn't it?'

'It's not quite proof ... Let's talk to him.'

'Confront him?'

'Why not? It's not like we're accusing him of being the murderer. I'd like to see what he says.'

'It would be nice to have one mystery cleared up,' said Nilima wistfully. 'Since we don't seem to be making any progress on the other one.'

'Don't be pessimistic. We're doing fine.'

Shwetha placed a call. 'Good morning, Sampath sir. Nilima and I wanted to ask you a couple of questions. Do you think you could meet us sometime today? ... Yes, if you come down to our office this evening before you go home, that would be perfect.'

Shwetha grimaced as she ended the call. 'I don't like this very much. He was so nice to us and welcomed us into his home. Now we're going to accuse him of being a thief.'

'If he is the thief, I don't know if I have much sympathy.'

'*You* wouldn't have any sympathy for a book thief?'

'Like the one in *The Book Thief*, sure,' said Nilima. 'In this case, no. To steal those books when he had so many choices is inexcusable.'

✍

A few hours later, Nilima walked out of Sandal Soap Factory Metro Station and hailed an autorickshaw. She hadn't been in this part of town before and looked around with curiosity at the wide streets that weren't very busy on a Friday afternoon.

The auto slipped into an even quieter road. Many trees were visible over the tall wall that lined the footpath. When the security guard waved the autorickshaw in, she stopped the driver. She was early for her meeting, and this was a lovely place for a walk.

It wasn't a very large campus, but she got lost anyway. She was reluctant to ask for directions of the few college staff she saw—a gardener hard at work and another security guard at the gate of a building—and happy to ramble aimlessly till it was time for her meeting. It was another sunny day and she was soon uncomfortably warm. Nilima rested her back against a tree, its leaves luminous in the sunlight. She watched a family of squirrels until they disappeared into the branches.

It was a minute to one when she stepped into the open-air cafeteria. Hafeeza had never been a punctual person, and Nilima settled down to wait, manoeuvring a V. L. McDermid paperback out of her capacious skirt pocket. But a few minutes later, Hafeeza and Sharmila walked up together. They weren't holding hands, but they were smiling in that engrossed way couples often do, like they shared a beautiful secret all their own. To Nilima's eyes they looked both smug and enviable.

Inspector Lamani caught sight of Nilima and stiffened into her usual stoic expression. Her holiday attire was of well-pressed navy jeans and a black collared T-shirt with only a thin blue line at the shoulder for embellishment—scarcely less austere or forbidding than her khaki uniform.

'Hey there.' Hafeeza smiled happily and settled onto a chair. The inspector condescended to give Nilima a nod.

Hafeeza made small talk, and Nilima tried to follow her lead. 'Are you enjoying your research?' Nilima asked, looking up at the branches they were sheltering under. 'It must feel so lucky to work here.'

'The campus is very pretty,' Hafeeza agreed. 'One of the biggest perks of my job.' Her large eyes rested in a wide face, a little flat nose giving it a pleasing symmetry and making her look younger than her thirty-two years. Her hair fell past her shoulders, straight and shiny and without a touch of grey, unlike Sharmila's, in whose hair—resolutely tied back in a ponytail—silver threads were apparent at a closer glance. 'The research is pretty fun too. But my advisor ...' She launched into a litany of complaints.

Nilima tried to maintain a sympathetic expression, but her mind drifted to her own near-decade of jobs—she couldn't really call it a career—in windowless offices and doing work she couldn't quite understand the purpose of—before Chikkamma, of course.

'It's not so bad,' Hafeeza concluded. 'I don't have the kind of stress Milly puts up with.'

Nilima blinked at the nickname. Sharmila's face was blank. Nilima wondered what she called Hafeeza. *Huffy? Fizzy?*

'She's taking a day off after weeks,' Hafeeza continued. 'I was hoping we could spend a weekend together, but no, she has to work all weekend.'

'That sucks,' Nilima said tentatively, avoiding looking at Sharmila.

'But I'm done with work for today,' Sharmila said. 'We're going to a movie later.'

'Sorry for taking up your time,' Nilima said.

'Don't be silly,' said Hafeeza. 'Now why don't you two chat while I get us some food? What do you want?'

Both Nilima and Sharmila were eager to leave the ordering to her—'You know the place better; order whatever you like,' Sharmila said firmly—and Hafeeza departed after promising them a great lunch.

Nilima and Sharmila awkwardly avoided each other's eyes. Now that she was out of the police station and in what

Hafeeza's presence made a social meeting, Sharmila seemed to have lost her usual self-assurance.

'Do you come here often?' Nilima said to fill the silence.

'No. I do not find the time. Only today because Hafeeza asked me to pick her up here. And this place serves better food than the mall's food court.'

'Yes, of course.' This was the longest personal statement Sharmila had ever made, and Nilima wasn't sure how to continue.

'You have questions for me, Miss Deka.'

'Yes, I was wondering about the alibis.'

Sharmila considered, and decided to answer. 'Dipen was with his wife all night. His wife confirms it.'

'And he doesn't seem to have a motive.'

'Correct. Mrs Veena Desai, as you know, was out of town.'

'And she seems grief-stricken.'

'You have spoken to her?'

'I talked to her domestic worker, Lotika. She said Veena is devastated by her husband's death. In fact, Lotika said she's afraid the murderer will come after her.'

'That's interesting.'

'I mean, I was thinking ...'

'Yes?'

'Lotika sees that Veena's scared. But maybe she's not afraid of being murdered. Maybe she's afraid of being caught.'

'Is that your theory? So that's why you were asking about her bank accounts?'

'She's scared and she's thinking of fleeing the state. What if she hired a hitman?'

'Why do you think so?'

'The timing of the murder, for one—like it was meant for the crime to have gone undiscovered for longer. That indicates someone close to him was involved, someone who knew his schedule.'

'That may be the case. But many people would have known that the shop is closed on Mondays and that Desai's wife and children were out of town.'

Nilima continued hastily, 'Also, consider the weapon.'

'We haven't found the weapon.'

'Exactly. Which means the killer took it with them. Going by that, and by the wound itself, it's something small and easy to hide. Like a dagger the killer could keep in their pocket. Which means they were prepared. And they didn't leave any clues—like it's a professional who's been very careful.'

Her theory seemed much less convincing here in the bright sunlight, with Inspector Sharmila's cool gaze on her. Nilima felt like a child who had just recounted a fantastical story to a sceptical adult.

'It's possible,' Sharmila said surprisingly. 'In fact, we have already taken this theory into consideration. We're looking into it.'

Or you are pretending to, Nilima thought, *because you don't want to admit I've thought of something you haven't.*

'But a professional would most likely have chosen a less messy method,' the inspector observed. 'This murderer would have got blood all over his clothes, unless he was very lucky. No one reported seeing anyone like that.'

'So the murderer must have had their own car. And maybe a change of clothes. That's the kind of planning a professional would do.'

'Maybe. Or it was an amateur—that's the opposite of professional, is it not?—who got lucky.'

Nilima got the distinct impression that Sharmila wasn't just referring to the murderer.

'I have already talked to the bank managers,' Sharmila went on. 'The one where the bookshop has its account and where Mr Desai had his account too, and another bank where he had a joint account with his wife. His wife had another account at a different bank—she's had it since before her marriage. And they had three credit cards between them.'

Nilima tried to absorb this sudden burst of information. So one bank account that Veena held alone, and one more she had access to. The credit cards weren't important; an assassin wouldn't accept a credit card payment, would they?

Sharmila went on, 'There are accounts in each of the children's names that, of course, the parents controlled. No withdrawals there, only deposits. Occasional transfers from the grandparents. There's gold and diamond jewellery belonging to Mrs Desai. Some at home, some in a bank locker. Mostly from her parents, I understand. And nearly two lakh cash in the house.'

Hafeeza came by with a plate of steaming medu vada. 'Everything else will take longer; they had some trouble with the gas running out and have to fetch another cylinder. I'll go back and stand by the counter, else he'll never get to us.'

'I'll go.' Nilima started to get up, feeling guilty at having Hafeeza, who was being so obliging and without whom she'd have received no help from the police, waiting alone for their food.

'Oh no, you two sit and talk.' Hafeeza hurried off before Nilima could extricate herself from the narrow gap between her chair and the table it was fused to.

'I was saying,' Sharmila continued so that Nilima only glanced longingly at the vada and didn't dare touch it, 'I asked the managers at all three banks about these accounts. Everything is above board, they said—nothing suspicious. I got them to show me statements.'

'And everything looked clean?' Nilima asked in disappointment. 'No large amount of money missing?'

In answer Sharmila pulled a neatly folded sheet of paper out of her back pocket.

Nilima opened the printout. 'This is Jagat's account? Okay, anything ... Hey, that's a withdrawal of six lakh rupees on the fourteenth. Five days before the murder. Why did he withdraw so much money? Did he need it for the bookstore?'

'He didn't withdraw the money.'

'What do you mean? This is his account.'

'I asked the manager what he knew about this. It's not an ATM transaction; it's far above the daily limit. Jagat would have to go to a branch to do this.

'The manager checked with an employee and confirmed that it wasn't Jagat who came for the money. It was his wife. She was carrying his cheque. I spoke to the teller; she's worked there for a long time and recognised Mrs Desai. I showed her a photo to confirm.'

'What did Veena do with the money?'

'She says she took it to Surat with her. Her brother was facing financial difficulties and her husband had agreed to help. Apparently, both families lent each other money when it was needed. She left for Surat the next morning, so it's a plausible explanation.'

'Do you believe her?'

'I think it is surprising she chose to carry cash all the way instead of transferring money to her brother, or even transferring it to her own account and withdrawing it in Surat. But then it's a lot of money to me. To Mrs Desai, it may have seemed like just a little bit of extra cash.'

'Did the brother confirm her story?'

'Hmm. I talked to him on the phone.'

'But he may have lied for her.'

'It's possible. She may have told him she just wanted a little money for shopping and her husband's death might make the police suspicious. It's also possible she did, in fact, use the money for an innocuous purpose.'

'But you can't be sure.'

'The timing is a little suspicious. And it's difficult to track cash, especially as her brother said he used all of it to pay off various debts and was vague about who all it went to. It's a little early to push harder, you understand. I would like to know more first, and I have enough to occupy me here without taking a trip to Surat on a wild goose chase—or sending one of my sub-inspectors.'

Nilima changed tack. 'What about the other suspects? Do they have alibis?'

'Let's see. Sampath's wife says he reached home soon after ten. The son had gone to Coorg with friends and only got back Monday morning. Three of Maniram's roommates say he was home by ten-thirty. Mehnaz was at a party till one-forty and went straight home in her Uber. We talked to the driver, he remembers her.'

'Pallav?'

'He claims he was out drinking. Several friends vouched for him, but none of the waiters recognised him—my men showed them photos. And none of his friends remember exactly when Pallav left. They were drinking heavily. They had started early in the evening at a brewery before moving to this cheap bar.'

'So he could have left in time to kill Jagat. And the accountant, Mohan? He seems to have been the last person to see Jagat alive.'

'Correct. He said they went over the finances for the month—a little early for that, if you ask me. When he left the store at ten forty, Jagat was still working. Mohan bought a dosa at a roadside stand before going home to his wife; she confirms he arrived before midnight. We haven't been able to find the dosa stand—and he doesn't remember the name on the board.'

'Yet it's the kind of thing people do all the time, don't they? Buy a dosa on the street.'

'Less often than they used to. Nowadays it's all cafés and breweries and big-chain darshinis. Anyway, let us enjoy our lunch.'

A beatific smile appeared on Sharmila's face. Nilima looked around to see Hafeeza approaching the table with a laden tray.

✍

'I think your theory of a hitman makes a lot of sense,' Shwetha said hotly when Nilima got back to the office and filled her in. Poorna was out of office today—she had a tour all morning and was now making the rounds of hotels with a new batch of flyers. 'Sharmila should take it seriously.'

'How easy would it be to find a hitman? You can't exactly ask for recommendations on Facebook.'

'I don't know,' Shwetha said. 'It probably isn't all that difficult to find someone who'd be willing to do this at a price.'

'I Googled "hire hitman Bangalore". I got a lot of leads. There are websites, even an app. But if you did find someone, how would you trust him? What if he goofed up? What if he blackmailed you later?'

'So how did Veena know whom to hire?'

'If she did.'

'If she did,' Shwetha conceded, 'it must have been based on a personal recommendation, no? Someone she trusts might have referred him.'

'I read this news piece about women in a small town hiring assassins to get rid of their husbands ...'

'That kind of thing isn't likely to stay secret, though.'

'You're saying it's a big risk?'

'Not exactly. Something being an open secret and being acted on by the police are two different things. The police may not get to hear the gossip.'

'But you would.' It wasn't a question.

'I could try. We can't ask Mrs Jadhav for help—her mother has been very ill, so she divides her time between here and Mumbai, where her mother lives.'

'That's unlucky.'

'Especially for the mother,' Shwetha retorted. 'I've been trying to work out who else might know the Desais. I got the Desais' old address—from back when Samudra was *the* Desai—and realised I have an old schoolteacher who must have been their neighbour. She still lives there, so we can talk to her.'

'Would she talk to us? I mean, would she even remember you?'

'I ran into her at a school reunion last year, and she asked me to visit. It'll be fine.'

Nilima opened her mouth to ask a question, but the doorbell rang. Sampath.

'Let's do this,' Shwetha said.

Sampath came in, simpering as usual, tossing off enquiries into their health and barely waiting for the answers before supplementing them with his observations on how tired they looked. Nilima was surprised that she suddenly disliked him; his politeness came off now as obsequious, not kind. She remembered Pallav and his description of Sampath as a turtle. *Not a turtle,* she thought, *a toad. He's a toady.*

Sampath sat, his smile faltering before the stern faces of his interlocutors. Nilima tried to turn her grimace into a polite smile, with limited success. But Shwetha—who was always so gracious—was, for once, not attempting to be polite.

'Why did you steal from the store?' Shwetha asked bluntly.

Sampath looked stricken. He tried to recover quickly, to paste his usual ingratiating smile on his face.

'Nonsense, nonsense, madam. Who told you that?'

'Don't lie to us. We know you're the thief.'

'I'm not ... I didn't ... It's my shop too. I have worked here for so many years. Jagat did not pay me as I deserved. All my loyalty counted for nothing.'

'You stole to prove your loyalty?' Shwetha asked. Nilima suddenly realised why the usually polite Shwetha was now so hard and unyielding; she would consider an employee stealing from her as a betrayal. Nilima felt a rush of tenderness and a paradoxically simultaneous stab of annoyance.

'It was hardly anything,' Sampath was saying. 'Just a few books here or there. I wanted my son to have books. I didn't take that much ...'

'It wasn't just books. You stole money too. And stationery.'

'You have to understand, they didn't pay me enough! And they laughed at me! All my years of experience. All the sweat I've poured into the shop. They thought I was stupid. I showed them! They never guessed it was me!'

'Who's they?'

'Jagat and Dipen. Impudent boys! I knew them since they were this high.' He raised his hand to the level of the arm of his chair. 'They used to call me uncle. But after he started working here, Jagat never let anyone forget he was the owner. He was the owner because his father and I worked so hard all those years! And Dipen, he took his friends home to play games ...'

'What games?' Nilima asked.

'Children's games! Video games and darts! They'd play games even in the office. When Jagat wasn't around, they would be on their phones playing some pub game—all shooting and killing people. They used to laugh at me. They played silly games, and they would mock me and laugh. How dare they disrespect me?' His voice rose to a shriek.

Shwetha said quietly, 'Did you kill Jagat because he found out you were stealing?'

Sampath jumped in his chair. 'No, no, madam, what are you saying? I wasn't here when he died.'

'You could have come back,' Shwetha said remorselessly. 'After you saw Maniram leave, you could have gone back to the store to talk to Jagat and then killed him when he threatened to fire you.'

'Illa, illa, I would never do that! I've known him since he was a child. He didn't respect me, but he was Desai sir's son. I could never hurt him. I could not hurt anybody!'

Shwetha turned to Nilima. 'Do you believe him?'

Nilima nodded wordlessly, less stunned by the tears now pouring freely down Sampath's face than by Shwetha's transformation. She looked as fierce as a goddess—and as ruthless.

'All right,' Shwetha said to Sampath. 'We'll assume for now you haven't killed Jagat. Don't lie to us again or we'll tell the police about the thefts.'

'Yes, madam. I'll do whatever you say, madam.'

Nilima thrust a box of tissues near his face. Sampath took one, not looking at her. 'I'm sorry,' she said ineffectually. 'It's just ... We wanted to know the truth.'

'Now you do,' he whispered. 'I hope you're satisfied.' He backed out of the office, eyes still averted, and shut the door gently behind him.

'What?' Shwetha said sharply when Nilima continued to stare at her.

'What got into you?'

'I'm tired of being nice.'

'I know he lied to us, but he was under no obligation to tell us anything, Shwetha. We're not the police.'

'So you're on his side now?'

'Don't be stupid. I just don't think that was necessary. He was crying!'

'You think he'd have told us all of that if we'd asked him politely?'

'We won't know now, will we?'

'We got results. I don't see what you're complaining about.'

'We were already sure it was him. He didn't really tell us much we didn't know.'

'Are you saying I shouldn't have tried to get the truth?'

'I'm saying ...' Nilima took a gulp of air and continued, 'I'm saying he's a frustrated, underpaid employee who found a petty way to get back at his employer. I don't think it has much connection to the murder. And I don't think we had any right to be so mean to him.'

Shwetha looked like she was going to explode in anger. Instead, she placed her head in her hands.

'Shwetha?'

A hand reached out and grasped Nilima's. 'What are we doing, Nili?' Shwetha said plaintively.

'I don't know. Does it feel real to you, that a man died? That someone stabbed him and watched his life bleed out of him? That this murderer is probably someone we know, someone we have talked to?'

Shwetha removed her other hand from her face. 'Do you want to stop?'

'I'm fine with going on if you are,' said Nilima, very aware of the hand still holding hers.

'Yes. I want to keep going. I want to finish this.'

Nilima's phone pinged. She picked it up with her free hand and went still.

Shwetha abruptly let go of Nilima's hand. 'New girlfriend texting you?'

'It's my sister. She sent a photo of her baby.'

'Oh, wow. She had her baby already?'

Nilima shrank into herself. 'When my mother called yesterday, she told me Protima was in labour. Protima had told me months ago that she was pregnant. It's just ... I hadn't spoken to my mother for a long time, and I was ...'

'You don't have to explain, Deka.' Shwetha leaned over and hugged her. 'Congratulations! You'll have to grow up and be a wise aunt, won't you?'

Nilima looked at her phone again. Shwetha quietly picked up her handbag and left the office. Nilima only looked up when she heard Shwetha's car drive off.

CHAPTER 9

The Girl with the Leaf Toe Ring

'He always had bad luck with women, that poor boy,' Miss Joanna said.

Joanna Rebeiro—Miss Joanna to all her students, current and past—had taught Shwetha in Class 6. Miss Joanna still taught in the same school, and she had lived in the same house most of her life. For some twelve of those years, ending nearly two decades ago, Miss Joanna had been a neighbour of the Desais, who had lived in the house four doors down.

Nilima and Shwetha had calculated that Miss Joanna was likely to be home on a Saturday afternoon, and she appeared delighted to see Shwetha again. Her round glasses were perched on a sharp nose, and her thinning hair was cut short. Bony limbs poked out of her floral print sheath dress.

'We had a meeting in Malleshwaram,' Shwetha had told her, 'and I said, "Miss Joanna's house is down that lane, I wonder how she is doing," and Nilima suggested we should pay you a visit and find out.' Miss Joanna had smiled warmly at Nilima and said, 'I'm glad you did.' She was evidently lonely—the eldest of four sisters living alone in the house they had grown up in. The other three had got married and moved away—the youngest just last year, to Australia.

'Jagat?' Nilima asked in response to Miss Joanna's declaration. Shwetha had mentioned the murder and skilfully encouraged the teacher to talk about the Desais.

'No, the younger one,' Miss Joanna answered softly. 'Such a handsome boy he was too, much younger than me, of course ...'

Nilima stared. Could Miss Joanna have had a crush on Dipen?

'He was a child when they moved here,' Miss Joanna said, as if to refute Nilima's suspicion. 'Twelve or thirteen maybe, a little younger than my youngest sister Rosie. He had beautiful manners, very charming for such a young man. Once or twice, I'd ordered books for the school from his papa, and the boy had brought them over himself and put them in the autorickshaw for me. It was a big carton, but he said it was nothing. Very strong he was, athletic too. Very into sports. Tennis, I think, and cricket. His older brother—he didn't know his manners. Always acted so arrogant.'

'Really,' Shwetha said sympathetically.

'The parents were nice, but they kept to themselves. Mrs Desai was always busy, poor thing. Always cleaning and cooking and ironing clothes—they had no servants. I think they weren't well off. At least not back then. They only rented the house. When she had any time, she'd be gardening. They did have a lovely garden—nice tomatoes, I remember. She used to send the boy, Dipen, over with a few sometimes. We sent her mangoes once every season, from our big tree. That tree was cut down with the others when the road was widened.'

Shwetha made another murmur of sympathy, and Miss Joanna continued, 'The boy was especially fond of mangoes. He lost his heart too easily, I thought. I saw him at the park near his school—he didn't go to our school, of course.' She smiled at Shwetha. 'He went to a boys' school in Richmond Town. I saw him there a few times with a girl.'

'At the school?' Nilima asked.

'At the park. It's where I get off from the school bus and walk my way home. I think he was besotted with her. And then she went off to college in Chennai.

'I've seen him with a couple of other girls over the years; he was just a healthy red-blooded boy. Girls are so fickle these days. They have so many expectations. My own sister Rosie had this very nice boyfriend when she was in college, but she refused to marry him ... There was an engagement once.'

'Your sister Rosie?' asked Shwetha.

'No-no-no, the boy Dipen. Just before they moved away—it might be one of the reasons the move was welcome to them, though the reason they gave out was that they were moving into their own flat.'

'But they did move into their own flat?' said Nilima.

'I think so. One of those new buildings. Mr Desai obviously couldn't afford one of these lovely old houses.'

'What happened to Dipen's engagement?'

'It was quite a scandal. Months after the engagement, she eloped with someone. Broke that boy's heart, I thought—though he put a good face on it, always cheerful, "Hello, miss, you look so pretty today" and "Let me carry your bags" and "You should join my band, you're a much better singer than most of the young girls." I used to sing while I was gardening sometimes—not any more, of course, I don't have the voice—and he'd stop and listen. And I'd scold him when he said such things, but he would always say he meant it.'

Miss Joanna shook her head, smiling. 'I heard he got married last year. Mrs Sabbarwal—she was their next-door neighbour and has a boy close to Dipen's age—she says this girl also doesn't seem to care for him much. That she spends more time back home with her parents than here with her husband. Girls don't have much conception of wifely duties anymore, do they?'

'We really don't,' Nilima said cheerfully. 'It doesn't make sense to us.'

Miss Joanna was taken aback but went on, 'His mother wasn't like that though. Not very educated, poor woman. Absolutely devoted to her husband and children. It was unhealthy, I felt. She never spent a night alone in that house; her husband was always there, and they always had dinner together even if he came home late from the shop. The boys—when they grew up they spent less time with their parents, of course, that's only healthy. If you ask me, that explains why she just gave up and died after her husband passed on. She just couldn't make it on her own. She practically wilted.'

'Didn't her husband die after they'd moved away from here?' asked Shwetha.

'Yes, but I saw her once, at Mrs Chandrashekara's daughter's wedding. Mrs Chandrashekara is our neighbour down the lane. She had come alone—Mrs Desai, that is—neither of her sons accompanied her, not even her daughter-in-law. And she looked so thin and pale, like she was wasting away. I am sure she didn't know what to do with herself once her husband passed on.

'It's not good to be so dependent,' Miss Joanna added solemnly. 'No man likes that. You can't be hanging around his neck.'

'Did Mrs Desai hang around Mr Desai's neck?' said Nilima.

'I meant metaphorically. She was the clinging sort.'

'And you think Mr Desai didn't like that?'

'What man would? You can't expect a man to come straight home every night and have dinner with the children. He needs to go out for a drink sometimes, or if he's home then he likes to nurse his drink, watch games on the TV, not take his wife out for a walk every night and for an outing every weekend. He always looked so tired too, poor man, and no wonder.'

'Did he work very hard?' Shwetha asked. 'Did Jagat not help?'

'That boy.' Miss Joanna's lips were pressed thin. 'He was never interested in anyone except himself. All these years he lived here, he never visited me. He would only visit Mr Ahmed—his house is right opposite mine—because he was this movie producer. Not that Mr Ahmed gave him much attention. This Jagat barely even greeted me when he saw me, and once when he did, he called me Joanna, can you believe it? "Hi, Joanna," like I was one of his employees!'

Nilima wondered if she had got the lady's name wrong—was she not called Joanna?

Shwetha stepped to the rescue. 'How impertinent! He didn't call you Miss Rebeiro or Miss Joanna?'

'No indeed, can you believe it! I had half a mind to tell him off, "Young man, haven't your parents taught you any manners?" But you know how I am, Shwetha dear, I've always believed in turning the other cheek. So I just nodded coldly at him.

'*He* married young. His wife, now she wasn't the clingy sort. She went off to visit her parents in some small town in western India every few months. She was bored here, no doubt.'

'You don't think she liked it here?'

'She didn't grow up here, you know. She'd come to live away from her home. She didn't have friends. But she did become quite friendly with that lady in the house next to theirs, Mrs Nair. She moved away when her husband died.'

'But he died ... Oh, you mean Mrs Nair's husband?'

'Yes, he had an accident—his car was quite smashed up. I wonder if he drank, though everyone said he didn't—people don't like to speak ill of the dead, do they? I believe in being frank; it saves so much trouble. This Nair boy drove home from his office—right across the city—quite late every night, but this one night he never got home.'

'This was before the Desais moved away?' Nilima asked.

'Oh no, this was just last year—or maybe the year before. As I said, young Mrs Jagat Desai was friends with Mrs Nair. She used to visit her here sometimes—I saw her after Mr Nair died; she had come to offer condolences as well. And then Mrs Nair moved away with her daughter to a smaller house; I believe she couldn't afford to stay here anymore.'

After they said goodbye to Miss Joanna and went back to the car, Nilima thumbed through her phone. 'It's as Miss Joanna said,' she said after a few minutes, 'this Sowmya Nair is friends with Veena on Facebook, and her husband died nearly two years ago. Accident. The news reports just say the car was found smashed up on the road, and no one seems to have seen anything. It looks like a heavy vehicle crashed into it, and then kept going.'

Nilima looked up when she didn't hear a response. 'This is good, right? We've got a lead. A friend of Veena's killed in an accident—this could be the work of a hitman too.'

'Yeah. I don't know how we'll find out more though.'

'I don't think we need to. I'll just tell Sharmila. She can dig into it.'

Nilima waited till they hit a red light and then asked hesitantly, 'Are you upset?'

'What, Miss Joanna's comments on wifely duties?' Shwetha shook her head. 'Actually, she's not really Miss Joanna. I heard there was a husband once. He abandoned her, and she came back to living with her sisters. She never even got a divorce, it seems.'

'So now she preaches the responsibilities of matrimony,' Nilima said thoughtfully, 'to a divorcee and a lesbian.'

Shwetha giggled, and Nilima sat up a little straighter. She finally noticed her surroundings. 'Are we going in the right direction?' Nilima asked.

'I thought we could look in at the National Gallery of Modern Art before we go back to the office. They have an exhibition on Amrita Sher-Gil that started today.'

'Really? I love her work!'

'I know.'

'How did you know that?'

'I listen when you tell me what you like.'

Nilima's cheeks blazed.

Shwetha continued, 'You know a tad about art ...'

'Not much,' Nilima protested.

'More than Poorna or me, and I've been thinking we should add an art tour to our repertoire. Let's look at this exhibition. Tell me how you feel and take notes so you can do your research later. I've got a group of tourists who are interested in an art tour next week. And yeah, you can think of a couple of other art galleries you can take them to as well.'

'Ooh, there are a few I like. I'd have to see what they're showing right now ...'

'It'll take some work,' Shwetha conceded. 'You focus on this for the next few days, and, if it works we'll make it a regular offering.'

'What about the murder?'

'That's not part of your job,' Shwetha pointed out. 'You are doing that because you want to.'

'We need to find out what happened.'

'And we still have a business to run. Spend as much time on the murder as you want, but I need you to do the tour on Tuesday.'

'In three days?'

'Just a two-hour tour, Deka. It'll be easy.'

Nilima narrowed her eyes. 'You said we're just going to look at the art so I can think about it. You've already booked the tour, haven't you? That too on our day off?'

Shwetha looked sheepish, but quickly recovered. 'That was the only day they have, and anyway I was sure you could do it,' she said grandly, looking away at the street, an effect that would have worked better if she were actually driving—maybe steering across a turn—and not peering through the windshield at the vehicles stalled ahead.

A horn erupted and set off a concert—autorickshaws and motorcycles and cars and buses contributing loudly. Shwetha's hands clenched on the steering wheel. Nilima considered how circumscribed her life usually was; she took the metro or an autorickshaw to office in the morning, and after work she usually walked to a place nearby for a quick dinner or for supplies she could cook on her one pan over her induction stove. Her occasional days off were for browsing books on Church Street or carrying a book and some snacks to Cubbon Park for a solitary picnic. Occasionally, she met a new acquaintance or date at a bar—a friend of a friend, or someone she'd talked to on Bumble—an awkward stilted evening that never transformed into a second meeting. She had tried a couple of queer events before giving up; she'd never be someone who was comfortable walking up to a group of people and chatting away.

This driving around town and getting her ears assaulted wasn't an experience she was unequivocally enjoying, but it was out of her routine, and she was getting to spend time with Shwetha outside the office. Before this week, Nilima hadn't even sat in the front seat of a car for a year. She pushed her seat back and put her legs up on the dashboard, and turned up the radio to drown out some of the honking. A Bollywood dance song was on, and she swayed along to it.

'You're enjoying this,' Shwetha said, her expression a familiar cross between amused and annoyed. 'Being stuck in traffic like this. We only have an hour before the NGMA closes. My stupid old car is overheating too. If it breaks down, we're screwed. We won't be able to move for hours.'

Nilima looked out of the car, not at the vehicles stranded all around them but up at the rain trees making a green canopy. 'Do you know where I lived before I moved here?' she shouted over the ad now playing on the radio. 'Gurgaon. DLF Phase 2, to be exact. It was only for a year, but I don't know how I stood it. I used to go to South Delhi every weekend just to stand under a tree.'

Shwetha laughed. 'Tell me about it. I lived in Bombay for five years. I was so glad to come back home.'

'Is that why you came back? Because you missed Bangalore?'

'That was one reason.'

Nilima leaned back and closed her eyes. Shwetha had never talked about her life in Bombay, why should she start now? Another song started; Rahat Fateh Ali Khan's dulcet tones filled the car.

Shwetha's voice was so soft it was almost part of the music. 'It wasn't the most important reason. I left because I got divorced and wanted to escape. There was too much baggage for me in Bombay. I wanted to come home and be the person I used to be.'

Nilima froze. What could she say that would tell Shwetha it hadn't been a mistake to confide in her? Should she hold Shwetha's hand the way Shwetha had held hers yesterday? Her arm wouldn't budge; her hand lay leaden on her lap.

'Did it work?' she asked, and immediately wondered if she had been too blunt. 'Are you happier?'

'Much,' said Shwetha. Nilima opened her eyes to see Shwetha sitting back as well, her arms folded across her chest, looking out at the trees.

✍

After their visit to the art gallery, Shwetha dropped Nilima off near the office and drove on to a meeting. Poorna was out conducting an evening tour.

Dusk had fallen. Instead of switching on the lights, Nilima opened the window that looked out on the front gate. There wasn't much to see except the occasional bookshop customer walking into the building, oblivious to the window behind which Nilima lurked in the shadows. Mosquitoes tumbled in and Nilima hissed and fidgeted ineffectually when the bites itched, resisting the urge to slap at her skin for fear of drawing attention to herself.

Her head was churning with the details of the plan she had made this morning. Should she risk it at all? She could get arrested or, worse, murdered. Preeti would be horrified if she knew.

Nilima shut the window, switched on the lights and settled in to wait. She typed a report on the interview with Joanna, occasionally consulting the audio recording she had surreptitiously made. Then she researched and planned her art tour, keeping an eye on the time.

At eight-thirty, she locked up the office before walking up to the bookshop. To her relief, Maniram was not at his seat by the door. There was a longer queue than usual at the cash counter, and Sampath was buried in orders to ring up.

There was no one on the upper floor except for Mehnaz, who didn't look up from behind the counter as Nilima slipped into an aisle. Nilima peeped over the shelves; the door to the office was shut. Was it locked or could she get inside?

What if Dipen was in there? *Not likely,* she told herself; at this busy time, if he were in the shop he would have been working downstairs. She had just decided to risk it, and thought of an excuse if she did open the door on him, when she heard a noise and ducked down.

Mehnaz was moving around, placing stray books back on a shelf a few aisles over. Nilima crept over to a stool and hunkered down on it, desperately hoping that Mehnaz would not come nearer and see her.

Mehnaz's high-heeled shoes clacked over to the stairs and made their way down; she must have gone to the bathroom. The upper floor was entirely empty: this was Nilima's chance.

She was about to make a dash for it when she heard a familiar voice. Dipen appeared on the stairs, turning back to talk to someone below. Nilima dropped onto her stool again.

Dipen's voice was softer and happier than usual. He made a joke that he himself laughed at, and invited his companion into the office. Through the gap between the shelves, Nilima could only see their feet—his narrow leather shoes, beautifully polished; his companion's feet in royal blue kolhapuri chappals, a silver leaf glistening on one toe.

The office door opened, and all four feet disappeared through it.

Should she give up and try another day? But she had picked Saturday night because it would be busy; it would be difficult to find another chance to slip in unobserved. She decided to wait. She softly pulled a couple of books down, wishing she had had the foresight to hide in the crime aisle instead of in poetry again. She could hear only a low murmur of voices, the shut door rendering the words unintelligible.

Mehnaz clattered back and resumed her station behind the computer. It was another sixteen minutes—sixteen agonisingly slow minutes during which Nilima tried to breathe noiselessly—before there was movement in the office again. A tinkly laugh faded as the door opened, and blue sandalled feet came out, followed by bigger brown shoes. Dipen was commenting on how the bookshop was doing—badly, but his voice didn't indicate any worry; he sounded carefree, cheerful, even giddy. He said he'd see if they needed help at the cash counter downstairs before he went home. He wasn't like his brother, he chuckled; he didn't need to personally make sure the till was locked every night.

The door shut, but Nilima heard no jangling of keys, and she peered between the shelves as their feet moved towards the stairs. Once Dipen's voice faded, Nilima got up and looked at the counter. Mehnaz was deep in her book again.

Nilima plunged across the aisle and into the office, softly turning the lock behind her.

The room was crammed with furniture. At one end was a big metal desk with a bulky computer and some loose papers, and on the other were two low cupboards. Three chairs sat around the desk, and on the wall behind it hung a big black-

and-white photo of a man standing in front of this same building—Samudra Desai, Nilima guessed. His figure was too small to make out his expression—all she could see was a thin man standing ramrod straight, the building looming ominously behind him.

Nilima gently turned the lock in the door. If Mehnaz or Sampath came by, they would think Dipen had locked the office. Just in case Dipen came back, or someone else had a key to the room, she curled up on the floor behind the desk. Now she wouldn't be visible from the door, but what if Dipen came inside? He would probably call the police, and she would have to depend on Sharmila to get her out of trouble. Her detecting career would be over before it started.

Her phone lit up with a call, and Shwetha's name flashed. Nilima's phone was on silent as usual, but even the glow might alert someone to her presence. As soon as the phone stopped ringing, she turned on airplane mode.

The door rattled, and Nilima's body froze for one awful moment. Then sharp footsteps receded, and she let her breath out again.

Her feet had gone numb from sitting in the same spot when the light leaking in from under the door was cut off. The place had been locked up for the night. Nilima waited for ten more minutes before creeping to the door. She listened for sounds of movement, then opened the door and poked her head out. She was alone in Jagdip Book House, with an entire night ahead of her. She shut the door again and turned on the light.

She opened her handbag and laid out her supplies on a chair. A bottle of water, a bag of banana chips, a bar of chocolate, several resealable plastic bags, hand sanitiser, a camera along with its charger and extra batteries, and a charger and power bank to make sure her phone stayed on all night, in case she needed to call for help. She pulled on thin disposable gloves to avoid leaving fingerprints. Her phone alarm was set for eight in the morning.

She took a picture of the desk so that she could put everything back as it had been. The papers on the desk seemed innocuous—the latest electricity bill, a couple of salary slips, publishers' catalogues, a letter from a publisher expressing regrets at Jagat's death. She took photos of everything.

The drawers held the expected jumble of stationery: notepads, pens and pencils, stamp pads, paper clips and staples, a stapler. There was also a small stack of currency notes—a bunch of hundreds, a few five-hundreds, a couple of two-thousands—and a few sets of keys.

She switched on the computer. Of course, it was password-protected: the username was Jagat. She tried 'password123', then the names of his daughters, Priyadarshini and Sanjeevani. She looked around the desk for a note that might indicate a password: nothing. She typed in 'Veena123' and pressed Enter. The message on the screen said the account had been locked due to too many failed log-in attempts.

Should she try the computers at the cash counters? If she ended up getting all the accounts locked, they might suspect something.

Still, she went to the counter on this floor. The computer had not been shut down—Mehnaz had just turned the monitor off. The username here was Jagdip. Nilima tried 'Jagdip123', then 'Password123', and was too afraid of getting the account locked to try a third time. The drawers were locked. She tried the keys she had found in the office until one opened both of them. The smaller drawer on top contained piles of rubber bands and bookmarks, pens, a stapler, a bowl full of coins, and a sheaf of fifty-, twenty- and ten-rupee notes. The larger one had a bunch of things that looked like they belonged to the employees: an old lunch box, a shawl (probably Mehnaz's), a raincoat, a roll of mints.

She went down the stairs, turning on her phone's flashlight—she didn't want to risk a neighbour noticing that the shop lights were on this late. Beyond the white spotlight she was waving, the shop seemed eerie, like she had wandered into a forbidden forest at midnight.

The computer at the downstairs counter had the same account name: Jagdip. She didn't try to unlock it. The drawers too yielded nothing interesting. *It's okay,* she told herself. *I know there are clues in the office. There have to be.*

Back in the office, she used the keys she was carrying to unlock the cupboards and rifle through them, bringing out the paper files to the desk in batches. A cursory glance revealed bills and other expense records from the past year. Some of the older files also contained book lists and sales records, but not from the last few years. All that must be on the computer. There was nothing related to any real estate deals.

All this effort for nothing. Tears spilled. Her head sank onto the desk.

After a while, Nilima sat up and wiped her face on her T-shirt. She had forgotten to include a handkerchief in her carefully packed handbag.

Stop snivelling, she told herself sternly. *I need to finish my work. Just because I haven't solved the case in one go doesn't mean I shouldn't keep on following the plan.*

It was warm in this windowless room, but she didn't dare turn on the ceiling fan and risk any papers flying off. She took a gulp of water and ate a few banana chips, more to keep herself awake than because she was hungry. When she was done, she carefully removed all traces of the snack from the desk (and congratulated herself for having had the foresight to pack banana chips instead of biscuits—fewer crumbs).

Nilima's attention was flagging; her eyes got heavier. She could barely read the printed pages, let alone the handwritten notes: the letters were blurring together. She gave up trying to make sense of anything and concentrated on taking pictures of every page. She could look at all of it after a good night's sleep.

She fell asleep before she was done, her head dropping to the desk. Her alarm woke her up a couple of hours later. The big room outside was filled with sunlight. It was still quiet downstairs. She shut and locked the office door.

After she had photographed all the papers, she shone her phone flashlight behind the cupboards, then got down on her knees and groped under them. She scooped up what she found: a few small things encrusted in dust.

Anjali obviously doesn't sweep under the cupboards very often, she thought as she placed each item in a separate transparent bag. She tore a page off a notepad, used it to shovel up the dust she had stirred up and shoved the paper (and the dust) under the cupboard. She doused her filthy gloved palms in hand sanitiser and rubbed them on her skirt.

She switched off the light. There was now enough daylight creeping in under the door to see by. She had another half hour to wait before the shop would open and she could sneak out. She sat upright, refusing to lean back or put her feet up on the desk for fear that she would fall asleep again. She tried to focus on the clues, to think of anything relevant she had seen or heard in the last few days, but her mind kept going back to Shwetha. She must be conducting the Sunday heritage walk now, but would be back in office in a couple of hours. Nilima would see her soon.

At nine-thirty, Nilima unlocked the door, listening for sounds from downstairs. It was a Sunday, so hopefully there would soon be enough customers that she could slip out without being noticed. She stood by the door till a grating noise told her that the shutter over the main door was being pulled up. Soon, she heard Sampath's voice, and then Maniram's answering him. Finally, she could pull off the gloves and rubbed her hands together in relief. She padded to the stairs, staying out of sight in case Sampath or Maniram looked up. Sampath was walking around downstairs; his tread was heavy and she could hear every step. Now he was talking again—she wasn't sure whether to Maniram or to himself, or to someone on the phone. It sounded like a monologue; he was griping about the road near his house being dug up. 'It's a dangerous thing, yes-yes,' he said.

A door opened and shut; he had gone into the bathroom. This was her chance. She walked softly down the rest of the stairs.

A woman and a child entered, looking for a last-minute gift for a birthday party, with Dipen just behind them. Nilima hid in an aisle. Dipen handed the customers over to Sampath, who came to the front now, and went upstairs; from her hiding place Nilima saw his legs slowly disappear. Anjali walked in and grabbed a duster from the back of the shop, not far from Nilima. Crouching, keeping an eye on Anjali, Nilima started moving towards the front.

A few more customers wandered in. Sampath was busy ringing up a purchase, and Nilima made for the door. Maniram looked surprised to see her, but another customer was walking up, so he raised his hand in response to her shaky smile and said nothing.

In the Chikkamma office, Poorna was typing away jerkily at her desk.

'You don't look too great,' said Poorna. 'Are you feeling okay?'

'Couldn't sleep much last night,' Nilima said honestly. 'Have a headache.' Her voice was hoarse, her arms red and itching from the dust, and her T-shirt stiff with dried sweat. She hadn't looked in a mirror since yesterday morning. How badly was her hair sticking up? Was her face smeared with dust?

'Go back home and rest,' said Poorna. 'I'll inform Shwetha. Just let me know if anything urgent needs to be done and I'll do it.'

Nilima hesitated. She did need sleep—and food. And she wanted to sort her thoughts out. She thanked Poorna and asked her to follow up with a couple of prospective customers—everything else could wait.

When she was at the door, Poorna said, 'You have a handbag.'

Nilima whirled around.

'You never carry a handbag,' explained Poorna. 'You just carry your stuff in your pockets.'

'I don't carry a lot of stuff in general,' said Nilima. 'Wallet and phone and flat keys. Notebook and pen, maybe. Cigarettes and lighter, sometimes, though I keep a stash in my drawer.'

Poorna nodded.

'I like pockets,' Nilima said defiantly.

'Who doesn't?' agreed Poorna. 'I keep thinking of asking you where you get your clothes. Most of mine don't have pockets, except for my jeans.'

'I had a tailor in Delhi. He made some of my skirts. And I don't buy clothes that don't have functional pockets.'

'I'll ask my tailor if he can put in pockets in my kurtas.'

'I'm carrying water,' said Nilima.

'Ah.' Poorna didn't look baffled by the seeming non sequitur.

'Because of my headache,' explained Nilima. 'In case I need to take a painkiller.'

'And it's so hot today,' said Poorna. 'I hope you don't mind my asking. I was just curious.'

'No, I understand being curious.' Nilima felt no resentment, only a mild admiration at Poorna's powers of observation. Poorna didn't seem to have noticed she was wearing the same clothes from yesterday—or she was too polite to comment on the fact. Nilima should have carried a fresh T-shirt to change into.

Nilima walked out to the street and waited for an autorickshaw. Kamath's hadn't opened yet; a broken bottle on the road indicated that last night had been busy. She carefully nudged the pieces closer to the bar's outer wall with her shoe.

It was only when she got into the autorickshaw that she remembered to take her phone off airplane mode. Immediately, she got a text from Shwetha, sent last night: 'Called because I had a suggestion about the art tour. Not urgent. We'll talk tomorrow. Good night, Nili!'

She wanted desperately to talk to Shwetha, to ask her ... what? How could she confront Shwetha with her suspicions? Didn't what she had seen in the shop mean Shwetha could not be trusted?

Nilima stared at her phone all the way home.

CHAPTER 10

The Wrong Attitude to Rain

'You did what? Are you mad?'

Nilima blinked dazedly. Instead of catching up on sleep yesterday, she had spent all afternoon visiting art galleries in the rain—the heat had broken, and Nilima finally had the grey, breezy and, she realised, extremely wet weather she had been waiting for. At home, she had made herself a dinner of toast, fried egg and sautéed spinach before climbing into bed to look through her photos from the bookshop office, and soon falling asleep instead. She still felt exhausted this morning, and even less equipped than usual for a conversation with Shwetha.

'Why didn't you tell me?'

This time, Nilima succeeded in getting some words out. 'I wasn't sure if it would work. I wanted to do it and then surprise you.'

'That you have! So? What did you find? Any clues?'

Nilima reached into her handbag. 'I don't know. Here, look at these.'

'What's going on?' said Poorna a few minutes later, walking in on Shwetha hunched over an array of transparent bags. Nilima summarised the events of Saturday night again.

'Wow,' Poorna said. 'That's so brave of you. I wish you'd told me; I'd have helped.'

'I will next time,' Nilima promised, and was surprised to realise that she meant it.

'What's in the pouches?'

'Loot from under the cupboards in Dipen's office,' said Nilima. 'I don't know if any of it is important.'

'Why did you take all this?'

'I would have loved to have taken everything to examine later, but if I'd stolen something from a drawer they might have missed it. I figured this stuff would be safe to take, since it was out of sight anyway.'

Poorna nodded and arranged the items in a row: a single earring (eight pearls set like a bunch of grapes), a medicine tablet, a handkerchief embroidered with the letter P, a visiting card, part of a handwritten note with a column of numbers on it and a bill from a stationery wholesaler.

Poorna picked up the earring first. 'This is pretty. Any idea whose it is?'

Shwetha shook her head immediately.

'Mehnaz?' guessed Poorna.

'No, it's not her style,' said Nilima. 'Dipen's wife, maybe.'

Poorna held up the medicine pill in its bag. 'I can't tell what it is. I can ask my neighbourhood pharmacist. He's nice.'

'Okay.' Nilima's mind felt slow, like an ant that had walked through honey. She was glad that someone else was making decisions, even though that someone was Poorna.

'Here's another puzzle.' Poorna pointed to the handkerchief. 'Who's P?'

'Pallav?' guessed Shwetha.

'I thought this was a ladies' hanky.'

'I don't think handkerchiefs have genders, Poorna.'

'Shut it, Deka. You know what she meant.'

'It's okay,' Poorna smiled. 'She's just teasing.'

Both Shwetha and Nilima looked at her in surprise.

'I have two siblings,' Poorna explained. 'That's sort of how we express affection.'

'My sister and I used to get on each other's nerves all the time,' Nilima acknowledged. 'Before I moved out, I mean. Are you an only child, Shetty?'

'And feeling this sudden urge to call my parents and thank them.'

Nilima opened the handkerchief bag and sniffed deeply. 'Mostly dust,' she pronounced after sneezing. 'Maybe a whiff of perfume. I might be imagining it.'

Poorna leaned in and sniffed too. 'Men's cologne, smells like. I have a good nose. In school, I could tell who'd brought what before they'd opened their tiffin boxes. Maybe you could ask Mehnaz if she recognises it.'

'Good idea,' said Shwetha, moving her chair closer. 'Now the business card.'

'It's a publishing sales rep,' said Nilima without looking.

'Could that be important?' asked Shwetha.

'I don't see how. Normal for reps to visit the bookstore, isn't it?'

'I guess. What are these bits of paper?'

'A bill for several kinds of notebooks; it seems straightforward enough. That scrap of paper—looks like some calculation. Expense for something? Can't tell without the rest of it. It looks fresher than the others; the paper's quite clean, see? It can't have been under the cupboard long.'

Shwetha examined the scrap through the bag, holding it carefully with two fingers.

'What do you think?' asked Poorna.

'No idea.' Shwetha placed the bag and its contents back on Poorna's desk.

'I thought you recognised something,' Nilima said carefully. 'The handwriting, maybe?'

'The numbers reminded me of something, but I can't think what. What else did you get?'

'I photographed every piece of paper in that room.' Nilima dug out the camera from her handbag. 'Everything's in here.'

'You have an actual camera?' Shwetha looked amused.

'Not everyone has an iPhone,' Nilima said snidely, pulling out the memory card. 'I've had this camera for nearly a decade now because my phone camera was never as good. It's all in there. I don't know what we'll find, or even what we're looking for.'

'Were you hoping to find something specific when you decided to search that room?' Poorna asked.

'No, not anything specific, just something that would point us in the right direction. We know so little at the moment.'

'Did you go through the papers when you photographed them?' said Shwetha.

'Cursorily. Nothing jumped out at me. Most of it was numbers—expenses, sales, payslips, that kind of thing.'

'We should find an accountant to look at it for us,' Shwetha suggested. 'If there's something interesting in the finances, they should be able to find it.'

'Don't we have an accountant?' Poorna asked.

'Naah, can't afford it. I do the paperwork myself. I did get some advice from someone when I started, but that's it. I don't know her well enough to tell her what we're doing here, especially since we got this illegally.'

Shwetha plugged the card into her laptop. 'Let me look through it. Maybe something will make sense. Give me a couple of hours.'

'Did you find anything on Mohan?' Poorna asked. 'Isn't he our main suspect?'

'I thought Veena was our main suspect,' said Shwetha.

'I don't know,' said Nilima. 'I feel whoever it is has a more direct connection to the bookstore.' She glanced at Shwetha, who was downloading the photos onto her laptop.

'Why?' asked Poorna.

'Call it a hunch. I feel all our answers are in there.'

Poorna nodded sagely. 'Hunches are good. I am a firm believer in intuition.'

'Of course you are,' Nilima blurted out.

'I guess we all have our favourites,' Shwetha said hastily.

'Like in fantasy football.' Poorna grinned, apparently unoffended. 'I've been getting into that ...' She stopped at the looks on her colleagues' faces. 'Fine, continue with your joyless existences.'

'Speaking of,' Shwetha turned to Nilima, 'don't you have to write that post for the Bangalore history Instagram account? It's due on Wednesday.'

'Almost ready,' said Nilima. 'I just have to, you know, write it and find pictures to go with it. I'll do it tomorrow.'

'Tomorrow's Tuesday, Deka. You've got the art tour. And I thought you'd take Wednesday off to compensate.'

'That's okay, I don't need a day off. And I'll have time tomorrow, after the tour. Right now, I want to find out more about all our suspects.'

'We could shadow someone,' Poorna suggested.

'What? Who?'

'I don't know, we should be following suspects, doing something.'

'I *am* doing something,' Nilima said coldly, in what she hoped was an imitation of Poirot. 'I am thinking, mon ami.'

Poorna replied with a string of unfamiliar sounds, of which Nilima only managed to recognise 'oui'.

'Hold on, you speak French?' Nilima cringed at the decidedly unFrench way she had pronounced her own two little words of contribution to this exchange.

'Yeah, I won a semester of free classes as a prize at school, when I did well in my 10th standard. I continued as long as they kept extending it—two more semesters—and by then I was too busy studying for my board exams to ace the French tests, so they said I could only continue if I paid the fees. I couldn't, so that was that.'

'What?' she asked when Nilima continued to stare at her.

'You must have been brilliant. Academically, I mean.'

Shwetha spoke up. 'Of course she's brilliant. Do you think I'd hire losers?'

You hired me. Nilima stopped herself from saying it. 'I didn't think you were listening.'

'I'm afraid I can't quite help it, given that you two are talking within five feet of me, not even bothering to keep your voices down. I have work to do.'

Nilima involuntarily glanced at the tiny room next to Shwetha's but didn't dare suggest she should use it if she wanted quiet.

'What do you think?' Poorna asked Shwetha, ignoring her outburst. 'Shouldn't we be following the suspects, finding out what they're up to?'

'Anything that will get you out of the office so I can work in peace,' said Shwetha, not looking up from her laptop. Neither Nilima nor Poorna seemed to care that yesterday had been the first Sunday in months that they had had to cancel the all-day tour. Three people had turned up for Poorna's temple tour on Sunday evening, and the group of tourists who had signed up for Nilima's private art tour tomorrow had already paid up, but the three upcoming public tours languished on Facebook with few sign-ups or comments. That was why Shwetha was desperately poring over her task list, sending off emails and messages, looking for a glimmer of hope that had so far refused to appear.

'Nilima, since you're working on Wednesday, you can take the lake tour if we don't get more people. Only two have signed up so far: it's a good way to practice.'

Nilima's jaw dropped in dismay. 'I need time to prepare!'

'Nonsense. You've gone with Poorna before.'

'You can practise when we're doing our detective work,' Poorna said kindly. 'We'll multitask!'

Shwetha added, 'I'll never get this done if you two are yakking away in here all day. If you're not going to do any actual work, by all means, carry on.'

'Come on, Nims, let's go.' Poorna put on her jacket. 'We'll talk on the way.'

'I need to prep for my art tour,' Nilima said, hanging back.

'You said on the group chat yesterday that you were all ready.'

'Yes, but still ...'

'Don't overprepare, you'll just be more nervous. Come on, taking your mind off it will help.'

Nilima rubbed her heavy eyelids and followed Poorna to a hot pink scooter with yellow daisies painted on the side. Poorna pulled out a helmet, saying, 'Sorry, I don't have another.'

'What? Are we going on this?'

'Yes, of course.' Poorna placed her handbag inside the storage compartment. 'What did you imagine, we'd follow someone around in an Uber?'

'I wasn't imagining following anyone at all,' Nilima muttered, but when Poorna, ears now covered by her helmet, turned her head and said loudly, 'What?' Nilima merely yelled back, 'Nothing!' and climbed on.

Nilima couldn't remember when she had last been on a scooter. The closest was a friend's motorcycle in Delhi last year; she had been scared at first, but after she had settled herself it had felt exhilarating.

But this was much bumpier, and her legs were stretched out so wide her thighs hurt, and she couldn't find anything to hold on to and there wasn't enough space and she was pressing too close to Poorna.

'Are you okay?' Poorna shouted.

'Yes, of course!'

'Who should we start with? I'm thinking Veena. If she hired an assassin, she may meet him again, no? To pay him the rest of the money or something.'

'No point,' Nilima yelled against the wind. 'The police are on this. Sharmila's interested in the money.'

'Mohan, then?'

'Mohan,' Nilima agreed. 'Let me pull up his office address.'

Nilima consulted Google Maps and Poorna obligingly changed direction. A fine drizzle thickened into a light shower. Poorna was protected by her helmet and jacket and jeans, but Nilima was in a knee-length cotton skirt and T-shirt, and the wind soon had her shivering.

They were in Banashankari soon enough. Nilima tapped Poorna's back when they were opposite the building that housed the accountant's office, but Poorna kept going, making for a tea stall just ahead. They got off the scooter, took shelter under the narrow tin roof and accepted little glasses of sweet milky tea. A couple of other customers were engaged in an enthusiastic conversation in Kannada with the stall proprietor about a recent movie. Nilima caught the movie's name, though she could follow little of the conversation.

'Now what?' Nilima whispered, suddenly aware that they had no plan.

'I don't know. Which floor is his office, do you know?'

'Ground floor.'

Poorna put her glass down on the counter. 'Let me check if he's in.' She stepped across the street before Nilima could stop her.

This lane was probably bustling on most afternoons with its row of commercial buildings—Nilima saw printers and photocopiers, a liquor shop, 'Spoken English' classes. But now most pedestrians had taken shelter indoors, and even traffic had thinned down to an occasional vehicle.

She checked Twitter for news about the torrential downpour. Occasional gusts of wind threw ribbons of rain into Nilima's face.

A bus loomed out of the blur, and the two men sharing the stall with Nilima ran off to catch it. The owner fastened a tarpaulin across the back of the stall and lay down for a nap.

Being effectively alone made her feel less awkward. She leaned back against the counter and lit a cigarette. A man came out of the photocopier's in a raincoat and pulled the shutter down before walking off into the rain. A large car stopped by the building she was watching, and two men went in.

It was raining too loudly to listen to music on her earphones. She shook the raindrops off her glasses and rubbed her eyes. Her back emitted a dull ache, and her feet were wet and cold inside her sneakers.

The world seemed to melt into water. Nothing seemed real except her own body and the metal box she was standing next to.

Hunger gripped her stomach. Would she have to miss lunch again? Was this why crime shows always had footage of cops eating on stakeouts?

Where was Poorna? How long had she been inside the building?

Nilima carefully pulled her phone out under cover of the tea stall's roof. It had only been twelve minutes.

Poorna loped back, sailing over a large puddle.

'You were gone a long time.' Nilima paused to excise the whining note out of her voice. 'Did you get anything useful?'

'I was talking to guys in other shops. This young fellow left Mohan's office while I was at the photo printing shop, and the guy there said he works for Mohan. There are no other employees, and this fellow seems to have left for the day. Maybe he works part-time.'

Nilima gestured at the rain. 'Must be going home. There are flash flood warnings.'

'There are warnings? My grandmother will be calling me now.'

'What about Mohan? Did you see him?'

'He must be in his office because the other fellow didn't lock the door. I went into the wholesale furniture place. There were only two people in there—the owner and an employee, I think. I asked if they knew Mohan's office—I had already seen which one it was, that's how I saw the door was unlocked. But I needed something to start the conversation. I told them I had just started a new business and need an accountant and would they recommend him? They said their shop doesn't work with him, they have someone else. His office doesn't get a lot of visitors, they said; they don't know if he's not doing well or if he's picky.'

'That seems a polite way of *not* recommending him.'

'Yep. And they also mentioned that the police paid him a visit a couple days ago.'

'Yes, Sharmila told me they took him to the station to take his statement.'

'I asked if they knew why the police were talking to him and they told me about the murder. I kept them talking, in case they'd seen Jagat visit or something. They didn't know what Jagat looked like, so I described him—I said I know him from the bookshop. They didn't remember seeing him. Then two men walked by in the corridor and this furniture guy said, "Hey, I've seen that big bald man go to Mohan's before" and the other guy slapped his shoulder, as if he was warning him. After they'd gone past, he said, "You fool, that's Madhura Shetty."'

Poorna clearly expected her to know the name, so Nilima ventured, 'An uncle of Shwetha's?'

Poorna snorted. 'No. They're not remotely related, I hope. Madhura Shetty is one of the big builders in the area. He's also, like, a crime boss.'

'What, like the mafia?'

'Yeah, the goss is he's one of the players in the land mafia. Owns quite a bit of the land south of the city, and some commercial buildings in this part of town. Not this one though. I asked the furniture shop guys.'

'You think he's related to our case?'

'Could be ... I don't know.'

'Jagat's real estate dealings,' Nilima said slowly. Both Pallav and Sampath had mentioned them, and this was the first tangible, if tenuous, link.

'He's probably just another of Mohan's clients and never knew Jagat at all,' she added pessimistically.

Poorna didn't respond. Her eyes were trained on the building gate.

They waited for the gangster to come out, Poorna fidgeting as usual, tapping her hand on her thigh. Nilima drew her body in tight, trying to avoid being splashed by the drip from the corner of the roof. She looked longingly at the portable gas burner, but the tea shop owner lay prone on the floor, a blanket keeping him warm enough to stay asleep.

Nilima fished out her last cigarette and generously shared it with Poorna.

Nearly an hour later, the two men finally walked out of the shop. Nilima found it difficult to make out their features in the driving rain, but they went to the car she had seen drive up. One was tall and muscular, and walked with controlled energy, as if he could run all the way to Whitefield without pausing for breath. He got into the driver's seat. The other man, Nilima realised when he came up to the car, was also tall, though he hadn't looked it next to his taller colleague. He was broad, with a paunch that was noticeable even through the screen of rain. His hair snaked down to his shoulders. He got in next to the driver, and the car rolled away.

Poorna uncoiled from her slouch against the counter. 'Let's go after them.'

'What? Why?' Nilima grabbed Poorna's arm to stop her from getting on to the scooter.

'We might find out something. Quick, before we lose them.'

'What's the point of following them?' Nilima demanded. 'They might just be going home. We don't know if they have any connection to the murder.'

'But ...'

'Mohan is our suspect. We know next to nothing about him. Shouldn't we stick with him?'

'All right.' Poorna allowed herself to be herded back under the tea stall's roof. 'But he's just sitting in his office. How will we find out anything? Do you want to wait till he leaves and then break into his office?'

'That might take hours. Hold on, I think I've got an idea.'

Nilima called up Inspector Lamani, who didn't sound thrilled to hear from her, and grew progressively less thrilled as Nilima outlined her request. 'If you call and frighten him, threaten him maybe, he may talk to an accomplice or try to hide evidence. We can follow him and see what he does. Maybe we'll find something out.'

'I have actual work here, Miss Deka.'

'Have you ruled Mohan out then?' Nilima asked pointedly. 'Do you know he's not connected with the murder? We just saw Madhura Shetty come out of his office—tell me that's not shady.'

'Fine,' Sharmila said abruptly. 'Just don't do anything foolish, madam. If you see anything suspicious, you call me immediately. Don't let him destroy evidence.'

'Yes, ma'am,' said Nilima, wondering how they were to stop him.

'Hmm, I will tell him to come to the police station in the morning. I will say some new documents about Jagat's business have come to light, and he needs to look at them and make a statement.'

'That's all?'

Sharmila chuckled. 'That will be enough to scare him—accountants always have something to hide. Hopefully, he is not very smart, otherwise he'll see it's a trick. I'm not stupid enough to warn him and leave him to himself all night to destroy any evidence or even leave town.'

'I hope not,' Nilima said, now worried.

'Listen, you text me your location every half hour, else I will send a man to look for you.'

'That's not necessary, ma'am.'

'It is,' the inspector responded darkly. 'If anything happens to you, Hafeeza will never forgive me.'

As she put her phone back in her pocket, Nilima said nervously, 'Sharmila will call and scare him, then we can see what he does. But she says Mohan might destroy evidence. What if he starts shredding papers or something?'

'I'll go and see.'

'No, you've already been in there talking to people. You'll be far more noticeable. It's my turn.'

Nilima stepped into the building, swiping at her glasses ineffectually with her damp T-shirt. The sign for Mohan's accountancy office was at the far end of the corridor. Someone was locking the door. Nilima stared at his back, matching his hazy figure to her memory of the photos she had found online. Mohan was short and stocky, his hair ringing a bald patch on the top of his head. His loose shirt was cuffed at the elbows.

She ducked into a stairwell, waiting out of sight until she heard his footsteps go past. Then she followed him out of the building.

Poorna already had the scooter running. Nilima had barely balanced herself on the seat when they lurched forward. Mohan, also on a scooter, was fast fading ahead.

If Nilima had been uncomfortable earlier, this ride was a lot worse. Muddy water splashed up at them; the scooter bounced in and out of potholes; and Poorna was going faster, trying to keep Mohan in sight. Nilima's legs pressed against the sides of the scooter, and her hands gripped the back of her seat. It was still afternoon, but the heavy rain made it hard to see. Other vehicles' lights dazzled her eyes, and water trickled down her glasses. She bowed to place her forehead against Poorna's back.

'You okay there, Nims?' Poorna asked.

'Yeah. Just can't see much.'

'Don't worry, I won't lose him. You just hold on.'

After what seemed like hours of thudding over bumps and puddles, Poorna slowed to a stop under a large tree. Nilima immediately pulled out her phone. It was only four; they had been riding for fifty minutes at the most.

Nilima clambered off the scooter, her legs feeling less than solid under her. 'Where are we?'

'Don't you recognise it?' Poorna got a clean rag out of the scooter's compartment and handed it to Nilima, who promptly wiped off her phone and her glasses, and merely pushed her dripping hair off her forehead, ignoring the trickles running down her neck.

'I've not even been here,' Poorna boasted. 'I remember the address from your notes.'

The lane did look familiar. A granite plaque on the wall proclaimed the name of the building: Minerva Mansions.

'He's come to Jagat's flat?'

'He's come to meet Veena,' Poorna said grimly. 'She must be in on whatever shady business he and Jagat were cooking up together.'

Nilima's phone flashed with a text:

> Where r u?

'It's Sharmila,' she whispered, and typed back.

She showed Poorna the next message:

> Dont move. Stay where u r

'For how long?' Nilima muttered furiously. 'What does she mean? Is she going to do something?'

'She will tell us, I hope.'

Another text appeared. 'I was hoping for an answer, and she's just creating more mystery.' Nilima held up the screen to Poorna again.

> Stay hidden. Dont let them c u

'Who's "them"?' Nilima said exasperatedly.

'Mohan and ... Veena, maybe?' Poorna suggested.

'Why doesn't she explain?'

'Should we squat behind the tree? To hide?'

Nilima's back and legs were sore. She repressed a shudder at the thought of huddling behind the tree, and it turned into a shiver. The breeze was mild, but in her wet clothes it seemed to go through her. 'The building watchman is out of our line of sight. Let's just stay here.'

'You're right, if someone sees us behind the tree it will look suspicious.'

They leaned casually against the tree, trying to act as if they'd stopped for shelter from the rain. Nilima's phone rang. All Poorna heard was 'Yes' and 'Okay' and once, 'Yes, ma'am.'

'Sharmila,' Nilima explained unnecessarily. 'She's afraid Veena might be in danger, if Mohan is the murderer.'

'Oh.' Poorna's eyes grew round. 'Like she might know something and Mohan came to kill her.'

'Or threaten her.'

'What do we do?'

'A couple of policemen are coming. That's who we're to hide from. And she called Veena. She says Veena didn't sound afraid. Sharmila told her she was sending policemen to return some of Jagat's things that they had taken to the police station.'

'What kind of things?'

'Documents—bank passbooks and flat papers and stuff. She said they were planning to return them anyway since they have been inspected and copied, so it's a good excuse.'

'Excuse for what?'

'For the police to visit. She asked Veena if anyone else was in the house. The children, Veena said, and Mohan had just arrived. So Sharmila asked to speak to Mohan. She kept him talking; she said she was looking through the documents and asked him foolish questions—her word, not mine. She wanted to keep him on the phone as long as possible while her policemen get here. And she told Mohan to wait for them and not leave.'

'She's trying to scare him.'

'And give him less of an opportunity to destroy evidence or hurt Veena, if he were so inclined. Look! Are those policemen on that bike?'

The motorcycle stopped at the building gate. 'Yeah, they're in uniform,' Poorna said. The security guard waved the riders in.

Nilima answered Sharmila's call almost before it rang. 'My men say they're on their way up to the flat. Is Mohan still there?'

'He hasn't left.'

'Good. You girls can go now. I'll tell you if they find anything.'

Nilima thanked her and relayed the conversation to Poorna. Neither of them moved; by unspoken accord they waited until Mohan rode out on his scooter and went past without noticing them. It grew darker and the wind rose up. At least it had stopped raining. Nilima hugged herself and wished again that she'd carried a jacket. Farther away, noises of traffic started up again, but this little street remained mostly undisturbed except for an occasional vehicle or a stray walker with a dog. The streetlights came on, the bleary yellow struggling to get through the wide canopies of the rain trees marching down the lane.

Nearly an hour later, the policemen rode out again.

It took three tries before the inspector answered Nilima's call, and she did not seem pleased. Nilima pressed the speaker button so Poorna could listen in. 'Yes, everything is certainly fine. Otherwise, my men would not have left. Mrs Desai seemed fine, the children seemed fine and Mohan was not carrying anything—they searched him. They also did a quick search of the house to see if anything has been hidden or destroyed.'

Nilima frowned. How could the police officers have known for sure if something had been hidden in the flat in the minutes before they arrived—something small, like a document or even a dagger?

'Did they find out why Mohan came here?' Nilima asked aloud.

'Both Mohan and Veena said it was a social call.' The inspector chuckled. 'Mohan says he comes to see Mrs Desai when he can. I am sure he came to warn her that we've found new documents. What they're afraid of us finding, I don't know. Was he carrying anything when you saw him?'

Poorna pictured Mohan walking out of his office building, his short shirt untucked, his pleated trousers crumpled. 'Nothing in his hands,' she said with certainty. 'He didn't put anything in his scooter, and even his helmet was locked onto his seat, so he didn't take out anything. And I'd have noticed anything bulky in his pockets.'

'Thank you, Miss Poorna. Now go home, you two. You've done enough today.'

Nilima looked at her phone: the call had ended. *That didn't sound like a commendation.*

✍

Nilima came out of the office bathroom, legs rigorously scrubbed to remove mud stains, to find Poorna carefully adjusting a bucket to catch drops of water plopping down from the ceiling. Poorna looked like a wet kitten. Her long hair, now unplaited, was dripping nearly as much as the ceiling. Shwetha was on the phone in her office; her voice drifted in through the open door, uncharacteristically brittle and harsh.

Nilima placed a box of tissues next to Poorna, who accepted the offering and rubbed her head vigorously. Nilima was plucking shreds of tissue off Poorna's head when Shwetha came out into the bigger room.

'Nice evening?' said Nilima. Shwetha gave her a dark look and got herself a cup of tea.

'So much for your boss being happy that everyone's back in to work through the evening, even though the city is waterlogged,' Nilima said softly.

'You didn't have to come back,' Shwetha retorted. 'It doesn't make much difference anyway.'

'Are you saying our hard work does nothing for this place?'

'If you haven't noticed, business hasn't been great recently. All we've been working on is the case. No one turned up for my tour this evening. I waited and kept calling the two couples who'd signed up. They didn't even answer.'

'Oh, that's why you're back early,' Nilima realised. Shwetha flinched; neither of them had bothered to ask—they had probably not even remembered she was supposed to be on a tour.

'It's been raining all afternoon,' Poorna put in mildly.

'It had stopped raining,' Shwetha said. 'And it's a monsoon walk.'

'Still,' Poorna said cheerily, 'who wants to go walking in this weather?'

'Better than out walking in the searing sun,' Nilima mumbled.

'Or out walking at all, for you,' Shwetha said sharply. 'You'd always prefer to laze indoors with a book, wouldn't you? I don't know why you wanted to work here in the first place.'

Shwetha settled in behind her desk, apparently not noticing Poorna's mouth fall open in consternation and Nilima's face become blank and taut.

'Because I didn't have a job,' Nilima said softly. 'Because I was tired of working in soulless corporate offices, and I don't have the skills to start something cool on my own. Because I thought *you* were cool and would be fun to work with.'

Shwetha sat up, looking stricken. She opened her mouth to apologise, but Nilima spoke first. 'Looks like I was wrong.'

For the rest of the evening, it was quiet in the office. The phone didn't ring, and Shwetha didn't make any more calls; when she asked Poorna or Nilima a question, she was punctiliously polite, and they answered just as politely. All three sat at their desks, working or pretending to—Nilima, for one, was just staring at her notes, thinking unhappy thoughts.

What if the business did fold? Or Shwetha decided she needed to reduce expenses? As the newer employee—and also the less enthusiastic and, let's face it, less competent one—wouldn't Nilima be asked to leave? How long could Nilima make it on savings already much depleted by moving cities and not earning for six months?

No point thinking about this, she told herself firmly. *I have a murder to solve. I can look for a job later if I have to.*

But her thoughts about the murder were no better. *Why is Shwetha in such a bad mood? Is it just the business or is she hiding something? Did she lie about that scrap of paper I found? She seemed to have noticed something. Did she take it so I wouldn't dig into it?*

Who could have written those numbers? Could it have been Shwetha herself? It didn't look like her handwriting. Or maybe she recognised the handwriting. Is she covering for someone?

Suddenly her mind presented her with a memory: Shwetha leaning over Jagat's body as Nilima came up the stairs. How much time had Shwetha had with the body before Nilima and Poorna had joined her—a few seconds, a minute? She had had the opportunity to remove evidence.

She wouldn't have done that, Nilima told herself. But her mind stuck on the possibility. Nilima knew Shwetha hadn't told the truth about her connection to the Desai family. What else had she lied about?

Nilima couldn't imagine why Shwetha might want to shield Jagat's murderer. But she had also realised she didn't know Shwetha very well at all.

CHAPTER 11

The Case of the Bunch of Pearls

That night, when sleep eluded her, Nilima pulled her phone out from under her pillow. Her art tour was in eleven hours. New questions her clients might ask popped into her mind, and she looked for the answers on her phone.

She woke up to her phone digging into her cheek and a rough voice yelling outside her window. She couldn't make out the words, except for a refrain of 'hear ye, hear ye, hear ye'. He was advertising something through a loudspeaker—unless she had gone back in time and it was actually a megaphone. She drew the curtain aside. The lane below had only the usual parked scooters and cars. The voice was fading, but she could still hear, faintly, 'hear ye hear ye hear ye'.

On her phone was a text from Shwetha:

> Hi, sorry, I won't be able to come with you today. I've got an unexpected meeting with a blogger who wants to write about us! He's coming to the office at noon.

Nilima, who had been as nervous about being under observation from Shwetha as she was about conducting the tour, wrote back sincerely:

> No problem at all!
>
> Good luck with the blogger!
>
> Tho are you sure he isn't looking for info on the murder?

Shwetha's response came at once:

> I did my homework, Deka!
>
> He's a travel blogger who focuses on places in south India
>
> Doesn't care about murders

And then:

> Good luck for today! Go kill it!!!

Most mornings, Nilima was too groggy—and more often than not, running too late—to care much about what to wear. It helped that she didn't have a lot of clothes, partly because she disliked shopping—a dislike born from the fact that most shops didn't carry much in her size—but mostly because she hadn't had a fixed home for longer than a year or two in over a decade. Moving frequently motivated you to have fewer possessions. She was also bigger than she used to be, while Poorna still wore clothes she had had in high school. And of her limited wardrobe, between half to three-quarters was either in her laundry bag or drying in her bathroom window at any moment, which further restricted her choices. Her process of selecting clothing, therefore, typically consisted of fishing out whatever was nearest and reasonably clean and pulling it on.

Growing up, *Jane Eyre* had been Nilima's favourite book, and she had modelled herself on that lady's brooding moroseness. It had seemed natural, therefore, to covet not the brightly coloured, Bollywood-influenced, embellished clothes her peers wanted but Jane's small wardrobe of colourless dresses. She remembered, on more than one shopping trip when she was a teenager, looking in vain for 'silver-grey' fabric for a skirt, and failing to find anything that hadn't brought to mind her school uniform.

From black and blue jeans with black and grey T-shirts in college, Nilima's wardrobe had somewhat expanded in recent years to include several dresses and skirts in black and grey (in varying shades of nearly black to light ash—none, however, had succeeded in being convincingly silvery). She had one set of black and green mekhela sador—cotton, not silk—for special occasions, as well as what Nilima was currently feverishly hunting for and finally pulled out from the bottom of the cupboard: wide-legged pants in charcoal grey linen, and an emerald silk top with a bow at the neck.

Since she had started working with Shwetha and Poorna, she had simultaneously disapproved of and envied their colourful, feminine wardrobes. Shwetha seemed to float in her palazzo pants and long kurtas, wispy dupattas that trailed after her and silk saris that glowed like jewels. Even with jeans she wore peasant blouses that emphasised her softness. Poorna wore what to Nilima seemed more comfortable clothes: jeans with shirts, short kurtas with leggings. Any of her ensembles probably had as much colour as was in Nilima's entire wardrobe.

Nilima screwed her only pair of earrings—garnets, a parting gift from Preeti—into her ears, and slipped her feet into maroon leather moccasins instead of the old grey sneakers she habitually wore.

Now for eyeliner. She was so out of practice that she failed to make the barely visible line she wanted, and once she put on her glasses she looked like nothing so much as an owlet. *Owlets are cute though,* she consoled herself. She had worn glasses with the thinnest frames for years, trying to make them invisible, hating how they made her fleshy face look flabbier. But the last time she had replaced her spectacles, she had tried on thicker frames and liked how they looked on her face. Her glasses now were rimmed in thick cobalt blue, drawing attention to their presence.

She had described herself as round ever since a friend in college had joked that her height wasn't much more than her width. When she had got her hair cut short a few years ago, it had been partly so that she didn't have to comb her frizzy tangled locks anymore and partly in acceptance of her resemblance to a big ball.

Her pants were crumpled and the bow at her neck sagged dispiritingly, but her clothes still lent her an air of competence. She thrust her hands into her pockets, and her shoulders settled into their usual slouch. She nodded at her reflection in the bathroom mirror.

She arrived early at the NGMA and was pacing the driveway nervously, pretending to admire the sculpture garden, when she saw her clients at the gate—a large family of Australians. She gulped and awkwardly introduced herself. Once she settled in after her initial nervous floundering, she was surprised that her group seemed to be enjoying themselves. Her delight rapidly descended into contempt when they didn't ask her difficult questions. Some of them walked across the rooms without stopping to adequately appreciate the best pieces. She remembered Shwetha's strictures and tried to remain polite. Not out of loyalty to Shwetha, she told herself, but because she felt more invested in doing this tour well than she had been in doing anything at her job.

She even managed to have a long chat about the portrayal of women in women's art with a teenage boy whom she had dismissed, at the beginning of the tour, as not being interested because he had stood apart and not met her eye. It had been so long since she had been a teenager that she had nearly forgotten what it was like, and she felt an unexpected rush of tenderness towards this awkward young man. This conversation made her feel better, though she wasn't ready to admit it was because she had connected with another person. She was happier to admit the other reason: the success of her tour was a reminder that she had useful skills and she could handle life, even though life was looking very confusing at the moment.

✍

Back at the office, Nilima gave an oral report of the tour to a very appreciative audience. She hadn't expected Poorna to be in today, but by unspoken agreement their weekly day off seemed to be temporarily suspended. Nilima brushed off their compliments and went to her desk. She had to write that Instagram guest post that was due in the morning.

Behind her, Shwetha and Poorna discussed ordering in a celebratory lunch. 'I'm paying,' Shwetha said before retreating to the inner room.

When the doorbell rang, Poorna went to fetch the food.

'Hey, Nili,' Shwetha called as she came out of her room to see Nilima huddled over her computer. 'Turn on the AC, I'll shut the window. It's so hot today!'

Nilima hadn't noticed the sudden change in the weather. Her precious silk top was damp with sweat and clinging to her skin. She wondered why Shwetha cared now, why she was being so cheerful and friendly. *It's because I'm doing extra work,* the voice in her head snarked. *It's not like she pays me overtime, so she turns on the charm when she needs something.*

Poorna set out the food on her desk. As she ripped open a paper bag, she said to Shwetha, 'I keep forgetting to tell you, that's a delicious dress!'

Shwetha's yellow kurta was embroidered in silver thread, as was the coral skirt beneath. She was as radiant as the sun. Nilima blinked and helped herself to a few fries.

If Nilima wore something like that (let alone the near impossibility of finding it in her size, though she supposed she could get it tailored—and it would probably cost about a month's rent), the colours would wash out her skin. That shiny fabric stretched taut over her torso would make her look ridiculous, she told herself. But on Shwetha, what you noticed was not the colours but how they made her skin glow, how the sheen of the silver thread was reflected in her eyes.

She realised Shwetha was looking back at her. 'Nice outfit,' she said roughly.

'You're dressed up too. I could get used to that.' Shwetha winked.

Nilima wheeled her chair around to face Poorna. 'You didn't tell us what your chemist said, about the tablet I found.'

'Ugh, he's on leave,' Poorna said through a mouthful of burrito. 'He's gone off to his village for a wedding. I tried to ask the other chemist in the shop, and she said she'd check up on it. He's supposed to be back in two days; I'll try again.'

'I have an update.' Shwetha reached into her drawer and held up the transparent bag with the single earring. 'I found out who this belongs to.'

'Who?' Poorna asked excitedly.

'Veena. Anjali saw it on my desk this morning.'

'Our cleaner?' Nilima said.

'Yeah. Anjali said she had noticed the earrings on Veena because they were so pretty. She's only seen Veena a few times in all these years, but she knows who she is.'

'Because Veena doesn't come in the morning,' guessed Nilima. *Like me. I hadn't met Anjali till last week.*

'Here, look at this photo of Veena on Facebook'

Poorna and Nilima bent over either side of Shwetha's desk. On the laptop screen, Veena was frozen in laughter, barely recognisable as the sad, severe woman Nilima had met last week. Shwetha's long finger was pointing at an earring with eight pearls dangling in a bunch. The time stamp indicated the picture had been uploaded last July.

'Mystery solved!' said Shwetha, playfully slapping Nilima's arm. Nilima flinched and deliberately wheeled her chair back across the room. The hurt on Shwetha's face made Nilima's stomach constrict. Luckily, Poorna was still staring at the screen and hadn't noticed the exchange.

'What now?' Poorna asked. 'Like, this doesn't help us. Veena must have dropped the earring when she came to meet Jagat at the shop.'

'Now we get back to work,' Shwetha said briskly. 'I hate to remind you that our actual jobs need doing too. Bookings this month are at an all-time low.'

'Why don't you give your North Indian friend a call? That fellow, what's his name ...'

Shwetha looked blankly at Poorna.

'That guy who got us that nice gig—full day with a whole lot of Americans. We made more money that day than we did all of last month.'

'How do you know how much money we made last month?' Nilima asked.

'Shwetha told us on Friday. When she said we need to work harder and get more business because we're not making enough.'

'Oh. I tune out when that speech starts.'

Poorna said hastily, 'Anyway, what's that guy's name? Amit? Or is it Sumit?'

'You mean Rahul,' Shwetha said coldly.

'Right. Can't he get us more gigs like that?'

'His American colleagues only come here once a year for the annual management meeting. He can't change that for us. He's only VP of HR.'

'Do you have any other friends who'd like to do a spot of nepotism for us?' Nilima asked brightly.

'Rahul is my uncle's friend. And do you think I'm not trying?'

'It just seems to me that that part is your job,' Nilima said. 'We're doing our work, aren't we?'

Shwetha abruptly got up, picked up her handbag and left, shutting the door carefully behind her.

'Do you have to do that?' Poorna said. 'If Chikkamma closes down, you'll be out of a job too.'

'I know. It won't be the first time.'

CHAPTER 12

Peril at Trendy Mall

Nilima had been so afraid of being late that she got to the lake twenty minutes early. She paid off the autorickshaw, arching her back in relief after the long bus ride where she had been hunched over on the hard, narrow seat followed by the short, bumpy autorickshaw ride. She walked in through the open gate. The footpath inside was already bustling with runners and walkers. She stepped off the track and stood within view of the gate. There were birds all around, birds whose names she didn't remember, even though she was sure Poorna had told her some of them. They were flying overhead and perched on the trees at the water's edge and congregated on a tiny island. She couldn't hear the roar of traffic—only birds chirping and screeching, and some schoolchildren shrieking nearby. Getting up so early, after barely three hours of sleep, seemed quite worth this.

A sudden sting on her palm: a large ant. Several were running down her arm and, by the feel of it, the back of her neck. She jerked forward and looked around. The tree she had been leaning against was covered with them.

She was shaking her body wildly, trying to get the little pests off herself, when she saw Poorna.

'Good morning,' Poorna said cheerfully, ignoring the dance she must have witnessed. 'One victim's cycling his way here; the others are in the car and should reach soon.'

Nilima had once referred to a group she was guiding as victims—of her commentary, she had meant, and of the tourism industry in general. Poorna had quickly adopted the term, to Shwetha's disapproval.

'I'm so glad Shwetha dropped her demand that I take charge of this latest group of victims,' Nilima confessed.

Poorna slapped her shoulder—in camaraderie, or was she dislodging a stray ant? 'You had your debut as a tour designer yesterday, you can relax today!'

Not too much, Nilima cautioned herself. *I wasn't paying enough attention when Poorna did this last month; I need to be prepared the next time Shwetha wants me to do this tour.*

They stood looking out at the lake. It had rained last night, but the sky was clear now. Even Poorna was stunned into silence by the sight of the rippling water turned golden by the sun.

The moment ended soon enough. The clients arrived and everyone introduced themselves, shouting to be heard over the loud family moving past them. Unprompted, the group formed a neat circle around Poorna, who talked about the lake and local conservationists' efforts to save it from development and have it cleaned up, and about the birds that made it their home. She led them onto the narrow track that circled the lake with Nilima bringing up the rear.

'Look, there are herons,' Poorna said, and the tourists immediately moved up to the fence, pulling up cameras they wore around their necks. Poorna was explaining the difference between night herons, grey herons and purple herons. Nilima was tempted to take a photo too, but the sight of these large cameras put her off; they made her feel like a paparazzo, and she put her phone back in her pocket.

'When commercial fishing started a few decades ago,' Poorna said, on the move again, 'this lake was stocked with tasty fish, and lots of pelicans and other birds started coming. In the last few years, an infection has been killing them off. But come back in September, and hopefully you can see some pelicans!'

The track was muddy and uneven; at some places the fence was worn away and there was a clear drop into deep water. The sun was higher now, and Nilima's face, neck and arms were burning.

On the far side of the lake were trees that sank right into the water and housed colonies of birds. In spite of the heat and her skin still itchy from the ant bites, she could have stood here for hours, just looking up at the birds circling above or down at the unexpectedly joyful sight of a duck diving in to fish, its black bottom quivering in the air before it disappeared.

The others had gone ahead, and she was here on work after all. She trudged after them carefully. She wasn't used to rough ground and spraining an ankle here would be embarrassing.

Afterwards, they had hot idli and vada and filter coffee at a crowded little eatery. Nilima was on her third tiny steel tumbler of coffee when the clients left, and she got heavily to her feet to say goodbye. Then she and Poorna sank back into their seats and finished their coffee in silence.

A grey-haired server placed the bill on the table and walked off. Poorna scrutinised it and counted out the money. Then she said, 'Let's look up Pallav.'

'What, now? Why?' Nilima failed to keep the dismay out of her voice. After this active morning, she had been looking forward to going back to the office and doing a little more online snooping on Jagat's colleagues and family.

'You said he was shifty, and his alibi isn't solid. Maybe he was mad that Jagat fired him.'

Nilima waited until they were out of the busy shop and couldn't be overheard, and said, 'Yes, he's definitely a suspect.'

'Let's go, then. See what he's up to, follow him around. He'll be at work now. He works in a shop nearby, doesn't he?'

'Yes,' said Nilima. 'But he'd recognise me.'

'You can stay hidden. And if he sees you, we'll pretend it's a coincidence. Come on.'

'I'll book a cab.'

'Don't be silly. My Activa is over there.'

'No, not your scooter. Let's take an autorickshaw instead.'

'Why, boo? This is so much more convenient. Plus, I can't just leave my scooter here.'

Finding herself out of arguments, Nilima followed Poorna to the parking spot. Her body could handle it; Poorna did this every day, after all. But riding pillion was surely more uncomfortable, with her legs stretched out. At least she didn't have to worry about navigating traffic and was free to gaze around her.

In the fifteen minutes or so it took them to get to the mall, Nilima wondered what they would do when they got there. If Pallav was at work, he'd probably be there all day. How would hanging around help them?

She shared her doubts while Poorna parked the scooter inside the mall gates. It was an old shopping complex that had evidently been renovated recently, and the sign outside proudly said 'Trendy Mall'.

'Yeah, I've been thinking that too. Could you ask your inspector to try the same trick she did with Mohan? Frighten him and see where he goes?'

'I don't know,' Nilima said miserably. 'It's a lot to ask. Especially when we haven't been able to help her much in return. It's not like we found out a lot from Mohan. And we may have put Veena in danger, and Sharmila had to send the policemen ...'

'Come on, Nims, we have to keep trying. Would your Miss Marple give up? If we keep going, we'll find something. Sharmila wants to help, no? She wants to solve the case too.'

Nilima didn't answer, but she followed Poorna into the building. The shops seemed to have just opened; as they passed a chain bookshop, an employee was desultorily tapping the shelves with a feather duster.

They took the lift up to the fourth floor. Nilima was still full of misgivings, but she couldn't think of anything to say before Poorna strode into the shop where Pallav worked.

Nilima went into the shoe shop next door, browsing the shelves nervously and fending off the enthusiastic young man who hurried forward to offer his assistance. She was nervously eyeing a pair of lime green high-heeled pumps she would never wear when Poorna came in. Poorna deftly got rid of the shop assistant by pointing to several styles and asking him to get them in her size. The man disappeared into the back of the shop; the only other employee was thumbing his phone at the billing counter.

'He's there,' Poorna whispered.

'You're sure it's him?'

'Of course I'm sure. He recognised me.'

'What?'

'Yeah. I was looking at the shelves—not too near him. He came right over and was like, "Hi, don't I know you?"'

'What?' Nilima's voice was high in panic.

'Relax, it's fine. I replied, "Do *I* know *you?"* and he said, "Don't you work downstairs from Jagdip Books?" and I'm like, "Yes, how do you know?" and he said, "I used to work at Jagdip. I remember seeing you." So I said, "Hi" and he said "Hi" back. I told him I was looking for towels, and he pointed me to a few and told me how great they are and I said they're nice, I'll think about it and come back, and I walked out.'

'Fuck fuck fuck fuck fuck. Why didn't we think about this? Of course he'd recognise you.'

'Relax, no? He doesn't suspect anything. You just call the inspector.'

'What? No! We can't continue now that he knows who you are!'

'Why not? This doesn't change anything.'

'But...'

'Come on, Nims, we can't back out now!'

Nilima stifled her retort; the shoe shop employee had come back out with a few boxes of shoes in his arms and was staring at them.

Poorna continued to talk in a low voice: 'And there aren't any other exits from his shop, so he must come this way to get to the lift. There are bathrooms at the end of this corridor; you can pop in and make your call and I'll stand outside to see if he leaves.'

Nilima gave in and walked out of the shop, leaving Poorna to look at the shoes and make her excuses to the shop assistant.

Nilima was so reluctant to owe another favour she almost hoped Sharmila would say no. But the inspector agreed, though she said, 'It would be better if you people told me in advance so I could send a policeman down instead of having you follow suspects on your own. Today is a bad day. There's a protest at Town Hall this morning and we're all here, as many of us as could be spared ... Will you be fine? I can send someone anyway, if you can wait for an hour. But it will have to be a uniform.'

Nilima considered Sharmila's offer. A uniformed constable would be visible and tip Pallav off; he was no fool. They could wait a day or two and get official backup, but Poorna would say they could do this better than any policeman. Nilima wasn't sure if she agreed; but after all this was Poorna's plan, and they were here already, so they might as well go ahead with it.

'Thanks, we'll be okay,' she told Sharmila. 'Could you ... could you not tell the store ... whoever answers, I mean, that you're you? That you are police, I mean? I don't want his employers to be alarmed unnecessarily, or to suspect him. He may be innocent, and it's not fair to make things difficult for him at work.'

The silence stretched so long Nilima began to say, 'Hello, are you there?' just as Sharmila answered, 'All right, Nilima.' It was the first time the inspector had called her by just her first name.

As she walked out of the bathroom stall, the mall worker cleaning the sinks looked curiously at her. Nilima had gone into the furthest stall and talked as quietly as she could—evidently not quietly enough.

'Done?' Poorna appeared outside the door, startling Nilima. 'Will she call the shop?'

Nilima nodded. 'I told her what you said—that he may not answer his cell phone at work.'

'And it's scarier getting such a call on your office phone, no? Now, let me go down and bring the scooter out. I'll keep it running near the gate so we can follow him more easily. You stay here and follow him out.'

Nilima wanted to protest, but Poorna was already walking to the lift. Besides, she was right; there wouldn't be time to go back for the scooter if Pallav hopped into an auto or a bus. If Poorna was late with the scooter, Nilima could follow him in an auto—if she could get a driver who would agree to follow another vehicle and not demand to know the actual destination. Maybe she could tempt him with more money.

She was counting the cash in her wallet when she saw movement out of the corner of her eye. Pallav had walked out and was going for the stairs right next to his shop, not the lift all the way across the floor. The door to the stairwell had already shut behind him by the time Nilima realised what was happening.

Nilima cast a longing glance at the lift—the red number over it said 0, so it would take some time to get up to the fourth floor—and then made for the stairs.

The door shut behind her, and she was plunged into darkness. She was reminded of Jagat, of his body lying on the landing all night. She hurried down, afraid of stumbling, her heart beating erratically.

She didn't dare unlock her phone; the sudden light might alert Pallav. She tried to listen for his footsteps. It was difficult to trust her ears, to hear anything above the general hum from the mall. There was a sound below—or was it above? Shouldn't she have reached the ground floor by now?

She halted at the next door. Should she continue going down? She took a few more tentative steps.

Her eyes had adjusted to the darkness. A large form hulked in the corner of the half-landing below. She stood still.

The form shifted. A man—Pallav. His arm moved, and she saw that it held something flat and wide and probably heavy, something that could knock her flat.

Nilima ran up the stairs, panting. Her body was weighed down with fear.

'Hello?' Pallav called below her.

She wrestled with the door in the landing. It didn't budge. *It's locked!* she thought.

Footsteps came up the stairs. She gave the door another pull; nothing. If she tried to run up to the next floor, she'd never make it in time.

A hand landed on her shoulder. She gasped and gave the door a desperate push. It swung open. It hadn't been locked; she had merely been trying in the wrong direction.

The sudden sunlight blinded her. She had been on the ground floor after all. The gate was right ahead, and Poorna was on her scooter, looking around impatiently.

Pallav pushed past her into the open. 'Hey, it's you,' he said.

Nilima made for the gate. It had rained since they had gone inside. The ground was slippery, and the puddle in front of the gate had grown larger. She looked around; Pallav was trotting towards her, keeping his balance effortlessly.

'Stop!' he shouted.

Nilima ran the last few steps and got on the scooter—sideways, since that was faster.

'Hold on,' Poorna said, and pressed the accelerator. They were immediately in deep water, and the scooter hit a rock concealed by the puddle.

The world tilted, and Nilima felt weightless, and then wet. She sputtered and spat out muddy water. Her left arm, trapped under her body, emitted a heavy ache.

She couldn't get up; her limbs didn't seem to work. Her knee now screamed for attention. Poorna was getting off the scooter, and the guard at the gate was gesturing frantically. Pallav carefully placed his package at the open doorway of the little security hut before wading over to her. By the time he leaned over to help her up, she realised what he had been holding all along. A bedsheet set, mauve with bright red flowers, shaped like a wide flat box in its plastic packaging. Not a weapon.

After Pallav and Poorna had helped her up and led her to dry land, where the security guard had placed his own chair; after Poorna had wiped her scraped knee with a handkerchief that Pallav offered and Poorna had wet with her water bottle; after Poorna had tied the now bloody handkerchief tightly around the knee; after they had debated whether Nilima needed an ambulance or if an autorickshaw could take her to the nearby hospital—'No hospital, I'm fine,' Nilima had croaked, but since she had been shaking with shock and had cried out in pain when Poorna had touched her arm, they had ignored her, Poorna merely offering her own jacket for warmth, and Nilima refusing with a brusque shake of her head, knowing she could at best wear it like a scarf, her arms would never make it through those sleeves; after the security guard had helpfully walked off in search of an auto, (Poorna had booked a cab, but it was fifteen minutes away, very likely more—the vehicles in the street had thickened into one of Bengaluru's inexplicable jams, and Nilima had looked up to see people gazing at her with interest from the windows of a bus and realised she was smeared with mud and blood and sitting on a chair on the footpath); after all this, when all they could do was wait for either an auto or the cab, Pallav asked the question Nilima had been dreading since he had waded into water to help her: What was she doing in there?

Nilima was relieved he had addressed the question to Poorna and not her—he apparently considered Nilima too invalidated to answer questions—as she had not been able to think of any answers in the several minutes since she had anticipated the question.

Poorna answered coldly, with just a hint of puzzlement, 'What, in the mall?' and Nilima was struck with admiration. What could, in fact, be more normal for two young women to do after their work outing than to go shopping? They didn't have any shopping bags, but they might have been window shopping. Even though Pallav had recognised Poorna, this wasn't much cause for suspicion; he knew they worked in the same office, so weren't they likely to be friends?

Pallav was more hesitant when he tried again: 'No, I mean on the stairs. She was behind me; then I called to her, and she just ran away like she was scared.'

'Yeah, she's claustrophobic. I shouldn't have left her alone; I didn't think it through. I went to bring the scooter up while she was in the bathroom ... Do you know her?'

Nilima recognised how smart this move was, taking the fight into enemy territory, showing an innocent if somewhat aggressive desire to protect her friend.

'We've met,' Pallav said. 'But why didn't she take the lift, if stairs bother her?'

'Lifts are worse,' Nilima managed to say out loud. 'Stairs are usually okay. But these were so dark, and I remembered finding Jagat's body ...' The shudder she exhibited was quite genuine.

Poorna touched her right hand. 'Cold,' she proclaimed, and rubbed it with both of hers.

'The hospital is close by,' Pallav said encouragingly. 'We'll get there in five minutes.'

'I don't need a hospital,' Nilima protested again, her voice quavering. 'I'm sure I haven't broken anything.'

'Probably not.' Poorna cast her a worried look. 'But I think we should X-ray that arm. We have a long way to go to get you back home and it would be nice to know for sure so we don't make it worse. And your knee should be bandaged up properly. You should probably get a tetanus shot too.'

An auto stopped and the security guard stepped out. Nilima got in, and, despite her protests, Pallav joined her. Poorna got on her scooter and followed them.

Pallav's presence continued to unsettle Nilima, even though he was being kind; he hovered over her, walked with her to the rows of seats in the hospital's lobby and offered to get her water. Once Poorna had got Nilima registered at the hospital, she came up to them and dismissed Pallav, asserting she had the situation well in control and hinting that more of Nilima's friends would be arriving shortly.

Nilima assumed that was a sham, but an hour later, when she had been X-rayed and was waiting for the doctor to see her, Shwetha arrived, resplendent in a peacock blue sari. After asking how Nilima was, Shwetha took out wet tissues from her bag and gently scrubbed Nilima's face clean of mud. Nilima's knee had already been cleaned and bandaged; she—and Poorna, going by her tense nail biting—were much more worried about the throbbing pain in her arm that was now spreading to her shoulder.

The doctor, a tall man with a trim moustache who looked nearly as young as Poorna, declared no bones broken: 'Just some muscle strain. It'll heal up by itself, just rest it for a couple of weeks.'

'Does she need bed rest, doctor?' Shwetha had asked, while Nilima's heart leapt to her mouth. She couldn't be confined to bed, she couldn't. Not with the murder unsolved, and she couldn't afford to take unpaid leave, and who would get her meals, wash her clothes ...

'No need for that,' the doctor said pleasantly. 'Just no unnecessary exertion. No more motorcycle stunts or whatever it is you were doing.' He grinned at Nilima and wrote out a prescription. 'Oh, and apply an ice pack twice a day for a week. Come back if it doesn't get better by then.'

I don't have a fridge, Nilima thought sullenly. *How do I get ice packs?*

Nilima stewed in gratitude and resentment throughout the long ride home in Shwetha's car. Shwetha had come over as soon as she could, got Nilima a snack and paid the hospital bills. Not a word of reproach at Nilima's carelessness and foolhardiness. She wasn't even trying to make small talk—she had turned the radio on low and was looking straight ahead through the windshield. Nilima shut her eyes and pretended to sleep, though every bump in the road sent pain shooting up her shoulder. Once she cried out, and Shwetha said 'sorry' softly and touched her hand. Nilima didn't react, didn't turn her palm up to meet Shwetha's, and Shwetha moved her hand back to the gear stick.

After manoeuvring her car through the narrow lanes of Halasuru to Nilima's apartment, Shwetha accompanied her up and offered to help her change. Nilima refused curtly and waited for Shwetha to leave before she plugged in her phone, pulled off her clothes and got in bed.

Finally left to herself, Nilima tried to sort through her emotions. Anger at herself for being persuaded into an adventure she hadn't been convinced of. Anger at Poorna. Anger she felt a little guilty for, because she knew it wasn't Poorna's fault. Blaming someone felt easier than confronting her disappointment and pain.

Nilima had learned a long time ago that the only person she could really depend on was herself—or she should have learned it. How could she have trusted Poorna—her judgement, her scooter-driving prowess, her planning? Of course she had been let down; that's what happened if you trusted someone before you knew them well enough.

Poorna had apologised for losing control of the scooter, but not for scheming Nilima into a plot she hadn't wanted to take part in. And indeed, why should she apologise for that? Nilima should have said no firmly.

That's just like her, Nilima thought childishly. *Riding roughshod over my wishes. I should never have stopped disliking her.*

The most humiliating part had been being helped by Pallav—Pallav whom she disliked, Pallav who was a suspect, Pallav who had turned out to be kinder than she'd expected. Moreover, she had ruined any chance of being able to spy on him; he would definitely be suspicious if Nilima turned up in his vicinity again. She wasn't any good as a detective—just like everything else.

But Shwetha! Shwetha had been so helpful today. And Nilima had chosen to hold on to her resentment and her suspicions. She was being unfair to Shwetha—steadfast, loyal Shwetha, Shwetha who seemed to like holding her hand ...

She was just slipping into a daydream in which she was standing in front of Shwetha under a tree in Cubbon Park, Shwetha pulling her closer, a smile blossoming on that perfect mouth, when her phone rang. Inspector Lamani's name was on the screen. The inspector had texted in the afternoon, and, receiving no answer, had then called Poorna, who had briefly explained the fiasco of the mission.

'How are you?' The inspector's gruff voice held surprising concern. Nilima reassured her, even though she was slurring her words by now. The painkillers had begun to affect her sleep-deprived body.

'Can we meet?' Nilima asked. 'I'd like to go over a few things with you.'

To her surprise, Sharmila invited her home that evening. 'Hafeeza is going out for dinner with some colleagues, so you and I can talk,' she explained. Nilima accepted reluctantly; she had wanted a quick meeting, not an evening of socialising with a person she suspected only tolerated her presence.

Why is Sharmila even willing to meet me? she wondered after the call ended. The inspector's voice had been placid, but she couldn't have been pleased at Nilima's failure. Nilima imagined her cursing amateur detectives in her head. Perhaps she just wanted more details so she could recount the story to Hafeeza and laugh at Nilima's incompetence. 'She may have goofed up the entire case,' Sharmila would say to Hafeeza when they were in bed together, 'but don't worry, I can save it. I've solved so many cases, what do these civilians know?'

The thought blended into a dream, because even though it was only five in the evening, the medicines had taken effect and Nilima was asleep.

Her alarm woke her up a couple of hours later. Sleep tugged at her, but she went to the bathroom and splashed her face with water to wake herself up. As she extricated her wallet from the pocket of the skirt she had tossed onto the floor, her fingers touched something unfamiliar. She fished out a handkerchief, damp and bloodstained, and shook it out. In one corner was an embroidered P.

✍

Hafeeza and Sharmila rented a flat in a recently constructed building in Hebbal whose dull beige exteriors proclaimed its understated class. The letterbox downstairs had the owner's name on it, but on the flat door was a wooden sign with both the women's names in bold letters. Sharmila opened the door with a rare smile that softened her face. She invited Nilima to sit, switched off the cricket match she had been watching on the TV and went into the kitchen.

The living room was spacious and airy, and painted a mango yellow. A large sofa faced the TV, and there were various knick-knacks on the wall: a japi, a Warli painting, a brass ornament in the shape of a sun. The curtains at the window were bright red, tie-and-dyed in yellow.

Nilima walked restlessly around the large room, standing in front of each wall ornament and examining it before moving on. She suddenly realised what was missing: books. The shelf on the wall held photographs and a plant, and a few newspapers were stacked neatly in the lower shelf of the glass coffee table.

Sharmila emerged with a silver tray. It held glasses with ice already in them, a bottle of whiskey, and a plate heaped with murukku.

'Hafeeza says you like whiskey,' Sharmila said, sitting on the easy chair at a right angle to the sofa where Nilima had hurriedly plonked herself. 'I have wine if you prefer it.'

'No, whiskey is perfect.' Nilima shrugged off the thought that she shouldn't mix alcohol with the pills she had already had. Instead, she took a large gulp and came directly to the point. 'We have been blundering about lately,' she said apologetically. 'Did anything we get you help at all?'

'You have some advantages we don't. People are less scared of you. They tell you things they may not tell us, at least not until we ask the right questions.'

'That's the idea.' Nilima took another sip and continued, 'I don't know. I don't feel like we've got much that's helpful.'

'Madhura Shetty,' the inspector said. 'We hadn't thought of him in connection with the case.'

'Is he connected, though? All we found out was that he met Mohan.'

'Correct, but that gave us the right questions to ask. We interrogated Mohan at the station yesterday. We pretended we knew more than we did. He got scared and told us everything.'

Nilima wondered if the police had done more than ask him questions. Had they intimidated him in some way? What if they had hit him, tortured him? How could she ask without offending the inspector and cutting off her help? And did she even want to know—could she deal with an undesirable answer and the ensuing feelings of guilt?

'Madhura Shetty was involved in a deal with Jagat. Mohan told us all quite beautifully. Enough for me to talk to Madhura.'

'You talked to him?'

'Hmm. Mohan would have told him I was asking questions, you see. Better for me to get to him directly. I know him a little from a previous case. He was very cooperative. He told me he wasn't involved in this.'

Nilima sat up. 'Did you ask him that straight up?'

The inspector chuckled. 'Not exactly. I started by asking if he knew of Jagat's murder, and he immediately admitted he knew Jagat. He told me—off the record, he said—that Jagat was going to sell him some land outside the city quite cheap. Not Jagat's own land, of course. He was only the middleman. That means Madhura didn't have a motive; he wanted Jagat's help.'

'What happens to the land now that Jagat is dead?'

'Hmm, he's getting it anyway. Madhura says he managed to get in touch with the owner.'

'Who's the owner?'

'Some old friend of Jagat's who lives in the States. The father used to live on the farm. He died last year so this friend wants to sell.'

'How did Madhura get to the owner?'

'Mohan sorted it out for him. He explained the case to Veena, and she handed over the contact info.'

'Just like that? No brokerage?'

'She hasn't asked for it, but Madhura says he'll give her a couple of lakhs anyway, and a lakh to Mohan. The fee Jagat had bargained for was five lakh rupees, so it doesn't leave Madhura enough of a profit to want to kill him, especially as he is trying to turn into a respectable politician. I don't think he did it, Nilima.'

'And did Mohan tell you why he'd gone to Veena's that evening?'

'Yes, to tell her to keep the information about Madhura's involvement to herself.'

'He could have told her that over the phone. Why did he go all the way there?'

'You're sharp!' Sharmila refilled Nilima's glass. 'I asked him the same thing. He said he went there to make sure there were no documents relating to this property in Jagat's house. He called Veena and said he'd come and look through all of Jagat's papers with her. Both Veena and Mohan said they didn't find anything.'

'And you took their word for it?' Nilima bit her tongue; antagonising the inspector was not a good idea.

'Of course not, my men searched the flat before they left. They found nothing. Anyway, we would have found any such papers the first time we searched the flat, the day you found Jagat's body.'

'There was nothing in the bookstore either?' Of course, she had looked through all the papers herself—except for anything the police had already removed.

'We had gone through the shop very thoroughly already. Nevertheless, I sent two men again that evening. They didn't find anything.'

'Was Dipen there? He can't have been happy.'

'He has been quite cooperative.'

'You said Mohan gets a lakh from Madhura. Doesn't that give him a motive?'

'He says Jagat would have given him that anyway, and Madhura confirms it.'

'And Madhura says he will pay Veena part of the fee?'

'He doesn't want to cheat a grieving widow.' Sharmila chuckled. 'He's developing a conscience, that's funny. But that's small change to him.'

'And to her?'

Sharmila looked appraisingly at her. 'Both Mohan and Madhura were pretty sure Mrs Desai didn't want a fee. In fact, she gave Mohan the contact details, saying she didn't want to be bothered with business, but the friend who owns the farm is still interested in selling.'

'Seems clear enough. Unless, of course, everybody is lying.'

Sharmila leaned across the coffee table and slapped Nilima's poor left shoulder, which throbbed painfully. 'You're just like us,' Sharmila said. 'Suspect everyone! That's good!'

'Is there any evidence at all that someone visited Jagat after Mohan left?' She continued hastily, as the inspector frowned, 'I know I've asked you before. I just wondered, now that you've had more time, if you know more than you did?' Nilima was hoping that, as Sharmila seemed inclined to be friendly today and was currently halfway through her second glass of whiskey, she would divulge details she hadn't before.

'The situation is the same. We didn't find any fingerprints on the outside of the door that shouldn't have been there, just Mohan's and Jagat's. There were also fingerprints of Dipen Desai and the maid Anjali—those were smudged, like they were older. Inside the shop, of course, it's hopeless, and Jagat's office didn't have any new unknown prints either. Any that were usable belonged to someone who worked there, or the wives, or Mohan.'

'Uh, doesn't that imply there was no meeting? No unknown person came in after Mohan. Surely, however careful someone was, you'd be likely to touch something.'

'Hmm. I wouldn't say it was impossible.'

'What about Jagat's phone? Did you get anything from it? If he had a meeting, wouldn't there have been a phone call or a text?'

'Nothing, not even an SMS. The last thing was a WhatsApp message around nine from his wife, asking him to call the children in the morning. We checked his Facebook as well—he was logged in on his office computer. We found no evidence that he used any other such sites. We asked his wife too and she couldn't help.'

Nilima nodded abstractly.

'We looked at everyone else's mobile phones too.'

'Are you allowed to do that?'

'They all seemed very eager to help,' Sharmila said, with such a faint emphasis on the word 'seemed' that Nilima wasn't sure she had heard it. 'They all handed us their phones for a quick look—recent calls and messages. And for Dipen and Pallav, we did a little more digging on our end. To see if they really were where they said they were.'

'And?'

'The GPS data backed up their stories. Dipen's cell phone didn't leave his house after it got there around 9.15. Pallav's was in various places in Indiranagar and not anywhere near the shop.'

'Any interesting calls or messages?'

'We found nothing suspicious. Anyone would be smart enough to delete incriminating evidence.'

'But you're telling me this anyway,' Nilima observed. 'What did you find?'

'How well do you know that partner of yours?'

'My partner? Shwetha, you mean. I'm only an employee. She's my boss.'

Sharmila was watching Nilima's face intently. 'There was a message from her.'

'A message? In whose phone?'

'Dipen's.'

Nilima wished she hadn't been drinking; she felt confused, woozy. She tried to keep her voice light: 'She messaged Dipen? They know each other, of course; they work in the same building...'

The inspector cut in: 'It said, "Better not, Nilima is getting suspicious."'

Nilima went still. The inspector tactfully got more ice and refilled their drinks. When she sat down again, Nilima asked dully, 'What was the message in response to?'

'I don't know. There was only one message. Nothing else from her or to her. He must have deleted them, and forgot to delete this one.'

Nilima stared at the little table by her knees and thought of what to say. Sharmila pushed her drink forward, and Nilima gratefully grabbed her glass and took a swallow.

'It may have nothing to do with the murder,' Sharmila said kindly. 'In fact, it probably doesn't. We haven't found anything else to link Miss Shwetha to this. But I thought I should warn you to be careful.'

Nilima nodded, still looking down at her drink. 'Thank you,' she said. And then, 'I think I should go.'

Sharmila did not attempt to dissuade her. *She's probably glad I'm leaving,* Nilima thought, and then chided herself for being unfair—however reluctant she had been to tolerate Nilima's interference in the past, the inspector had been undoubtedly friendly today. She walked unsteadily down the stairs, gingerly touching her sore left arm with her right hand.

She waited in the unlit lane for her cab to arrive, silently running through the conversation with Sharmila, every shift in tone, every nuance. A little voice in her head that sounded suspiciously like Preeti said *I always suspected ...* Something else lurked in her brain, something Sharmila had said earlier. *Suspect everyone,* she had said. And then, soon after, she had told her about Shwetha's message to Dipen, warned her—of what? Did Sharmila suspect Shwetha?

CHAPTER 13

The Adventure of the Sale Agreement

Nilima stood on the landing outside the bookshop where she had found the body. It felt like something was missing, like she'd expected to find a body there, but not Jagat's. Jagat, of course, was long dead.

The door was ajar. She had never seen this door open before. She stepped in.

The shop was quiet. No one was at the counter. The lights were off, but she could see, if only in greys: moonlight flooded in through the windows. She walked between the bookshelves. Everything felt different, unfamiliar. Her heart was pounding.

She turned a corner and stepped into another aisle. Here was what she had been looking for. On the floor, just ahead, was a large lump that could only be another body.

Moonlight glinted off the white clothes, the dupatta fanning over a shoulder as if it had been styled for a photoshoot.

Dread filled Nilima's gut as she crept closer. Thick curls shrouded the face, and Nilima knew what she would find before she leaned over and gently brushed the hair off Shwetha's face ...

She shifted in her sleep. The dream changed.

It wasn't Shwetha lying before her, but Sampath. Sampath was smiling softly as if he was sleeping, his face ghastly pale. His shirt was soaked dark, as Jagat's had been. Leading away from the wet pool over his head were bloody footprints.

Nilima gulped and clutched her T-shirt at the stomach. She knew what she would find now would be the worst yet. But she didn't consider turning back and walking out of the shop. She followed the footprints, taking care not to step on them.

She turned another corner. She had never seen this part of the shop before. There were tall shelves, dusty and looming. She caught flashes of white, of thin long things that might clatter to the ground if she brushed against them. *Bones,* the word formed in her head, even as she resolutely kept her eyes from focusing on them and confirming her guess. She walked on and saw something ahead that was also white but bigger.

It was Shwetha. Nilima came to a stop and whimpered in relief. 'You're okay.' She sagged against the nearest shelf, not caring anymore what was on it.

Shwetha turned and smiled at her. Her smile that was always full of promises was tonight brighter—demonic. Nilima looked down and saw Shwetha's white clothes splattered with something dark, and in her hand a long knife ...

Blood gushed from Nilima's shoulder, and she felt a pain so sharp that she woke up. She had turned in her sleep and was lying on her tender left side. It took her a long time to stop shaking.

She checked her phone for the time: 3.41. She had only slept for a few hours. She took another painkiller to ease the throbbing in her shoulder, and lay back down.

When she woke up again, the sun was beating down through the thin curtain, making her head ache. She slipped her phone out from under the pillow and saw a text from Shwetha:

> Hope you're feeling better. You're to rest and not come to work today, okay? That's an order.

The text had come at 9.02; it was now nearly noon. Nilima would have liked to go back to sleep, but she was ravenous and light-headed. She hadn't eaten since the upma Shwetha had foraged in the hospital, twenty-two hours earlier, except for a couple of murukku at Sharmila's. She was out of bread and the thought of dry biscuits made her choke.

She still had on the stretchy cotton dress she had worn last night to visit Sharmila. She couldn't face the ordeal of showering or changing with her injured arm, which had begun to throb painfully again. It was raining hard, so she settled for a perfunctory wash and ordered a cab to the office.

'I told you not to come in, Deka,' Shwetha said as Nilima struggled to close her umbrella with one hand, finally just dumping it open on its pole next to the bathroom, while Poorna hovered anxiously and offered to order lunch.

'I can still use my phone,' Nilima said curtly and a little untruthfully; bending her left arm brought on a stab of pain, but she could, slowly, use her phone with her right.

The others' solicitousness annoyed her. It was worse when she tried to work and realised they were right after all; typing on the keyboard with her left hand was agonising, and typing with one hand was frustratingly slow. She had missed a full day at the office and had a flurry of emails and messages to respond to.

Hi, how r u? Hope ur arm is better!

Nilima grimaced at the computer.

'What's wrong?' Poorna asked from across the room as she emptied three sachets of sugar and two creamers into her coffee. Shwetha had shut herself into the small room to make calls.

'Nothing,' said Nilima. 'It's a Facebook message.'

'What, did someone leave a dirty message on our Facebook page again?'

'No, it's not on our page, it's for me.'

'Someone sent you a dirty message?' Poorna walked over.

'No, not that. It's Pallav.'

'He sent you a—'

'No! No one's sent a dirty message! He just asked how I am. Look.'

Poorna leaned over to look at the screen.

'That's nice. Why are you upset?'

'Not upset, just embarrassed. It was not my finest moment.'

'Don't be silly. It wasn't your fault.'

Nilima felt something like gratitude.

'Anyone can have an accident, there's nothing to be embarrassed about. You think too much.'

Poorna skipped back to her seat, leaving Nilima looking after her resentfully. She had been told many times in her life that she tended to overthink things; being reminded of this fact never made her feel better or more capable of stemming her flow of self-reproach.

Tentatively, using only her right hand while her left forearm rested on the desk in a position that caused her least pain, Nilima typed out a response. Soon, she was typing faster, and her left hand kept twitching closer to the keyboard before she winced in pain and pulled it back. The day rolled on. Poorna said bye as she left for her afternoon tour. Shwetha was in the inner office gesticulating into her phone.

Nilima opened her notebook and started writing, looking up every few minutes to make sure Shwetha hadn't moved closer.

> Suspects
>
> J. Mohan: Last person to see Jagat. No alibi. Did he kill him before he left? Motive: Was one of them double-crossing the other? Did something go wrong with the deal with Madhura?
>
> Veena Desai: Foolproof alibi. Suspicious circumstances: mysterious withdrawal from Jagat's account. Mohan visited her, so she had some knowledge of Jagat's dealings. She could have hired an assassin. She has the strongest motive: she inherits most of his wealth, as well as the life insurance, and spouses are obvious suspects.
>
> Ramesh Sampath: Has a motive if Jagat found out about the thefts. (Did he?) And he disliked and resented Jagat. Alibi only corroborated by his wife (and by Maniram circumstantially, but Sampath may have doubled back).

Pallav Shastri: Was fired—why? Did Jagat suspect him of being the thief, or did Pallav uncover a secret in Jagat's private papers? Did Jagat threaten him? Did he want revenge for being fired? (All speculation; we need to find out more. He was kind to me, but that says little.) Alibi: he was apparently at a bar with friends. But he may have left his phone with a friend to help establish his alibi. Would a friend cover for him and become an accessory to murder?

Dipen Desai: No apparent motive. Could have had a disagreement with his brother (after all, everyone seems to have had one), but why kill him now, after working with him apparently amicably all these years? Also, his wife says he was home with her, and his phone location checks out.

Ronita Parekh: If Dipen killed Jagat, Ronita must be an accomplice. Or perhaps they did it together. No apparent motive so far. Must find out more about her.

Madhura Shetty: Did he have a financial motive for Jagat's death? Can we find out where he was that night? Also, most likely of all the suspects to have sent a hitman.

Shwetha Shetty: Has been cagey about connection with Dipen. She keeps trying to 'handle' any clues that point to him, like the Saima thing, and maybe that note with the numbers? Did she have a motive? Did she do it for Dipen?

X: We still don't know who—if anyone—was meeting Jagat after Mohan left. This person might well be the murderer.

Owais Kalburgi: Our landlord may have wanted Jagat out of the way because he was blocking the sale of the building.

Anjali Bopanna: No motive that we know of. Gave the police a solid alibi; she was at home with her family, and several neighbours saw her come home before eight, and no one saw her leave again.

Mehnaz Siddiqui: Seems above suspicion. Pretty solid alibi—there are photos on Facebook and an Uber trail.

Lotika (last name?): Disliked and resented Jagat, but his death may leave her out of a job. Extremely unlikely, and police have checked up on her alibi—her daughter and mother-in-law.

Poorna Radhika: No motive or suspicious behaviour.

Maniram Bora: No motive or suspicious behaviour.

Once she was done writing this out, she read it over. Then she tore out a fresh page and made a list of tasks.

Nilima

Ask Sharmila if Madhura Shetty has an alibi.

Talk to Pallav and find out why Jagat really fired him.

Shwetha

Find a way to interview Ronita.

Look into our landlord Kalburgi. Does he have any history of violence?

The door to Shwetha's office opened and Nilima hastily shoved her notebook into her drawer. She waved the task list at Shwetha.

'What's that?' Shwetha asked, before taking the paper and reading it. 'I already asked my dad about Kalburgi. My dad is friends with his cousin's husband. No hint of anything unsavoury; owns several properties that his parents had bought years ago, and has never seemed to want for money.'

'Some people want more money even if they don't need it,' Nilima commented.

'Yeah, but Kalburgi apparently shows no sign of avarice. I mean, he's been happy enough renting to us at a low rate just because he knows my father. I shall look into Ronita. She is only a few years older than me—I'm sure I can dig up a friend or an acquaintance who's connected to her.'

Nilima grunted.

'What's up, Deka? You look glum.'

'It's this case. It's eating at me.'

'What's wrong?'

'Everything.' Nilima bit off each syllable in anger. 'We haven't got anywhere. We're no good at this. We have vague theories and no proof. We've done nothing except get in the way of the police. I fucking locked myself into the store overnight and still found nothing worth finding. I'm so bad at this, I went to shadow Pallav and he ended up taking me to the hospital!'

Shwetha placed a hand on her shoulder. 'It's all right, Nili.'

Pain erupted in Nilima's shoulder. 'I DON'T NEED YOUR SYMPATHY!'

Shwetha moved back, stunned. 'Okay,' she breathed. 'I'm sorry.'

Nilima rattled open a drawer and got out a cigarette. Her hands were shaking so much she couldn't get the lighter to work. Shwetha eased the lighter from her hand and lit it. Nilima froze for a second, then took a deep puff.

Shwetha said softly, 'What's wrong?'

Nilima was quiet for a long moment. Then she said, 'Nothing, sorry. My shoulder's acting up, that's all. Leave me alone, I'll be okay.'

She spun her chair towards the screen and sat unmoving till, at last, Shwetha walked away.

✍

The cheapest sandwich on the café's menu, a cheese omelette sandwich, was a hundred and twenty rupees—much more expensive than the slices of bread Nilima had planned to toast for dinner. But she was hungry, and she had needed a place to talk to Pallav that wasn't her office or her bedroom, though he had appeared willing to visit either, warmly insisting on whatever was most convenient for her so she wouldn't, as he put it, 'exert herself'. Nilima had suggested this café because it was only a short walk from the office.

When he arrived—eighteen minutes late, Nilima noted silently—he seemed a different man from the Pallav she had met last week. He inquired solicitously about her arm all over again.

Nilima still didn't trust him, but she didn't trust anyone right now, and the possibility of finding out something important seemed worth the risk. She told him a version of the truth, strongly hinting that she was a friend of the inspector (almost true, after last night's hang) and that she was unofficially assisting her with the case (which was quite true, she argued with herself, though it was debatable how much Sharmila welcomed the help).

Pallav was suitably impressed. 'Oh, that's why you girls were at my store! You were investigating, right?'

Nilima nodded warily.

'And the inspector—what did you say her name was?'

'Inspector Lamani.'

'That's it! I got a call at the store from her that morning, just before I met you—she sounded so intimidating. Wait, did you plan that?'

'Yes, she was supposed to scare you and we would keep an eye on you to see what you'd do.'

Nilima was watching his face intently, but he only looked embarrassed.

'Guilty as charged!' He raised both hands in a mock gesture of surrender. 'I headed straight to the basement—there's an empty area there where I go whenever I have to make a private phone call.'

'You went down to make a call?'

'Yeah. I wanted to call my buddy Ash, to warn him to stick to the statement he'd given to the police. I was afraid they were trying to break my alibi.'

'Why?'

'Why?' he echoed. 'Why what?'

'Why did you think we'—Nilima boldly emphasised the word with a twinge of guilt—'would go after your alibi? It was false, wasn't it? Where were you really?'

'I was out drinking with my friends, just like I said. I didn't lie, it was just ... I met this girl and was with her for about half an hour, or maybe an hour. We were making out in her car and we smoked a few joints. I didn't want to give the cops her name; it might have got her in trouble, right? She had told her parents she was at a friend's wedding.'

'Why were you calling Ash in particular?'

'He is the only one who knows the real story. He told the others we were outside smoking—everyone else was too drunk to remember much.'

'So, did you call him? Before you saw me?'

'I didn't get to it, right? This security guard came up to me as soon as I got there, handed me this bedsheet set—it was one of ours, from my store, I mean. Said he'd found it that morning, dropped by one of the delivery fellows. They come in through the basement. The box must have broken. Anyway, I asked him why he didn't just bring it to the store, and he made some fuss about not leaving his post. He wouldn't leave me alone, so I grabbed the product and was coming up the stairs—I thought I'd step out of the mall and make the call, so no one could overhear—when I saw you. You were just standing there, not going up or down. I thought you needed help.'

Nilima did not want to relive that memory and quickly asked, 'Did you get around to calling Ash at all?'

'Yeah. On my way back to the mall from the hospital.'

'What did you find out about Jagat?' Nilima asked abruptly.

'What?'

'Jagat fired you for snooping into his private papers. You must have seen something.'

Anger flared briefly on Pallav's face before he burst out laughing. 'Wow, you *are* smart,' he said in admiration. Nilima struggled to keep the pleased smile off her face.

'Is this yours?' Nilima held out the handkerchief she had found in Jagat's office, still in its plastic bag. She had tried to wash the bloodstains off its companion—the one her knee had been bandaged with—but had failed and tossed it into the dustbin.

'Yes, is that the hanky I gave you the other day? You didn't have to return it.'

'No, I couldn't get that one clean,' Nilima said, feeling ungrateful. 'I found this in Jagat's office, a few days after he died. It was under the cupboard.'

Pallav looked a little sheepish. 'You're right, I looked in the cupboard. That's where I found it.'

'Found what?'

'I don't know why it was important. I didn't understand why he was so angry. I told him I hadn't read anything. That wasn't completely true, I did glance at it, sure, but I didn't know any of the names. So how did it matter?'

'Names? You found a document?'

'It was a property agreement. For some land in Mallasandra.' To Nilima's mystified expression, he added, 'That's a little outside Bangalore.'

Nilima leaned forward. 'What were the names, do you remember?'

'Victor Lobo. That was one. The other ... I'm trying to remember.'

'Was it Madhura Shetty, by any chance?'

'The builder? No way, I'd have remembered that name. No, it was a woman's name.'

'A woman? Are you sure?'

'Absolutely.'

'You didn't take a photo of the paper, by any chance?'

'Naah. I told you, right, I didn't think it was important. I just looked for Jagat or one of the other Desais, but I didn't find their names. Then I lifted the papers to see if there was anything more interesting in the stack beneath, and that's when Jagat came in and caught me. Do you think it was important?'

'I'm not sure. Do you mind if I give the inspector a call?'

'Why not? Now I am on your side, right?'

Nilima cast a sceptical eye at him and called the inspector. To her surprise, she got a jovial response. 'How are you, Nilima?'

Nilima, who had started to say, 'Inspector, I want—' paused and stammered, 'I ... I'm very well, ma'am. You?'

'Good, good. Arm healing nicely?'

'Yes, thank you. I wanted to tell you something. I'm sitting with Pallav right now—'

'Pallav? Isn't that the chap you were trying to follow?'

Nilima winced at 'trying' but only said, 'That's right.'

'Following didn't work, so you're trying more direct tactics, hmm? You're a very persistent person, Nilima.'

'Thank you, Inspector.'

'Please call me Sharmila.'

'Yes, er ... Pallav says he saw a deed of sale in Jagat's office, for a piece of land in Mallasandra. Madhura Shetty's name was not on the document.'

'He would hardly buy it under his own name,' the inspector chuckled. 'Not him, the old fox! What name was on the deed?'

'Pallav says one of the names was a woman's, though he can't remember it. The other name was Victor Lobo. That must be Jagat's friend?'

At the police station, Inspector Lamani sat up straight and pushed back the files on her desk. 'A woman? Ask him if it's Kaveri Panchamukhi.'

Surprised, Nilima relayed the question.

'That's it!' Pallav slapped his hand on the table. 'That's the name!'

'You were right,' Nilima gasped into her phone. 'How did you know?'

'Because that's the name of Jagat's friend. The one who owns the land.'

'Oh, and Victor Lobo? Is he an accomplice of Madhura Shetty?'

'I don't know. I've never heard of him, and I know most of Madhura's stooges. Let me find out. Can you ask Pallav if the deed was signed?'

Nilima held her hand over the phone and checked with Pallav. 'No, ma'am—Sharmila,' she said slowly. 'He says it wasn't signed.'

CHAPTER 14

The Big Showdown

Nilima woke up when the painkiller wore off. She pushed herself upright even though her head felt heavy and her eyes kept falling shut. It had taken her a long time to fall asleep. *It's not hurting all that much,* she had tried to tell herself. After a couple of hours of lying stiffly, she had got up and groped for the pills on her table.

She cut up a plastic bag and tied it over her bandaged knee before getting in the shower. She turned the water up as hot as she could bear and gingerly sponged herself with her right hand. The heat soothed her left shoulder and arm. She waited for the steamed bathroom mirror to clear up while she dabbed herself ineffectually with the towel in her right hand. Her hair looked lank and felt crumbly. She didn't know when she could shampoo her hair again: touching her head, even with her right hand, made her shoulder send out radials of pain.

After liberally dousing her shoulder and arm with pain-relieving spray, she slowly put on her bra, wincing again as she reached both arms behind to hook it.

If I were thin, I could go braless, she thought, and immediately chastised herself. It had taken her long years to stop hating her body; she didn't want to relapse.

She sat on the bed again for a few minutes, feeling too tired to move. She pulled on the second of her two jersey cotton dresses, letting out an involuntary groan as she slipped it over her arm. The other dress went into her handbag to be given to the dhobi—she couldn't wash clothes for a while. Her arm hurt more in cold air, so she carefully pulled on a hoodie. Buttons were too difficult; back or side closures were out of the question.

She munched on a couple of dry biscuits just so she could take another pill, and brushed the crumbs off her chest as she got up. Her handbag with its cargo of dress, umbrella and more biscuits wobbled on her right arm as she struggled to lock the door with her right hand.

She didn't book a cab. The roads were bumpy, and yesterday's Uber ride had left her with a badly jostled arm. Instead, she pulled up her hood against the seemingly incessant rain and angled the umbrella carefully over her left shoulder. Pressing her left arm to her chest so it wouldn't get wet and cold, she set off on the slow trek to the metro station, dodging puddles and enthusiastic bikers. In the train, she stood with her left arm safely against a wall, but changing trains at Majestic was a scramble and the pain in her shoulder became a harsh buzz. The less crowded lanes of Jayanagar were a relief.

It was nearly noon, but Shwetha wouldn't tell her off for being late, and might even say she should have taken the day off.

How did it work, though, if she took the day off? She had felt too embarrassed to ask. She wasn't supposed to take any time off for the first three months, so would her salary be cut?

Her bank balance was next to nothing, and she had emptied out her fixed deposits over half a year of unemployment, and her mutual fund account had only a couple of lakhs from years of carefully squirreling away small amounts. What would happen if her arm didn't heal, and she needed more treatment? She was nearly thirty: she had imagined the days of living precariously would be behind her by now.

By the time Nilima entered the office, she was already tired, her left arm a bolster of pain she had to cart around. Shwetha was pacing like a caged tiger.

'Hi,' Nilima breathed, but wasn't sure if she was heard—wasn't sure if she could have been heard in the absence of lip reading, and Shwetha wasn't looking at her—so she went to her desk and sat down.

Nilima fidgeted with a pen while waiting for her computer to boot up, but couldn't resist the urge to look around. Shwetha wasn't pacing anymore; she was leaning against the wall with her eyes shut and her fists clenched.

Her pain was so palpable that Nilima cried out, 'What's the matter?'

Shwetha's eyes flew open. Nilima had never seen this expression in them before—or she had, just not directed at her. Shwetha had looked much like this the evening they had confronted Sampath about the thefts. It was grey outside now, not quite dark, but Shwetha's eyes sparked the same fire in the fluorescent lights. The drip from the ceiling beat a steady rhythm in the bucket below.

'You're asking me?' Shwetha's voice was gasping and harsh. 'What's the matter with *you*?'

Nilima made a sound that was approximately: 'Buh?'

Shwetha let go of the wall and pulled herself straight. She said more calmly, 'I found your notes.'

'What notes?'

'Your notes! I found your list of suspects, which includes me! I'm glad to know what you really think of me.'

Nilima opened her drawer. Her notebook was on top, where Shwetha had put it back neatly, even in her rage. Nilima had intended to surreptitiously tear out the pages and put them in her pocket, but Shwetha's presence had interrupted her, and she had forgotten about them.

'Why did you open my drawer?' Nilima pushed back memories of coming home from college to find that her mother had gone through her drawers and read her diary.

Shwetha's head reared back. 'Because it's *my* drawer,' she said, much like Nilima's mother had said, 'This is my home and you're my daughter and I have a right to know.'

'All the drawers in this office belong to me,' Shwetha continued imperiously. 'This isn't your home. And ... I was looking for a pen.'

She still had a pen—one of Nilima's pink gel pens—clenched in her fist as if she had forgotten she was holding it.

Suddenly, the enormity of what had happened hit Nilima. This was Shwetha, who was her friend—maybe more than a friend even, but she couldn't think about that right now—

who had driven her home from the hospital, whom she had told about her parents, who had indulged her play-acting as a detective. Now Shwetha knew Nilima hadn't trusted her, that Nilima had, in her most paranoid moments, wondered if she was evil. She was overwhelmed with guilt.

'Shwetha.'

'What do you have to say?'

'I didn't mean ...'

'You didn't mean it? Don't lie to me, Nilima. You put me down on your list of suspects. Were you planning to share that with your friend the inspector?'

Nilima shook her head, but Shwetha wasn't looking at her. 'All this time, all this time I believed we were in this together, that you were my friend, that we'd find the killer—you were suspecting me?' Her voice broke.

Nilima tried to speak several times before words came out. 'You ... you lied.'

'What?' Shwetha's voice was still harsh with anger.

'What were you doing with Dipen that night?'

'What?'

'Don't bother pretending. How long have you been friends with him?'

'What are you talking about?'

'I SAW YOU! The night I broke into his office! You were holed up with him for half an hour!' She remembered that it was really twenty minutes, but she was angry enough to exaggerate. She wanted to throw something, maybe her keyboard? Instead, she gripped the edge of her desk so hard it dug into her palm.

Shwetha said shakily, 'Is this why you've been acting weird around me?'

'What?'

'You've been different lately. Sort of quiet and sad and maybe angry.'

'You noticed?'

'Of course I noticed! I just didn't know whether I should say anything. I thought you were unhappy because we weren't making progress with the case. And then your arm ... Or maybe there was something going on at home.'

Nilima was taken aback. 'What do you mean, at home?' She pictured her little room with the curtain flapping over the bed. What could possibly happen there?

'Yes, with your parents. Or maybe with your sister and the baby.'

'Oh.'

'I did wonder if you were mad at me,' Shwetha said softly. 'I thought I should wait till you were ready to talk to me—like a grown-up.'

'And I was waiting for you to explain why you're suddenly friends with Dipen. I heard you laughing with him. I even recognised your feet!'

'What?'

'YOUR FEET!' Nilima pointed with her pen. 'Your pedicured feet with your leaf toe ring! You were wearing bright blue chappals!'

'You recognised my feet?' Shwetha seemed mildly amused, which made Nilima angrier.

'Yes! Haven't I spent enough time sitting here staring at your feet?! I'd recognise them even without the toe ring. So don't try to lie to me. What were you doing with him?'

'You were up there since then?'

'Hiding behind the poetry shelves. I sneaked into that room once you walked out with him.'

'I'm sorry. I should have told you.'

'You think?'

Shwetha was quiet.

'All the gossip that you gathered from your "network" about Dipen and his family—you already knew all of that, didn't you? You were lying when you said your aunties told you?'

'A bit. Not all of it.'

'So how long has this been going on? What were you talking about up there? Have you been laughing with your *buddy* about our stupid little investigation?'

'It's not like that,' Shwetha said desperately. 'I would never betray you like that. You know that.'

'I also knew you didn't know him. Because you said so.'

'I didn't exactly say that.'

'Oh? You're going to hide behind a technicality now? After I found the body, when we were wondering how to tell Jagat's family about his death ... You had his brother's number all along! All this time we have been questioning everyone and you didn't think to mention you're friends with Dipen?'

'I'm not.'

'You were plenty friendly that night!'

'I was trying to be friendly because of this murder. I thought he might tell me something.'

'Oh, that's all, is it? You don't know him from before at all, do you?'

'I do,' Shwetha admitted. 'We used to be lovers.'

'What?'

'Back when I was in college,' said Shwetha, almost pleading, her eyes bigger and rounder than ever. 'It was just a few months. We were never officially together.'

'And then?'

'And then we stopped seeing each other. It was mutual. I fell in love with someone else soon after, graduated, got married, moved cities, moved back ... I wasn't in touch with him. We were never friends.'

'So that night ...'

'We're friendly when we run into each other. I knew, of course, when I rented this office that I'd run into him. I wasn't looking forward to it, but I couldn't not take this place because of that. If I avoided all the places where I might run into someone I'd slept with, I wouldn't get out much.'

Nilima felt an urge to laugh. At least she wasn't shaking with anger anymore. But her exhaustion had returned, and her arm throbbed, and she felt unaccountably sad.

'When I came to the office that evening, we were both parking our vehicles—'

'Why did you come in at all?' Nilima interrupted. 'You were supposed to be out at your meeting.'

'I came by after it was over,' said Shwetha. 'I wanted to catch up on work.'

'Of course you did.' Nilima wanted to laugh again.

'When I got out of the car, Dipen was right there. We chatted. He invited me up. He seemed to want to show off. Like he was proud of running the place.'

Nilima nodded. Men tended to behave that way around Shwetha.

'I went along. I wanted to get him to talk, see if he would say anything that would help us. That's all.'

Shwetha was looking over Nilima's shoulder. Nilima turned around. Poorna was standing by the door, her body still, her usually expressive face blank. Nilima now realised Shwetha had been talking to both of them.

'And did you?' Poorna asked. 'Find out anything?'

'No, he was just bragging. Gloating, almost. About how much better the shop will do now that he's in charge.'

'It's not an empty boast,' Nilima said slowly. 'The store does seem to have got a new lease of life.'

'Do you think so? Do you think Jagdip will survive, then?'

Nilima looked at her.

'What's the matter?'

'We can't just go back to being friends like nothing's happened.'

'Why not?'

'You lied to me! How can I trust you now?'

'You're one to talk about trust! You put me down on your list of suspects!'

'Because you lied to me—to us!' Nilima waved to include Poorna. 'In fact, you're still lying to us!'

'What do you mean?'

'You know what I mean! How can I trust you if you keep lying to my face?'

'Nilima,' Poorna said gently.

'No, Poorna, believe me, she's lying!'

'I believe you, Nims,' Poorna said gently. Nilima looked startled.

Poorna went on. 'Tell me, what is she lying about?'

'She said ...' Nilima faced Shwetha again. 'You just said your relationship with Dipen was in the past. That you only accidentally ran into him that night.'

Poorna pulled her chair near Nilima before sitting down. Nilima went on. 'He is a suspect. You didn't tell us you were communicating with him.'

'She was?' Poorna asked.

'Inspector Lamani told me she'd found a text from Shwetha in Dipen's phone.'

'What? From when?'

'I don't know,' Nilima realised. 'I forgot to ask.'

'What did it say?'

'Better not,' Nilima quoted, the words having echoed in her brain countless times over the last day and a half. 'Nilima is getting suspicious.'

Poorna glared at Shwetha. 'How do you explain that?'

Shwetha's face sank into her hands. 'I've been afraid of this.'

'Afraid of what?' said Poorna.

'Of my texts being found on his phone. He was supposed to have deleted them. So the inspector knows? God, how embarrassing.'

'Knows what?' Poorna asked again.

'That I had been sleeping with Dipen.' Shwetha looked up.

'But that was ages ago,' said Poorna. 'How would the inspector find out?'

'Of course,' said Nilima. 'You're still fucking him.'

'No, not anymore,' Shwetha said. 'The last time was just a week or so before the murder.'

'What?' Poorna said with a deplorable lack of originality.

'We were both working late. He locked up the shop and came down here.'

'Wait, you did it in here?' Poorna jumped up from her chair. 'Dude, ew! I need to clean everything!'

'When did you send that text?' Nilima continued without waiting for an answer: 'Have you been warning him about my suspicions throughout? Did you tell him everything we were doing?' She heard her voice get bigger and louder but it felt disembodied, like she couldn't control it, like it belonged to someone else.

'Of course not.'

'What was it like? Did you enjoy gossiping about "stupid Nilima, she's trying to find out who the murderer is," in your post-coital state of bliss?'

'It wasn't like that! I told you, we didn't sleep together after the murder.'

'And why should we believe you? Haven't you lied to us enough already? Maybe you're still his secret girlfriend.'

'I'm not lying!' Shwetha sounded angry again. 'But I don't expect you to believe me. After all, you think I'm a murderer.'

Nilima shouted, 'That's not the point!'

'It is for me!' Shwetha shouted back. 'You spend all your time with me and you think I'm a murderer? You think all these things and you don't tell me? How dare you lecture me on honesty?'

'That's rich coming from you. You lied to us!' Nilima said again.

'And looks like I was right to not trust you with the truth!' For the second time this week, Shwetha grabbed her bag and walked out. This time she slammed the door behind her.

Poorna went to the water dispenser and drank deeply from a glass. She poured out another. Nilima was still gazing at the door.

'Here.' Poorna placed the glass in front of her. 'Drink up.'

'How could she do that?'

'Drink up,' Poorna said again. Nilima responded to the authority in her voice and obediently downed the water.

Paradoxically, she felt drained. She slumped in her seat, her head resting on the desk. Her arm had begun to pulse with pain again.

She felt Poorna sit by her, but she didn't open her eyes. Her body tensed, ready to yell again if a hand landed on her. Nothing moved. She couldn't even hear Poorna breathing next to her. Outside the office were the usual noises: two people talking cheerfully as they passed by in the lane, footsteps treading heavily upstairs—what were they doing, skipping rope?—the phee-phee-phee-phee of a car alarm.

Had Poorna moved away? Nilima raised her head. Poorna was sitting quietly, studying her nails—today they were a bright pink with golden dots on them.

'Your nails look nice,' Nilima said to break the silence.

'Thanks,' Poorna said absently.

'How could she have done that?'

'Done what, though?'

Nilima frowned in surprise. Poorna said deliberately, 'I saw two people say a lot of things.'

'What? What did I do?'

'Do I have to explain? You suspected her for what, a week? All this time you didn't say anything.'

'I thought—'

'You thought she could be abetting the murderer, even that she was the murderer. I know it's just a puzzle to you, you don't really care—'

'I do care!' Nilima cried out, stung.

'That just makes it worse. Shwetha trusted you, Nims. I've known her longer than you have, and she doesn't trust people easily.'

'She trusts you,' Nilima muttered.

Poorna paused, long enough that Nilima felt ashamed of what she had said. Poorna spoke up again. 'You look at this intellectually, because you pretend you don't care. You think people are less important than books.'

Nilima shook her head in protest, but Poorna continued, 'To Shwetha, people are what matter. She's had trouble trusting people since her divorce. It's not just her husband; so many people who she thought of as friends or family have cut ties with her or just been mean. She's found it difficult to find her place in her old world again.'

'She told you that?'

'Not in so many words, of course not. You think Shwetha would admit to struggling? But it's easy enough to see.'

Unsaid was the implication that Nilima should have seen it. She grew hot with embarrassment.

Nilima fumbled for the thread of righteousness that seemed to have slipped out of her hands. 'She was lying to us all along. What about that? If she was looking for trust, she should have trusted us!' she ended triumphantly.

'Maybe after all the gossip she's heard about herself, she wanted to keep her personal life private.'

'Oh.'

'Maybe she was embarrassed, who knows? Coming back to her old city, living in her parents' flat, driving her old car, taking up with her old college flame ... maybe she didn't want to talk about it.'

'Oh.'

'You hid stuff too. All this time you suspected her and you didn't say anything. As soon as she knew, she confronted you. She didn't keep it to herself and sulk over it.'

'Unlike me,' Nilima realised. 'You think she didn't tell us about Dipen because she didn't think it was relevant? To the murder, I mean.'

'Yeah. She still didn't think about it when she confronted you because she had compartmentalised it, I guess. If she had felt guilty, she would have kept quiet, no?'

They sat in silence for a few moments. Finally, Nilima said, 'All these days—ever since I saw her with Dipen—I have been feeling so betrayed.'

'You were jealous.'

'Huh?'

'You don't like Shwetha being involved with someone else.'

'I ... Why would I ...'

'Come on, Nims, your crush on her is pretty obvious.'

Nilima's heart stopped. 'To Shwetha too?'

'Hasn't she said anything?'

'No,' Nilima said, thinking of the times Shwetha had held her hand.

'You could ask her out. Better than resenting her dating other people.'

'I don't even know if she ... I mean, she's straight, right?'

'Who cares?'

'I care. I've been out of the closet too long to get shoved back in because someone I date isn't sure of who she is.'

'How will you know if you don't ask?'

Nilima sighed. 'I know. I've been too scared.'

'Scared of her saying yes or no?' Poorna said shrewdly. 'It's easier to pine for her than get into a real relationship, is it?'

'How are you so wise at so young an age?'

'I'm not, really. I'm just not as much of a fool as you think I am.'

'I don't think you're a fool!'

'At least have the guts to admit it. You're full of contempt and it comes out in your little taunts. You're so superior to us, your life's so sorted, your values all ironed out.' Poorna gave a little laugh.

Nilima sat frozen. Is that what Poorna and Shwetha had thought all this time? That she felt superior to them? All those jibes that she had told herself she didn't mean, all those bits of criticism—all Nilima had been looking for were ways in which she wasn't completely inadequate. And these had always paled in comparison to all the ways Shwetha and Poorna had seemed better than her. She had never thought her petty comments might have hurt them.

There was a sound at the door. Nilima jumped up, thinking, *Shwetha!* But Poorna was already moving towards the door, saying, 'It must be Mehnaz.' Of course Shwetha would just let herself in; the door was unlocked, she wouldn't knock. Nilima sank back into her chair. She should be surprised at Mehnaz flouncing in like she belonged here, but it didn't seem to matter.

Mehnaz was speaking rapidly in Kannada. Poorna listened attentively, but Nilima just gazed at her desk. Till one word penetrated the fog: 'police'.

Nilima looked up. Mehnaz turned to her, switching to English. 'Have you done anything yet? Why are you just sitting there?'

'She doesn't know,' Poorna said.

'You haven't told her yet? What are you waiting for? Why are you not doing anything about it? How dare you ... You guys came and butted in and put him in trouble, now you're just going to leave him in jail?'

'Hold on, what happened? Who's in jail?'

Mehnaz flung herself into a chair. Poorna answered, 'Sampath. He's been arrested.'

'What? Just now? The police were here?'

'I saw them take him away when I got here,' Poorna said. 'Mehnaz was ... uh, she was there ...'

'I followed them down,' Mehnaz said defiantly. 'They didn't listen to me, they just took him. I called you too. You didn't answer.'

Nilima's phone was face down on her desk. She flipped it around. Two missed calls from Mehnaz and a text: 'Call back, emergency!'

'Sorry, my phone was on silent.'

'Then I went back up to yell at Dipen and tell him to do something, but he just put his hands up, like what can I do. That asshole! If it was someone in his family, he'd be calling all his contacts, but of course he won't bother for Sampath.'

'Was Sharmila here?' Nilima asked Poorna, who shook her head. 'She didn't tell me anything.'

'Why should she tell you?' Mehnaz banged her fist on Poorna's desk. 'Do you think she'll ask for your permission? You are sitting right here and you have no idea? They just came and took him away, in front of all our customers, and, of course, Dipen made a joke and did nothing, his only concern was placating the customers. Poorna said you guys would do something. But you're just sitting around!'

Behind Mehnaz, Poorna made a helpless face at Nilima, like *What was I supposed to do? Tell you in the middle of your fight?*

Nilima wished Poorna *had* interrupted their fight. This was far more important. She called the inspector. Sharmila answered instantly but wasn't receptive to Nilima's protests. 'I'm working, Miss Deka. I can't talk now. We had evidence to arrest Sampath.' Sharmila paused to yell orders at someone. 'There's too much happening at the police station today. Call me tomorrow.'

Nilima looked at the screen—sure enough, the call had ended. 'She's refusing to talk to me. I've been downgraded to Miss Deka. We're screwed.'

'I thought Sampath was home by eleven,' Poorna said.

'The fool lied,' Mehnaz said bitterly. 'He went to Kamath's before going home. He does that often. He must have told his wife to lie for him.'

'That's bad,' said Nilima.

'This is all your fault,' said Mehnaz.

'Mehnaz, we were only trying to help.'

'How are you helping? You've only interfered and messed things up. Help Sampath if you want to help!' Mehnaz waved her arms angrily. 'But no, no one cares about him. Everyone laughs at him. He is the only nice person in that place. The only one who cares about anyone else.'

Nilima looked at Mehnaz numbly.

'How can the police have arrested him? He's an old man. He's worked for this shop all his life. Did you know what he told me as they took him away? "Don't worry, kanna, I'll be okay." He didn't ask for help, he wasn't angry, he comforted me.'

Poorna ventured, 'Are we sure he didn't kill Jagat?'

'What!' Mehnaz cried out in outrage.

'I can't picture him as a murderer, somehow,' Nilima answered. 'He is a pompous pest, but the bookshop is his life.'

'That gives him a motive, no? If he thought Jagat might fire him?'

Mehnaz stood up. 'I don't believe it. He didn't do it.'

'Then we'll prove that he didn't. Shwetha knows a lawyer. She'll be able to help.' Nilima's face fell as she remembered her row with Shwetha; she couldn't call her now.

'I'll call Shwetha,' Poorna said.

'And I'll go to the police station,' said Nilima. 'Sharmila will have to talk if I refuse to leave.'

'I'll come with you.' Poorna picked up her helmet and bag. 'You don't worry, Mehnaz. Go up, see to the shop.'

Mehnaz shook her head as she walked out. 'I'm going home. I'm not working here anymore.'

'Let's take a cab,' Nilima said. 'You can talk to Shwetha on the way.' Poorna shot a glance at Nilima's arm and put her helmet back down.

This time, there were more people at the police station, a few arguing loudly with police personnel seated at their desks. An officer pointed Nilima and Shwetha to a bench. Nilima curled up in a corner, away from the tired-looking man at the other end. Poorna sat upright next to her, fidgeting unceasingly and getting on Nilima's nerves, but she did not voice a complaint. She kept glancing at Sharmila's door in hope, but the inspector didn't come out, nor did anyone invite them in.

Poorna got up and paced, then got a phone call and stepped out of the building to answer it, and came back and paced again. A constable asked if they wanted tea. They refused, but Poorna took the opportunity to wheedle him in Kannada, asking when they could see Inspector Lamani. 'Madam is busy' was all he would say, though he smiled kindly at her.

At last, they were ushered into Sharmila's presence. Sharmila sighed audibly and gestured at the chairs in front of her. 'I told you we're having a busy day, Miss Deka.'

'You can't arrest Sampath!' Poorna burst out. 'We're very sure he is innocent, ma'am.'

'We have already arrested him.'

'Why?' Poorna protested. 'What proof do you have?'

'He has been stealing from the shop. For a long time, perhaps years. We think Mr Desai found out and fired him, and Sampath killed him in retaliation.'

'How did you find out about the thefts?' asked Nilima.

'We are the police, Miss Nilima. We find out things. Even if you choose not to tell us.'

Nilima's cheeks burned, but she continued to argue. 'He may have stolen, but that doesn't make him a murderer.'

'He lied about his whereabouts that night. We looked up his GPS records after we found out about the thefts. He didn't get home till after midnight. His phone was near the bookshop till almost eleven, then it was switched off. He didn't turn it on till he was home. A neighbour saw him enter his building. He—the neighbour—was walking home from a film that ended at 11.50.'

'Did Sampath say what he was doing?' asked Poorna.

'Now he says he didn't get into the autorickshaw after all. He changed his mind and went to a bar, and later his phone battery died. He drank till the bar closed, then he went home.'

'Have you verified this?' demanded Nilima.

'He just told us this, Miss Nilima. And you realise it's been almost two weeks now, and apparently he goes to this bar often. No one will remember one specific night. He paid in cash.'

'This bar—is it Kamath's?' asked Nilima.

'That's correct.'

'But that's the next building. That would explain his GPS location—if he was there the whole time. He may be telling the truth.'

'We had already interviewed the manager of the bar, and the waiters, to see if they had seen anyone leave the lane that night. They didn't report anything. None of them mentioned Sampath.'

'Did you specifically ask about Sampath?'

'How could we, when we didn't know he was there? Now he says he goes there often, so if he was there, someone should have mentioned it.'

People don't tell the police everything, Nilima thought again. 'You'll check up on his story?'

'Certainly, we will verify his statement. We're not villains, Miss Nilima. Right now, given how he lied to us all along, he's our best suspect.'

'What about Madhura Shetty? What about Victor Lobo? Did you even follow up on the information I gave you?'

'Hmm.' The inspector visibly gathered her patience. 'You were right, it was important. Jagat was trying to cut a deal—a more lucrative deal, for himself—with an upcoming builder called Ranjit Lobo. Victor is his brother. Madhura found out and paid Jagat a visit that night, around eleven.'

'Madhura was the mysterious visitor?' Poorna asked.

'Hmm. Mohan told us everything this morning when we brought him in again. Mohan made the appointment with Jagat, saying they had something important to discuss in private. He was to keep Jagat in the office late that night, so Madhura and his henchman could arrive unseen.'

'And intimidate him?' Nilima said. 'Hurt him?'

'Mohan swears they didn't touch him. And the post-mortem bears that out. No bruises, except for the back of his head. Our doctor thinks he must have hit his head on the door as he lost consciousness. There were threats, not just to him but to his family as well. Jagat backed off and promised to get the deal done for Madhura. That means Madhura and Mohan have no motive.'

'If you believe Mohan!' exclaimed Nilima. 'He's lied to you before, why would he be telling the truth now?'

'Victor Lobo confirms this statement. He said Jagat called him up that night, soon after eleven.'

'But you said Jagat hadn't made any calls that night!'

'Jagat had called from Mohan's phone. I assume Mohan had dialled to make sure there was no duplicity again. He doesn't seem to have trusted Jagat anymore, hmm. After Jagat told Victor the deal was off, Mohan got on the phone and told Victor to go through him for any land deals, not Jagat.'

'That sounds like a threat. I still think Madhura or Mohan might have stabbed Jagat, maybe in anger, maybe not meaning to kill ...'

'Your thinking doesn't make it true, Miss Nilima. There's no evidence.'

'But why didn't Madhura or his flunkey leave fingerprints?' demanded Nilima. 'You didn't say you'd found any at the store.'

'We didn't,' Sharmila said defensively. 'I asked both Mohan and Madhura about that and they had the same answer: Madhura didn't touch the doors—of the office and the shop—because Mohan held the door open for him each time. They were in there for only a few minutes; it's not surprising he didn't touch anything else. And the henchman, Raman, he didn't go into the shop at all. He waited outside the door.'

'You've questioned Madhura?'

'He's still here.' Sharmila jerked her head at the corridor. 'We're getting his statement typed now for him to sign. When I told you I was busy, I meant it.'

'What about Veena? Have you looked into her friend's husband's death?'

'Hmm. There's nothing to suggest it wasn't an accident.'

'I suppose Sampath is easier to go after,' Nilima said bitterly.

'Be careful, Miss Nilima,' the inspector said softly. 'Now should I call someone to take you to meet Sampath, or to show you the way out?'

Poorna grabbed Nilima's elbow—her right elbow, thankfully. There was nothing more to be done.

'We'll meet Sampath, please,' Nilima said.

Afterwards, they found an autorickshaw to take them back to the office. Poorna chattered away: did Nilima know this street, and hey, they had done a tour here, and oh one of her friends lived over there ... Nilima ignored her steadily until she fell quiet.

Nilima's left side was getting sprayed by stray raindrops, and her arm ached heavily. She didn't want to be rude—Poorna was her friend now, and she was helping—but her head was buzzing with thoughts and she couldn't take in any more. How had everything gone so horribly wrong? She was so close to the answer. She knew who the murderer was, or at least she was pretty sure she knew. But she had no proof, and she hadn't been able to come up with a way to get any. And now Sampath was in jail. He had been as polite as usual in his cell, saying 'Thank you for coming, madam,' just as he'd welcomed Nilima into his home—she closed her eyes to shut off the memory.

When she opened them again, the autorickshaw had stopped at a traffic signal. A motorbike stood so close that Nilima could have touched the man's back without straining her arm. The inevitable angry honking started up and quickly escalated into a hellish cacophony, barely muffled by the rain.

She had lost Shwetha's friendship. Shwetha, who had given her a safe haven after a decade of working at places where she had felt unwanted, even threatened. Nilima hadn't realised how comfortable she had been at Chikkamma until the comfort had shattered under the weight of her suspicions.

The autorickshaw was moving again. They were almost at the office. 'Stop!' Nilima called out. The driver obligingly pulled up at the curb.

'I'll be in soon,' she said to Poorna as she stepped out. She quickly turned and walked away, ignoring Poorna's questions. She scurried into the building before she could get drenched—or reconsider her hasty plan.

She was inside Kamath's for the first time.

It was smaller than she had expected; a low ceiling and no open windows making it claustrophobic. Most of the steel-and-glass tables were already occupied, even though it wasn't six yet, by men staring determinedly at their glasses. The fug of Old Monk and fried food filled the room. The tall black-shirted man behind the cash counter eyed her warily.

Nilima made for the winding concrete steps at the other end of the room. As she knew from looking at the building from outside, the top floor had a wide window overlooking the street. It was open now, and the room was awash in pale daylight, only slightly hazy from cigarette smoke. The inside walls were painted in the same magenta with turquoise trim as the outside of the building.

She took the empty table closest to the stairs, ignoring the patrons looking at her as if she had presented herself for their entertainment. She placed her hands nervously on the table, but it felt sticky, so she clasped them in her lap.

A waiter handed her a stained laminated menu on his way to other tables. He was heading back out of the room when she raised a hand and stopped him. He was young, his grey uniform accentuating his muscular, if short, body.

She ordered a small whiskey and a plate of chilli chicken. She wondered if Poorna was hungry. Neither of them had had lunch.

She smoked nervously for something to do other than looking back at the faces around the room. The man came back with her whiskey with no ice. He upturned the little steel bowl on the table and drew out a sachet from his pocket. A handful of peanuts burst forth into the bowl. Entranced by this performance, she didn't speak until he had reached the stairs, and her low cry of 'sir' went unnoticed. She dug her nails into her thigh.

What would Marlowe do? she asked herself. She poured a finger of water into her glass from the steel jug on the table and took a big gulp, but it didn't make her feel any braver. Marlowe would have walked in like he owned this place. He'd make friends with the patrons, he'd get all the information he needed out of the waiters, and he'd probably get into a fight doing it and go home with a swollen face and an air of smug satisfaction.

No amount of cigarettes or drink would make her into him. She lit another anyway.

Miss Marple, then. But Miss Marple wouldn't be caught dead in a place like this. She'd probably talk to that young waiter's mother and get her information that way.

The waiter came into view again, carrying plates of food. He lightly placed hers down without pausing and went on through the room. This time, when she waved her hand, he didn't break stride. Now the yellow lights came on, softening the pinks on the walls.

Her chicken was delicious, though so spicy it stung her mouth. She decided to give herself a reprieve and set to finishing every morsel. When the waiter made another lap past her, she managed to stop him by barring his way with her arm.

'Repeat?' he asked promptly.

She refused and asked for the bill. He nodded, already moving again.

The bill was for 110 rupees. She placed two hundred-rupee notes on the billfold and told the waiter to keep the change.

By the time his grin appeared, she was shoving her phone in his face. On the screen was a photo of Sampath. 'Do you know him?' she asked in Hindi.

He looked at her with no sign of recognition.

'He's my friend,' she tried. 'Did he come here last week Sunday, the nineteenth?'

'I don't remember,' he shrugged. Then, seeing her worried face, he added, 'Wait here.'

He came back in a few minutes with a man who looked older, bigger and more authoritative. A moustache, no beard. 'Yes, ma'am?' he said politely, folding his arms over his chest, and Nilima recognised him from the counter downstairs. She gestured to the chair opposite her, but he shook his head implacably.

'Sampath.' She waved her phone again. 'He comes here often? I work in the next building too, where Jagdip Book House is.'

The man straightened up by a millimetre. 'He's a frequent customer,' he admitted.

'Was he here on the nineteenth?'

'I do not remember, madam.'

'I've just come from the police station.'

'Police station?' His calm air seemed a little ruffled.

'About the murder at Jagdip's.'

He nodded. 'That was a tragedy. But it's nothing to do with us.'

'It might help the police if they knew for sure whether Sampath was here that night.'

'You're not from the police.' It wasn't a question.

'No, I'm a friend of Sampath's.'

'I'm sorry, madam.' He shook his head in seemingly genuine ruefulness. 'He comes here often, but that night? I'm not sure.'

'Can I ask your other waiters?'

He stared at her until she placed two hundred-rupee notes on the table. He pocketed them, still managing to look disapproving, and said he would send the waiters up. Nilima wanted to go downstairs with him, but he shook his head and hurried off.

The first man to come up was middle-aged and fat, whiskers covering much of his round face. He was monosyllabic and unbending, refusing her offers to sit down and not admitting he knew Sampath, not even when she showed him a photo. 'Nahi, nahi,' was all he said. Nilima bit her lip and wished again that she knew Kannada. But it probably wouldn't have helped anyway, she thought as the man escaped down the stairs.

The next waiter had grey hair and thick glasses. He had worked here for a decade and admitted to knowing Sampath. 'I can remember he wasn't here last night,' he told her, his hairy hands gesticulating wildly. 'But so many nights ago? Even when I was young my memory wasn't that good.'

The last man was younger, thirty-something, Nilima guessed. Heavy-set, with large eyes, a trim moustache and beard. When she introduced herself, he offered up his name: Hari.

He sat down in response to her invitation, and accepted a cigarette. With renewed hope, Nilima showed him the photo of Sampath and asked if he'd been here the Sunday before last.

'Haan, haan,' he said politely.

'You remember him?' Nilima asked in Hindi.

'You're not from the police?'

'No, nothing like that. I'm Sampath's friend. I'm trying to help him.'

'Yes, the night of the murder. He was here. I remember thinking about him when we heard the news the next day. We were all talking about it, wondering what he knew ...'

All? Of course, they'd have talked about it in the kitchen, it would have been big news.

'What do you remember from that night?'

'Nothing. It was the usual Sunday night. Crowded. Sampath came in late—ten, ten-thirty? He drank his usual Old Monk and stayed till we closed around eleven-thirty. In fact, he was still on the street when I walked out a few minutes later. He was looking for an auto. I found one and helped him into it.'

'Helped him?'

Hari chuckled. 'He could barely walk. I was glad he remembered his address.' Nilima's heart leapt in hope. Sampath had been too drunk to walk, which meant he had been too drunk to stab a man and not leave bloody footprints and fingerprints all over the crime scene.

'Can I have your number, sir? The police will want to talk to you.'

'Police?' He stiffened.

Nilima explained that Sampath was locked up under suspicion of murder.

'Nahi, madam. I can't talk to the police.'

'What? Why?'

'I have two little children, a wife. I cannot be involved in a police case.'

'But Sampath is innocent.'

'So am I, madam. I can't risk it. The police will question me, they'll call me as a witness, for years and years. My life will be tied up with this needlessly. And that's if I actually get to live and the murderer doesn't hurt me or my family.'

'Hari sir, please.'

'I can't do this. If you tell the police about me, I'll say I don't remember anything.'

Nilima didn't have the heart to push further. She passed him a five-hundred-rupee note—she was out of hundreds—and made for the stairs, not looking back at the roomful of men who were still staring at her.

CHAPTER 15

Kitty Party Night

The next morning, Nilima arrived at the office to see Shwetha's car in its parking spot and no sign of Poorna's scooter. She didn't feel up to facing Shwetha alone and made for the terrace instead.

She lit her first cigarette of the day. She settled into the shade provided by the building across the lane, and a middle-aged woman glared at her from a window. Nilima puffed on her cigarette and turned her eyes to the orange flames of the African tulip pushing a branch over the terrace.

'Hey,' said a voice behind her, and Nilima dropped her cigarette.

'Sorry.' Poorna held out her own pack. Both of them leaned against the low wall and stood contentedly for a few moments.

'Clear day for once,' Nilima offered, waving at the blue sky.

'It said on the radio that it won't rain again till tomorrow.'

'How was the tour?'

'It was okay. One person was outraged she had to bring her own bottle of water, one guy knew more than me and wanted to take over the tour ... The usual shit.'

Nilima shrugged her good shoulder in sympathy. Poorna was looking up at the sky, uncharacteristically quiet.

Then Poorna said, 'My pharmacist friend called me last night. About that tablet you'd found in the bookshop's office.'

'And? Did he know what it is?'

'It's a morning-after pill. Like, what you take after sex if you're not on contraception and don't want to become pregnant.'

'I know what that is. Just because I've never needed it ...'

Poorna grinned. 'That means someone probably had sex in there.'

'That doesn't help us much. No way to tell who it was.'

'Dipen?' Poorna guessed.

'That'd be my bet too, but it could have been anyone. Jagat, Pallav, Mehnaz ... Hard to imagine Sampath doing that, but who knows. As long as it isn't poison.'

'You thought the pill was poison? Why?'

'I didn't know, I thought we should check it out, just in case. If it was, it might have meant there had been an earlier murder attempt.' Nilima stubbed out her cigarette and put the end carefully in an empty cigarette box she pulled out of her pocket.

'Shwetha wants to talk to us,' Poorna said abruptly.

'Oh yeah? What about?'

'Come on, Nims. She's waiting. I came to call you.'

Poorna led the way downstairs. Nilima bent down to pick up a fallen flower before following her, tucking the bright velvety blossom in her pocket.

When Nilima entered the office, Poorna had pulled up her chair next to Shwetha's desk. Nilima stood in front of them, feet wide, hands in pockets. Shwetha's face was wary.

'What are we doing about Sampath?' Nilima demanded.

'I'm not doing anything,' Shwetha responded coolly. 'I'm doing my work.'

'We have to do something. He looked miserable even though he kept saying he's okay.'

Shwetha softened slightly. 'I called my lawyer friend,' she said. 'She's on her way to see Sampath now. The rest is up to her.'

'Thanks,' said Nilima unexpectedly, and turned to go to her desk. Then she changed her mind and said, 'I'm sorry.'

Shwetha continued looking up at Nilima through narrowed eyes. They eyed each other for what felt like five minutes, but was probably no more than five seconds.

'I'm sorry too,' Shwetha said at last, so low that Nilima leaned forward to hear her. 'I should have told you both about Dipen. I was too ashamed.'

'Ashamed?' Nilima said in surprise. 'Why?'

'I want to tell you what happened,' Shwetha said. 'I mean—anything you want to know.'

'You don't have to,' said Nilima.

'I want to,' Shwetha repeated. 'Tell me what you want to know.'

'How did it start?' Nilima asked. 'Back then.'

'It was over ten years ago—'

'Ten years?' Poorna spoke up. 'I was thirteen.'

'I was twenty, twenty-one?' Shwetha said. 'Anyway, it didn't last long, we weren't in love or anything.'

'How was he?' Poorna asked.

Shwetha tilted her head quizzically. 'Poorna, I'm not going to tell you details of how he ... how we ...'

'Ew, dude, no! I just meant, what was he like? Was he nice, was he mean? You knew him, right? That should help us.'

'You're right, Poorna!' Nilima said, settling into her chair. 'Why didn't I think of that?'

'You can't think of everything,' Poorna said generously. 'Come on, Shwetha. Tell us what you remember. You must have been quite young then, right? And he was much older? That's creepy.'

'It wasn't like that at all. He was ... you know he was in a band. I was a bit star-struck. One of the band members went to my college, so they used to hang out there. They played at a couple of college events. This was during my post-grad. Dipen was maybe eight years older? It didn't matter to me—boys my age seemed so immature. And he used to be really good-looking. He always had girls hanging around him. I was flattered when he chose me.'

'Did he treat you okay?' asked Poorna.

'He was fun to be around. Cheerful. Easy-going.'

'Were you exclusive?' asked Nilima.

'No. He saw other women—he would even tell me about them. He used to talk about free love and all that.'

'Asshole,' said Poorna, just as Nilima said, 'What a jerk.' They nodded at each other in agreement.

'No, he wasn't. He was fine with me seeing others too. It was kind of new for me, this casual sex thing. I'd always done what I'd been supposed to do till then—obeyed my parents, came home early every evening, got good marks. Now I was staying away from my parents for the first time, even though I was in the same city and went home every weekend. This was my way of exploring, of rebelling, I suppose.'

'That's what you should do when you're young,' said Poorna wisely.

'Says the twenty-three-year-old who goes home by eight at night.' Nilima rolled her eyes. 'Tell us more about Dipen, boss. Do you know if he had a job? How was he financing this lifestyle of playing music and hanging out on college campuses?'

'I had no idea at the time. Somehow, I never thought about it. They used to make a little at music gigs, but not much. I guess he must have been living on his inheritance. His mother was still alive then—he lived with her, so he never took me to his place.'

'How did it end between you?'

'It kind of petered out in a few months.'

'Why, because of your husband?' asked Poorna.

'No, I didn't start going out with Cyrus till late in my second year. I ended it with Dipen much before that. I got a tad tired of hanging around watching him play and get stoned, hoping he'd come back to my room with me. After some time, it got boring.'

'And later? How did you start up again?'

'It was last year. October, I think. I had been feeling lonely. One evening, I came back here after a coffee date.'

Poorna and Nilima exchanged a look that meant: *Of course she came back to work after a date.*

'It was a bad date. The guy had grilled me about my divorce. I told him off, of course, but I was feeling raw. I came back here to try to work and feel better. It didn't help. When I was leaving, Dipen was out there getting on his bike.

'When we'd run into each other before, we'd only exchanged smiles or a polite hi. This time, he came over and talked to me. He was charming and it felt just like old times. We came back inside. I didn't know then that he was engaged.'

'He didn't tell you,' Poorna said with contempt.

'Our time together felt like an escape from everything else, from worrying about Chikkamma and my parents and my finances. It wasn't often, just a few times—when we were both working late and everyone had left, he'd come over. Sometimes I stayed late hoping he would come over and he didn't. I told myself I was stupid.'

'Did you ever go up there?' asked Poorna, and unbidden, the image appeared in Nilima's mind: Shwetha and Dipen on the desk in that room she'd spent the night in, Shwetha's legs wrapped around his body ...

'No. Only that one time Nilima saw me, and that really was a friendly visit.'

'And he didn't tell you when he got married?' Poorna asked.

'We didn't talk much.'

Poorna sniggered.

'I knew he was getting married,' Shwetha continued. 'A friend had told me. He didn't come for a couple of months around his wedding, so I thought it was over. Then he came one night, and neither of us mentioned it, and we carried on as usual.'

'When did he send you that text?'

'It was a few days before the murder. He texted me asking to meet up that night. I was trying to break off this habit, so I said no. He pushed a bit, asked why, so I told him Nilima was getting suspicious. It was an excuse, but not quite untrue—it was harder once Nilima was also here working late. I was afraid you two would find out, and I was ashamed. He was obsessed about keeping it a secret.'

'I wonder why,' Poorna murmured.

'I thought that excuse would stop him. And it worked.'

'And that's the message he didn't delete and the inspector found when she looked through his phone,' said Nilima.

'And you thought ...' Shwetha didn't look angry, just sad. 'Nilima, how could you think I was involved in the murder?'

'I didn't know what to think,' Nilima said. 'I didn't really believe it, but I couldn't see any other explanation. Why didn't you just tell us?'

'Are you seriously asking that? Do you remember how you reacted to every mention of Dipen? You were so full of judgement.'

Nilima looked surprised. 'He's a murder suspect.'

'Come on! Everyone in the building is a suspect.'

'Sure, but ...'

'But what? You've always had it in for Dipen. What's your problem?'

'He's ... he flirts ...'

'Lots of people flirt. If you hadn't noticed, I do it all the time. Just because you're such a prude doesn't mean everyone should be.'

Nilima opened her mouth, but didn't know what to say. *It's different,* she thought. But she was sure saying that out loud would just make Shwetha angrier.

'What?' Shwetha said.

'Sorry. I didn't mean to imply you were doing anything wrong.'

'Nilima's right though,' Poorna said unexpectedly. 'You should have told us and not been such an ass about it.'

'Excuse me?'

'All right, if you want to be like that ... not been an arse.'

Shwetha's smile, never far off, rose to the surface. 'Fool.'

'No, you.'

'Why?'

'You should have told us,' Poorna said again.

Shwetha looked tired. 'It wasn't any of your business.'

'In what way?'

'What do you mean?'

'If you're speaking purely as our boss, the owner of Chikkamma Tours (Pvt.) Ltd,' Poorna said, making air brackets, 'you're right; it's not our business who you sleep with.'

'That's right.'

'But you're also our friend. Or do you not want to be anymore?'

Shwetha frowned. 'Of course I do.'

Poorna went on, 'And are we all investigating the murder together? Or are you our boss there too and decide what we do and don't need to know?'

Shwetha sighed. 'I'm sorry. I have been acting bossy, haven't I?'

'Often, these days,' said Nilima.

'I don't really know how to be the boss,' Shwetha confessed. 'I keep getting it wrong.'

'You're mostly okay,' said Poorna. 'It's only when you try to pretend you aren't unhappy or vulnerable that you get a stick up your ass ... sorry, arse.'

'I don't like you both seeing that I'm having trouble managing things. That's my job, you shouldn't have to worry about that.'

'We're a team,' Poorna said forcefully. 'We're here because we like you, because we're part of Chikkamma. Stop acting like we're not here.'

Shwetha looked tentatively at Nilima. Nilima wanted to agree, to take Shwetha's hand in hers, but her feelings and thoughts were all in a jumble and she needed time to unravel them.

'I have something else,' Shwetha said. 'Two things, actually.'

She waved a transparent bag with a piece of paper in it. 'This paper you found in Jagat's office, Nilima, I think I've worked out what it is. I was looking through all the photos you took of the files, and it had the employees' salary slips, and this number on top is the same as Sampath's salary. I think Jagat was planning to give him a raise. He was working out the numbers on this paper.'

'Does that help?' Poorna asked.

'It might,' Nilima said. 'If Jagat was planning to give Sampath a raise, and if Sampath knew, he doesn't have motive. It's not much, but it's something. I'll give this to Sharmila.'

'What's the second thing?' Poorna asked.

'I'm going to a party,' Shwetha began.

'Sweet!' said Poorna.

'We're only trying to catch a murderer,' said Nilima.

'And free an innocent man,' Poorna continued.

'And keep this business going.'

'You have a social life to maintain.'

'If your improv comedy bit is over,' Shwetha began again.

'We could go on for a while,' Nilima countered.

'I don't doubt it.' Shwetha looked amused. 'I suppose it's an improvement to having you two ganging up on me. This party—'

'Oooh, do tell us about it,' said Nilima.

'What sort of party is it?'

'Is it a costume party? A masquerade?' Nilima batted her eyes.

'Shut it for two minutes, will you?' said Shwetha more roughly. 'I'm helping my cousin Tina host it. Actually, Tina is married to my second cousin's son, but she's about my age.'

'Cradle-snatching?' inquired Nilima.

'Actually, her husband's a couple of years older than me. His grandmother is my dad's oldest aunt's daughter.'

'You've just named more family than I've talked to in a decade,' said Nilima.

'Tina is doing me a favour. She's getting Ronita there.'

'Ronita,' echoed Poorna. 'As in Dipen's wife Ronita?'

'How did you pull that off?' said Nilima.

'I found out Tina is friends with a neighbour of Ronita's, Bhuvaneshwari. She's practically Ronita's only friend in town, from what I hear.'

'And this friend's promised to drag her to this party so you can interrogate her? Hardly a surprise the poor thing is reluctant to make friends, if this is how her friends treat her.' Nilima was teasing now, the hard edges having fallen off her voice. Shwetha was in the clear, she hadn't done anything wrong and she had apologised, and they were friends again, and she was trying to solve the murder ... Nilima felt buoyant, like she'd fly off if she didn't hold on to the arms of her chair.

'What if Dipen comes?' asked Poorna. 'Won't that be awkward?'

'He won't. Only women are invited.'

'What kind of weird party is this?' said Nilima.

'Is it a baby shower?' asked Poorna.

'Is it a coven meeting? I always suspected you were a witch.'

'Is it a kitty party?'

Shwetha abruptly stopped smiling.

'Hold on,' said Nilima. 'It *is* a kitty party?' She burst out laughing.

'What is a kitty party?' asked Poorna. 'I've only heard of them in TV shows my grandmom watches—they are things rich society ladies go to.'

'Whoa,' said Nilima, still looking at Shwetha. '*You're* a rich society lady.'

Shwetha lobbed a pen at her. 'Actually, Tina and her friends focus on charitable causes. The kitty goes to the lucky recipient's favourite charity. They help each other out, volunteer in each other's organisations and connect people they know who might be of help.'

'Ah,' said Nilima. 'It's a kitty party for rich society ladies who think they have consciences.'

'So,' Shwetha continued loudly, 'Tina is pretending she wants Ronita's help for a charity she's involved in. They are trying to set up libraries in government schools, so she is going to make a pitch to Ronita about getting Jagdip Book House involved. Ask them to let Tina's people put up a donation box at the cash counter, give them a discount on old stock, things like that.'

Nilima recapped the situation: 'And when her only friend in Bangalore brings her to this party so the hostess can ask her to use her connection to her husband's business, *you'll* pounce on her and ask her about her connection to her brother-in-law's murder.'

'Are you judging me?'

'No, I think you're brilliant!'

'Yeah,' Poorna agreed. 'Good work, boss!'

'Not you too,' Shwetha groaned. 'It's bad enough that Nilima keeps calling me boss.'

'Hey, boss,' said Nilima at once, 'how many people are coming to this thing?'

Shwetha was so relieved that she and Nilima seemed to be back on their old terms that she smiled. 'Ten or twelve, I guess. They are all regular members except for me and Ronita. Tina's explaining my presence by saying I just moved back last year and want to get involved in some volunteer work. She's also hinted that my parents might be looking for a new cause to donate to. We had to make my presence look natural.'

'And in return for this favour you're helping Tina cook and clean and decorate?' asked Poorna.

'I don't think there'll be balloons, but essentially, yeah.'

'She's cooking everything?' said Nilima. 'Why not just order in?'

'That doesn't get you as many points as serving home-cooked food,' Poorna guessed.

'Yeah, the unspoken agreement is the hostess cooks. It's supposed to be easy finger food, but actually each host tries to outdo the others. Tina's counting on my help because the last time she hosted, she took the "simple snacks" suggestion seriously, and her reputation hasn't recovered since.'

'Take the rest of the day off and go prep for the party,' Poorna suggested.

'I'll go to the police station with that piece of paper,' Nilima added. 'You go help your cousin host a fabulous party. We owe it to her.'

✍

Shwetha walked into the spacious kitchen of Tina's airy flat that took up the entire first floor of a building in Indiranagar. Tina, her heart-shaped face creased in worry and her arms dappled with flour, was dressed in a faded yellow nightgown. She let out a cry of welcome and followed up with a steady stream of anxieties about the party.

Shwetha hugged her, carefully avoiding her floury forearms. Tina's toddler Appu was in the stroller, humming cheerfully to herself. The domestic worker, Gauri—tall, thin and intimidatingly stern—had gone back to cleaning the living room after letting Shwetha in.

Tina went to her bedroom to change as Shwetha tied an apron over herself. She was wearing an old silk sari, mustard with a green border, and didn't want to get oil splattered on it as she fried up the savoury snacks Tina had rolled out. A cake was spinning in the convection microwave, and one end of the table had platters laid out with little chunks of meat ready for grilling.

Shwetha bent over the stroller to coo at the baby. For a moment, Shwetha envied Tina, who didn't have to worry about whether she would be able to pay her employees next month or if she could afford to put off water-proofing the office for another season. Whether she had made the right decision in renting an office at all when she could have set up a small office in her living room instead—but the thought of having Poorna and Nilima in her flat all day was overwhelming. Whether the scandal of having a murder occur in the building would attach to her business, and how long people would continue to whisper, 'Of course she didn't have anything to do with it, but it's just sad how bad luck follows her.'

The doorbell rang, startling Shwetha—and Appu, who let out an aggrieved wail. Shwetha watched her for a second, but she merely resumed humming, so she went out to greet the guests.

Gauri had already opened the door and ushered the guests into the living room. Shwetha had hoped it would be Ronita; Tina had asked Bhuvaneshwari to come early, ostensibly so that Tina could talk to Ronita before the others arrived. But the two women who perched on the sofa were older, with matching linen saris and grey hair—one's in a bun, the other's cut stylishly short. Gauri disappeared into the kitchen. Shwetha sat on the blue velvet stool and introduced herself. One of the women responded, 'Oh, we've heard so much about you' in a way that made her wince internally.

The doorbell rang again, and Shwetha invited two more women in. The first was elegantly dressed in a cream sheath dress and golden ballet shoes, and had chestnut brown hair. 'You must be Shwetha,' she said, and added in an inadvertent echo, 'Tina's told me so much about you. I'm Bhuvaneshwari; this is Ronita.'

Bhuvaneshwari was loquacious, and Shwetha was compelled to focus most of her attention on her. She sneaked glances at Ronita, who had claimed the easy chair in the corner, away from the light thrown by the window and the brass lamp. Her pale pink churidar-kameez accentuated her daintiness and made her look almost fragile. Wavy hair cascaded down to her hips. She smiled shyly and fiddled with her silver bangles.

Bhuvaneshwari greeted the linen twins like old friends, but refused to sit down. 'I have to freshen up,' she said. 'Get the dust out of my eyes. You'd better comb your hair too, Roni. I wanted to take a cab,' she turned to Shwetha, 'but this one insisted on riding her scooter. I feel like all the dust of the city has settled on my skin. No, don't worry, I know where the washroom is.'

Shwetha promptly sat next to Ronita, abandoning the linen twins to themselves. 'You ride a scooter?' she said. 'I've always been too scared to learn. My colleague Poorna rides hers to office though, and all around the city; she prefers it to buses and cabs.'

Ronita smiled, visibly less nervous. 'I learned even before I started college,' she said. 'I used to ride my scooter to class every day. Of course, Pune, especially back then, was easier than Bangalore now.'

'Ah, you're from Pune!' The woman in the grey sari—Aruna—called from across the room. 'Did you move here recently?'

'December. When I got married.'

'Congratulations! Do you miss Pune?'

'A little. I'm not used to this city yet. I've been trying to explore it on my own.'

'Why on your own?' The woman in the blue sari—Tara—asked. 'Does your husband not have time to take you?'

'He's busy,' Ronita said easily. 'He runs a bookstore. There are no weekends.'

'Oh, that sucks!' said Shwetha quickly. 'I sympathise. I run a business too, and rarely take a day off. Which bookstore is your husband's?'

'Jagdip Book House. It's in Jayanagar.'

'Wow, that's a coincidence! My office is in the same building! You must be Dipen's wife.'

'You know Dipen?'

'Not very well. We just see each other sometimes around the building, that's all. I'm on the ground floor, below the bookstore.'

The linen twins were looking at them with frank curiosity.

'Are you talking about Jagat?' Bhuvaneshwari reappeared. 'What a tragedy.'

'Ronita is Jagat Desai's sister-in-law,' she explained to the others.

On cue, Aruna and Tara expressed their condolences. Ronita nodded awkwardly.

Tina came out at this opportune moment, having changed into a red lace dress and red lipstick. Bhuvaneshwari hugged her and kissed her lavishly on each cheek.

'Would you like to come in and freshen up too?' Shwetha murmured to Ronita. 'Comb your hair?' She thought to herself: *I'm being very rude, implying she needs cleaning up.*

Ronita seized the excuse to leave the room, and Shwetha ushered her not towards the nearest bathroom meant for guests but to Tina's bedroom, which was furthest from the living room. The doorbell rang again, but Shwetha shut the door behind her, and the sounds from the rest of the flat faded away.

'I thought you might want to get away for a bit. I'm sure you've had your fill of people offering condolences.'

'Oh, yes. Thank you. You see, we were not close.'

'Of course, you only got married recently,' said Shwetha. 'But your husband must have been close to his brother? I don't have any siblings; it must be so tough to lose one, especially when you work together.'

'They saw each other every day, yes.'

'Pardon me for asking, surely I have seen you at Jagdip too? You look so familiar.'

'Oh, yes. I go once in a while to help out. I don't have much to do at home.'

Shwetha sat back against a pillow on Tina's bed and waved at the large mirror opposite, and Ronita obediently walked up to it. 'It's almost an institution, Jagdip, isn't it?' Shwetha said. 'It's been around for so long.'

'I only moved here recently.' Ronita sat gingerly on the edge of the bed in front of the dresser and pulled a comb out of her handbag. 'Honestly, to me it's just a shop.'

Shwetha bent over to pick up a pair of used socks and hide them under a pillow. Tina clearly hadn't expected anyone to come in here. 'Do you like working there? I love running my business, but it can be stressful.'

'Oh yes, my husband gets very stressed at times.'

'That must be difficult.'

'I think he does find it frustrating, yes.'

'No, I meant for you.'

Ronita's hand, which had been combing her hair, went still. Without turning around, she said quietly, 'Oh, yes.'

'I'm not good at handling stress. It's one of the reasons I'm glad I live alone. I don't even have a cat. Sometimes after a bad day I just want to sob into my ice cream.'

Shwetha watched Ronita's reflection in the mirror; she didn't smile in response to Shwetha's light-hearted tone. 'He doesn't do that. But he gets very angry at times.'

Shwetha was hit by an awful conviction. She formed her next words carefully. 'On terrible days, I want to punch the walls.'

Had she gone too far? What would she do if Ronita clammed up—or worse, got offended?

Ronita replied slowly, 'He does that sometimes. Slams the table. Throws a plate.'

Shwetha was careful not to make any sudden moves, as if Ronita were a skittish kitten. 'Has he hurt you?'

Ronita shook her head in a childlike gesture. 'No, no.'

'But you're afraid he might?'

Ronita's big eyes stared at Shwetha in the mirror.

'I'm sorry if I made you uncomfortable,' Shwetha said honestly.

'It's okay. I don't talk about it much.'

'It must be difficult. You just moved here, it's not like you have friends to talk to.'

Ronita put down her comb and dabbed her face with a tissue she extracted from her handbag.

'Some years ago, I got married and moved to Bombay,' said Shwetha. 'I'd lived here all my life. It was strange to suddenly be in a new city—a bigger city—to be married to someone I realised I didn't know very well, to have a life that was so different from my old life.'

Ronita turned around to look at her.

'And then, my husband and I had troubles. I didn't know what to do. I was too stubborn to ask friends or family for advice; after all, I'd decided to get married and move away. How could I turn to them for help because I'd made the wrong decision?'

'It's not like that for me,' Ronita said. 'My parents arranged the match. But I was eager. I am thirty-four. I had lived with them all my life; I wanted my own family. I was in love with a man for a long time, but it didn't work out in the end. He married someone else. I felt this would be right for me.'

Shwetha continued, 'A new start, in a new city? That's what I hoped my marriage would be. I would be a new person. Everything would be wonderful. Only, I was the same person, just without the friends and family I was used to. There were still phone calls and all that, but no one to look at me and say, "Is everything all right? Are you happy?"'

Ronita bowed her head and tears dropped, making a pattern on Tina's pristine white sheet. 'They do ask me that,' she said, taking little gasps of breath. 'My parents. I went to see them last month. I don't know what to tell them. How do I tell them I'm already unhappy?'

'Better sooner than later. How will staying unhappy for longer help? It will only complicate things further.'

'I don't have a reason for leaving. Not really. It's not like he hits me. He's very nice most of the time. He even does housework—everyone I know complains all the time about their husbands not doing housework. Dipen washes dishes, does the laundry—without being asked.'

'You aren't happy,' said Shwetha gently. 'That's enough reason.'

'It's not so easy.'

'I know.' Shwetha laughed. 'Believe me, I know. But it's easier than it used to be. People do it all the time.'

'I never wanted to be one of those people.'

'No one does. No one walks into a marriage expecting it to not work out. That doesn't mean you have to stay if you're unhappy.'

Ronita rubbed her face with another tissue. Shwetha wondered what eyeliner she used; it barely smudged.

'The night Jagat died,' said Shwetha, 'I think I remember seeing you leave earlier in the evening. You and Dipen left the store together, didn't you?'

'That's why it was such a shock. We were just with him that evening, and in the morning ... Sampath called Dipen to give him the news. We were both stunned.'

'Dipen was home with you when he got the news?'

'Oh, yes.'

'Was this around eleven in the morning?'

'Yes, how did you know?'

'My colleague found him.'

'Oh. They said he was found by someone who worked downstairs; of course that would be someone from your office.'

'Yeah. It was quite a shock for her.'

'Oh, yes. Dipen wouldn't let me come with him to the shop then. I just sat at home and waited. I called my parents, then I called Veena. She didn't answer. I think she was too shocked. She was in Surat, you see, visiting her family. Her brother called me back later. He said she was getting on a flight, with the kids and her parents.'

'It's so sad, isn't it? To think of Mr Desai lying there all night ... I keep wishing one of us had been there, had been able to help him. But I was home by nine that night. I remember I got in bed early too, I was so tired.'

'Me too,' said Ronita. 'I had cramps—period, you know. It started soon after I got home, so I took a pill and went to bed. I didn't even have dinner.'

'Good thing Dipen was home with you. It's lucky he wasn't at the store too.' Shwetha hoped Ronita wouldn't notice she was contradicting herself—after all, she had just implied that if someone had been around, Jagat's life might have been saved. 'I keep thinking that Jagat must not have known what was going to happen, because he would have tried to make a call, right? Maybe to his brother?'

Ronita shook her head. 'Dipen said he didn't receive any calls.'

'In any case, if he had got a call, you would have heard it too, wouldn't you?'

'Oh, no. I was in bed. Dipen was watching TV till late at night.'

'Does he usually go to bed late?'

'Oh, yes. Never comes to the bedroom before one. Often even after that.'

'I find it so difficult to sleep when I'm cramping. Even if I've taken painkillers, I can't sleep through the night.'

Ronita nodded eagerly. 'Yes, that's how I felt. I'm normally a heavy sleeper, but that night I woke up a couple of times to sounds of the TV—he was watching a football match. Later, I heard him take a shower. I fell asleep again. I don't even know what time he came to bed. I just remember that the last time I woke up, he was in bed and fast asleep. I looked at my phone and it was past three.'

'Does he usually shower at night? I'm afraid of showering late in this weather—I'm sure to catch a cold.'

'He doesn't, usually, no. I take a shower every morning and evening; he only showers in the morning, if that.' Ronita shrugged, a men-are-weird gesture at another woman.

'And the next morning, you found out about ...'

'Oh, yes. I slept till late that morning. I was just having breakfast when he got the call about Jagat.'

Tina burst into the bedroom, Appu on her hip. 'Shwetha, what are you doing here? Everyone has come, we're starting. Oh, you must be Ronita.'

'So sorry, Tinu,' said Shwetha, as Ronita disappeared into the bathroom and Appu held out her arms to Shwetha. 'I lost track of time.'

✍

Nilima was typing an email with one hand, her legs up on the desk. The door opened suddenly, and her leg slipped, throwing her off balance. Shwetha bounded in, her face excited.

'What's up?' Nilima asked, righting herself. 'Why did you leave the party so early?'

'I made an excuse. I said there was a work emergency.'

'A tour emergency?'

'Where's Poorna?'

'She's not back from her exclusive couple's tour. What's going on?'

'I know who the murderer is.'

'And?'

'Don't you want to guess?'

'Dipen.'

'How did you know?'

'He's the only one who made sense. I wasn't sure though, it was only ...'

'A hunch.'

'How did you find out it's him?'

Shwetha told Nilima everything she had learned from Ronita.

'That's not much,' said Nilima. 'His alibi isn't foolproof, and he took a shower. It's not exactly evidence.'

'Now you don't think it's him?'

'Oh no, I do. But it's not enough to go to the police with. We have no proof. We barely have a motive. We don't have the murder weapon.'

'We don't even know what it is,' Shwetha admitted.

'Umm ...'

'What?'

'I have a hunch. For the murder weapon.'

'Say it,' Shwetha said imperiously.

'You know what game Dipen is fond of playing?'

'What?' Shwetha's face lit up with understanding. 'Oh my God. Darts!'

Nilima nodded. 'Both Pallav and Sampath told us about them.'

'How did you work this out? And why didn't you tell me?'

'I wasn't sure, and ... you hadn't reacted well to my suspicions of Dipen so far.' Shwetha pouted and Nilima went on hastily, 'I was thinking about the weapon, and whether it was really a weapon—I mean, if it was just something the murderer happened to have on him. So, I thought that's how the murder might have taken place. Dipen comes back to the office that night. Maybe he and Jagat have had another disagreement that day and he's upset. He has been playing darts by himself while the TV is on and Ronita is asleep in the other room, and he puts one in his pocket without thinking. He goes back to the office because he remembers something—maybe that they haven't put away the day's cash—or because he wants to confront his brother. Jagat is leaving and they walk out together. Maybe Jagat berates him again, and he still has the dart in his hand, and he isn't thinking, he just jabs his brother with it.'

'Suddenly, there's so much blood,' said Shwetha.

'Jagat falls backwards. He was lying on his back when we found him, and Sharmila said he hurt his head as he fell. Dipen is probably near the stairs, so he doesn't step in the blood, even though some must've stained his body and clothes.'

'And Dipen goes home, maybe still clutching the dart ...'

'He may have put it in his pocket,' offered Nilima.

'And he takes a shower to wash the blood off. Wouldn't his clothes have been bloody too?'

'His shirt, definitely, I'd think,' said Nilima. 'Maybe he takes it off and dumps it on his way home, and goes home in his undershirt. If he dirtied the shirt—wiped it on the ground, maybe tore it a little—and put it in that big dumpster on the main street, no one would notice it, and it would be emptied in the morning, before the police knew about the murder.'

'Or he could be wearing a dark shirt,' Shwetha said, 'that he washed off when he got home. If he put it in the washing machine with other clothes the next morning, who would notice anything wrong? The one nice thing Ronita told me about Dipen is he does the laundry. And Ronita was on her period.'

'This makes it culpable homicide rather than murder, doesn't it?' said Nilima. 'If we're right, it wasn't planned. And everything else—Jagat's body being outside the door rather than inside, it being a Sunday, Jagat's family being away, Ronita being asleep when he went out and came back in, not running into Sampath or anyone else near the office—was just luck.'

'Huh,' said Shwetha, 'he always was a lucky motherfucker.'

'Though, I don't know,' Nilima continued softly, as if talking to herself. 'Even if he didn't think it through, he probably knew, even subconsciously, that he'd be safe. That no one would discover Jagat till at least the next morning. After all, he knew Jagat's family was away, he knew it was a Sunday. Why else did he pick that night to lose it so badly, to let all his rage and resentment drive the dart into his brother's neck?'

Shwetha poured herself a glass of water and drained it. Then Nilima asked, 'What should we do now?'

'I was thinking ...'

'Yes?'

'I made Tina promise to keep the party going at least till eight. It's only six now. That gives us two hours, assuming Dipen doesn't leave the store before eight.'

Nilima grinned. 'Are we sure he's not home?'

'You could ask Maniram,' said Shwetha. 'Tell him to give us a heads up if Dipen leaves the store.'

'Cool, I'll call him on the way. Lucky Dipen lives nearby!'

'Can you walk on ahead?' Shwetha asked politely. 'I have to pick up something, I'll do that and walk over. My car might be too conspicuous. Let Dipen see it parked here if he comes down.'

'Hold on,' said Nilima. She rummaged in a drawer and threw a pair of clear disposable gloves at Shwetha, tucking a second pair into her pockets. 'Let's make sure to use these. If we're right, it might be important to not leave fingerprints.'

Nilima continued to rifle through the office drawers, pulling out odd things: her keys, a few pins and clips from Shwetha's drawer, a length of wire ...

'What on earth are you doing?' Shwetha said impatiently. 'We need to get going.'

'I'm looking for a way to unlock his door. One of those should work.'

'Do you think I'm a complete amateur?' Shwetha hissed. 'I've got the key.'

'What?' Nilima spun around.

'At least I hope so. It was one of only two keys in Ronita's handbag—the other looked like her scooter's. I made an impression on Tina's soap. The key maker in the next lane is making a duplicate. That's why I need to go there first, to pick it up—he said it'd be ready in half an hour.'

'You're brilliant, boss.'

'Yeah, yeah, let's go.'

✍

Nilima leaned against a wall around fifty metres from Dipen's building. It had been half an hour since they had left the office; surely the key should have been ready by now. She lit another cigarette. It had started to rain, and she didn't hear Shwetha's footsteps before she suddenly appeared out of the shadows between the streetlights, brandishing a key.

They walked past the security guard at the building gate, Shwetha nonchalantly saying 'good evening'. Nilima put on her gloves before she pressed the button for the lift, and Shwetha followed suit.

When the lift door opened on Dipen's floor, a family of four—two adults and two children—were waiting to go down. Shwetha smoothly slid her gloves off and hid them in one hand under cover of her seragu, opening the door with the other. Nilima thrust her gloved hands into her pockets as she stepped out. The toddler in her father's arms stared at her, and Nilima refrained from staring back.

After the lift moved downwards, Shwetha pulled on her gloves again. Nilima found the door marked 403. 'This one,' she said.

Shwetha inserted the key in the lock. She jiggled it and turned it this way and that. Nilima kept her eye on the corridor and the other doors for potential eyewitnesses while Shwetha took a deep breath and tried again; this time, the door opened. Nilima let out a breath she hadn't been conscious of holding. They crept into the flat and shut the door behind them.

Light leaked in through the kitchen windows; there was no wall between the living space and the kitchen. 'Do we dare switch on the lights?' Nilima whispered.

'I think so,' said Shwetha. 'Maniram and Tina should call us if either of them leaves, and it'll be much faster if we can see properly.'

Nilima found a light switch. A pale glow suffused the room from a pendant light overhead. She turned on another switch, and a sconce lit up. A grey four-piece sofa set took up most of the sitting area; a few shelves and coffee tables held photos and books. Nilima scanned the shelves, noticing a Murakami and an Asimov. A large cabinet separated the sitting area from the kitchen. 'Nice bar,' said Nilima.

A short corridor led off the living room. Shwetha opened the first door and switched on the light.

Posters of Nirvana and Linkin Park lined the walls between bookshelves, a big TV and a dartboard. Several easy chairs were strewn about, the leather stained and worn. A vinyl player rested on a chest of drawers, and low tables held mismatched lamps.

'His man cave,' murmured Shwetha. Nilima walked over to the drawers and opened one.

'Let's split up,' said Shwetha. 'You continue here, I'll do the bedroom and the bathrooms and meet you back in the living room.'

The drawers were stacked with records. Nilima ran her hand covetously over the rows of vinyl before searching the room. She felt the chairs to make sure nothing was hidden in the stuffing, shone her phone's flashlight under all the furniture, looked behind books and swiped the tops of tall shelves.

Shwetha banged a drawer shut in the next room. Nilima wondered whether to warn her, but speed seemed more important than silence. She was moving some books off a shelf and didn't turn around when she heard more noises in the living room, only looking up when a shadow fell on her.

Dipen was standing at the door of the room.

'Who are you? What are you doing in here?' His voice was a high shriek, his face livid; gone was the suave businessman she had seen in the shop. If she had been thinking properly, she would have reasoned with herself that someone who had just found an intruder in his home could be excused for not being polite and calm.

But Nilima's brain had gone quiet. She pushed herself up from the ground, too shocked to say a word.

'What are you doing in my house?' he yelled. 'Wait, I know you. You came to the shop. Don't you work at that stupid place downstairs?'

Nilima dimly felt a part of herself growing furious at the insult to her workplace. But fear had overwhelmed everything else, and she couldn't think or speak. She could only stare numbly at him.

'What the hell are you doing here?' He advanced threateningly. 'Are you spying on me? What do you know?'

He was almost on her; his arm reached out. He whispered, 'Tell me now, else you'll regret it.'

His hand closed around Nilima's neck. Pain exploded in her throat, and her tongue tasted bile. She wanted to move, shout, fight back. But her body refused to budge, and now the pain in her throat got worse. She couldn't breathe.

'Dipen?'

Dipen whipped around. Shwetha stood in the doorway, handbag in the crook of her arm, no unevenness in the pleats of her sari betraying the fact that she had just been crawling under the bathroom sink. He let go of Nilima and she collapsed against the chest of drawers, coughing weakly. Her arm was throbbing with pain—had she jerked it somehow?

'What is going on here?' Dipen looked from Shwetha to Nilima, and then back again.

'I'm so sorry, Dipen. I shouldn't have done this. I just ... I had to see you.'

'What do you mean? Why are you—'

'I can't stop thinking about you.' Nilima couldn't make out if Shwetha was genuinely on the verge of tears—*not surprising if she is,* thought Nilima, as she realised that she herself was shaking like a leaf. She pushed herself straight again.

Dipen now looked baffled, which was an improvement, Nilima recognised, from looking murderously angry. *Not a euphemism,* she added to herself.

Her next thought: *Ah, I can think coherently again.* She reached into her pocket, keeping the rest of her body immobile. Could she text Sharmila without Dipen seeing her?

'How the hell did you get inside?' Dipen demanded, and Nilima's heart lurched. This was the question Shwetha couldn't explain away.

'The door was ajar. I just knocked, and it opened.'

'What?' Dipen looked unconvinced.

'Had you locked it before you left?' Shwetha asked. 'I wondered if the flat had been broken into.'

'No.' Dipen considered. 'Roni was here when I left.'

'Maybe she forgot to shut the door properly?' asked Shwetha.

'What are you doing here?' he said yet again. Nilima almost sympathised with him, until she reminded herself that he was a murderer. She unlocked her phone.

'I met Ronita earlier today,' said Shwetha. *Good stalling, boss,* Nilima encouraged her silently.

'You met Roni?' Dipen seemed engrossed by Shwetha. 'Where?'

'At my cousin's party. I didn't realise who she was, at first. When I did ... I don't know. Suddenly, I felt so jealous. I had to see you at once. And since she was at the party, I came here. I thought I would get to talk to you alone.'

Dipen jerked his head at Nilima, and she froze. 'Why bring her then?'

'Shwetha didn't bring me to your flat, Dipen.' Nilima had wanted to sound firm and calm, but her voice came out high and panicked.

'I told her not to come! I said I was coming here to meet you, and she kept saying it was a bad idea. She said I should forget about you.' Shwetha sounded increasingly hysterical. 'I refused to listen, but she must have followed me here. She called for me from the door—I didn't think to shut it behind me. I hid in your bedroom—I thought if she didn't see me, she'd leave. But she came in here to wait, it seems.'

Nilima put her phone carefully back in her pocket.

'How did you know I would be home? I left work early.'

'I didn't know,' Shwetha said desperately. 'I wasn't thinking.'

'I don't believe you!' Dipen thundered. 'What are you two up to?'

Dipen took a step closer to Nilima. She opened her mouth to scream but all that came out was a whimper. *This is it,* she thought. *This is how I die. Preeti was right. And Shwetha ...*

The doorbell rang. Dipen's eyes narrowed. 'Stay quiet,' he threatened.

There was another ring, followed by an insistent knock on the door. And, blessedly, terrifyingly, Poorna's voice—loud, cheerful, normal. 'Nilima! Shwetha! Are you in there?'

'Who's that?' Dipen whispered.

'Poorna,' Nilima breathed, not noticing Shwetha's warning look.

'Who's Poorna?'

'Our friend,' Nilima said proudly.

'Come on, you guys,' Poorna called again. 'Stop fooling around. Is Dipen home? Tina just said Ronita is on her way home. We should go before she gets here. Awkward!'

Nilima looked intently at Dipen's face, trying to decipher his thoughts. His hand clenched, and she could almost feel herself choke again.

It sounded like Poorna was banging on the door with her fist. 'Come on, Shwetha! You are in there, right? The security guard said he saw you go in.'

Dipen seemed to make up his mind and strode towards the door. When he opened it, Poorna almost fell in.

'Take your friends home,' Dipen said, his mouth curled in a sneer.

Shwetha and Nilima eagerly shuffled out of the flat. When she passed him, Nilima saw Dipen's lip tremble. He was nervous. He had not bought their story, but he was letting them go because anything else was too risky. Nilima imagined him calculating whether he could kill all three of them and dispose of the evidence before his wife got home, and deciding against it.

They hurried to the stairs, too impatient to wait for the lift. As soon as the door of the flat closed behind them, they broke into a run. They ran down the stairs and out of the building into the now pouring rain and only stopped in front of a shop next to a streetlight on the main road. The shop was closed, and they collapsed against the metal shutter, the overhanging roof offering some protection from the rain.

Shwetha hugged Poorna. 'You saved us,' she cried.

'Both of you saved me,' whispered Nilima, too hoarse and battered from the shock to speak any louder.

'Hush,' said Poorna, pulling her into the hug. 'You're safe now.'

'How on earth did you find us?' Shwetha said when Poorna let them go.

'Oh, Nilima had texted me when she was waiting outside Dipen's building for you. I wanted to come straight here, but she wanted me to wait in the office. So I was at the window that looks out over the gate. I saw Dipen leave and I thought he might be going home, so I followed him.'

'Oh, good job!' cried Shwetha.

'I tried to call you. Your phone was switched off.'

'What?' Shwetha got her phone out of her handbag. 'Oh, it's dead. If Tina had tried to reach me ...'

'I don't think Ronita walking in on us would have been worse than Dipen,' Nilima croaked.

'Are you all right, Nili?' Shwetha asked. 'The bastard hurt her. He was strangling her when I got to the room.'

Poorna placed her hand gently on Nilima's head. 'Please tell us you're okay.'

'Yes. My throat still hurts a bit but I'm fine. Shwetha got there just in time.'

'I'd have killed him if he'd hurt you,' said Shwetha fiercely.

Nilima pulled her own phone out of her pocket. There were four missed calls from Poorna and one from Maniram. 'I forgot to take my phone off silent,' she confessed.

'We need to warn Inspector Lamani,' said Shwetha. 'We couldn't find the murder weapon, but we have to tell her our suspicions. Maybe she can find it before Dipen gets rid of it.'

'Um,' said Nilima, 'I did find it.' Her phone lit up with a call.

'What?' said Shwetha and Poorna together.

'Yes, Inspector,' Nilima said into the phone. 'Yes, we were in Dipen's house. No, we're out now, we're fine ... We should have told you, I'm sorry. We weren't sure ... No, we're sure now. I found the murder weapon.'

'What?' said Shwetha and Poorna again.

'It's a dart. Yes, the thing you hit a dartboard with. The box is in the lowest drawer in his TV room, below the record player. It's underneath some records—you'll find it easily, the records don't sit in a straight row because of it. I'm pretty sure one of them is the murder weapon.'

Nilima removed her phone from her ear. 'She was calling from the car. She's almost at Dipen's.'

'How did she—?' Poorna started at the same time as Shwetha said, 'When did you—?'

'I called her while you were talking to Dipen. Of course I couldn't directly tell her what was happening, I didn't want Dipen to know, not unless there was no other option ...'

'That's why you announced where we were so loudly!'

'Yes, after I saw she'd answered the phone. I was hoping she'd get it, though I didn't think she'd get there in time to rescue us. I had to take the chance. But then we didn't need her to save us, because Poorna got there first.' Nilima grinned at Poorna.

'And you found the weapon too! Good job, Nili!'

'I'm a genius in the shape of a potato,' Nilima said. 'It's the first place I looked.'

'How did you know it would be there?'

'As soon as I saw the drawer, I knew that's where it would be, with his precious vinyls, all his treasures together.'

'It's a weapon,' said Poorna, 'not a treasure. He killed his brother with it.'

'I think he treasured it though,' said Nilima. 'Because he seems to love darts and because I think he enjoyed killing his brother, even if he hadn't planned it, and he wanted to remember how that felt ...'

Nilima hadn't realised she was trembling again until Shwetha placed an arm around her. Pain shot through Nilima's left arm, but she didn't move.

'Thank God Dipen opened the door,' Shwetha said. 'I was running out of excuses to stall and I'm not sure I would win a full-on fight with him.' Nilima was both grateful and a little resentful that Shwetha hadn't included her in this hypothetical fight.

'I'd have told him I had the inspector on the phone,' said Nilima. 'He wouldn't have dared to hurt us then.' She wasn't sure of that; it might have seemed more prudent to Dipen to kill them all instead, so they couldn't testify against him. But she didn't voice this possibility.

'And if he hadn't opened the door,' Poorna added, 'I'd have rung everyone's doorbells, yelling loud enough to rouse the whole building. I wouldn't have left you both in there.' She grabbed Shwetha's other arm.

Then Poorna said, 'Look, there's a police car, maybe that's the inspector.'

They ducked out of the light and watched the white car—and yes, Inspector Lamani was in it—tear down the street and turn into the lane they had just left. Then they walked back to the office through rapidly forming puddles, arms linked all the way.

The long evening in the office didn't feel like a celebration. Poorna manoeuvred the bucket to catch the drip from the ceiling. Nilima placed an online order for Chinese food, and Shwetha asked her to add soft drinks. 'It will help with the shock,' she explained when Nilima raised her eyebrows at Shwetha welcoming sugar, 'and we can mix it with something stronger. I'll call the liquor store.'

'Let's not,' said Nilima. 'Sharmila might want to talk to us soon.'

So they made do with noodles and fizzy drinks. Poorna checked and rechecked the door and windows to make sure they were all fastened, and talked to several members of her family to explain that she was still at work and would be home late. Nilima kept wondering what was happening at Dipen's flat, moving abruptly from best-case to worst-case scenarios. 'We did it!' she said excitedly at one point. 'We nailed him! Now we'll be famous. People will be lining up for our tours. I will never have to write another Facebook ad again.'

A few minutes later: 'We broke into the apartment! What if he says we planted the darts? What if he says one of us—or all of us—killed Jagat?'

'Relax, will you?' Shwetha tilted her head to examine her nails, which she was painting sea green. 'It'll all go well, believe me. We've done what we set out to do.'

'Did you have that in your handbag?' Poorna pointed at the bottle of nail polish.

'Yeah, I'd dropped it in this morning thinking I'd do my nails at Tina's before the guests arrived, but we were too busy preparing.'

Poorna sat down next to Shwetha and held her hand out, and Shwetha coloured Poorna's nails green too. Nilima didn't want to ask to be included but was a little disappointed at being left out. She paused her pacing to take two paracetamols to ease the throbbing in her arm, washing it down with the last of her orange soda. Shwetha had reached for the Thums Up Nilima had ordered for herself, and Nilima hadn't stopped her.

Suddenly she remembered something. 'You went through Ronita's handbag? At the party?'

'It was easy.' Shwetha didn't look up from Poorna's nails. 'She left it in Tina's bedroom when she went to the bathroom. I borrowed soap from Tina's other bathroom and took an impression, and slipped the keys back into Ronita's handbag. Then all I had to do was take the soap to my key guy.'

'You have a key guy?'

'Yeah, you know I keep misplacing my keys. I've gone to him several times before. I said my sister was visiting and I'd given her my flat key after taking the impression. He even gave me a repeat of his lecture on getting duplicate keys made before you need them, but he agreed to do it quickly.'

'Of course he did,' Nilima chuckled.

'Why did you suspect Dipen? You've had it in for him since the beginning.' Shwetha smiled to show she wasn't resentful.

'At first,' Nilima said, 'I just couldn't figure him out. He seemed very happy to be managing the store, but by all accounts he had taken little interest earlier. That implied a man who wanted power, but how badly did he want it? What he did with Saima—it was nothing egregious, but it implied he wasn't very careful with other people's feelings. And then when Miss Joanna talked about him, I wondered. The story about his fiancée eloping with someone else, it might mean she changed her mind and it wasn't his fault, but it might also mean she wanted to escape him. And what you said about him too—he wasn't a thoughtful boyfriend. Of all the people I met who knew Jagat, I could most easily picture him killing and then looking perfectly calm the next day.'

'I feel stupid,' Shwetha said.

'For what? You handled Ronita so deftly—I could never have got the information out of her that you did. And then you swiped her key!'

'If you ask me,' said Poorna, 'we've all completely outdone ourselves today. We delivered the fucking murderer to the police. We make a pretty good team, huh?'

As they waited, rain began to seep in under the door and through a crack in the wall. Shwetha found a few rags and they mopped the floor up until the rags were too soaked to be of any use. They turned the fans on high, hoping that would help dry up the floor a little, and shivered in their wet clothes. Poorna pulled off her T-shirt and put her dry denim jacket on, and Shwetha wrapped her seragu around her shoulders. Nilima heated up a mug of water and pressed it against her arm.

At nearly two, Inspector Lamani called Nilima and asked why they had been in the flat. Nilima offered the rehearsed excuse: they had gone to confront Dipen, to ask him about the darts, and found the door open. She was sure the inspector didn't believe her, but Sharmila said abruptly that she would meet them in the morning, and ended the call.

Now they were free to go home. Poorna valiantly declared she would ride her scooter home, but Shwetha said, 'Nonsense! It's still raining. I'll drop you all home.'

Nilima's place was nearer, but she hopefully suggested accompanying Shwetha to drop off Poorna: 'You shouldn't drive all the way back from Yeshwantpur alone.' Shwetha firmly refused, and Nilima got into the back seat. The breeze tickled her face. The city was quiet as if tucked in to sleep for the night. In the front seat, Poorna began to snore softly. They had solved the case and found the murderer. The inspector had said she'd release Sampath immediately. But Nilima felt no euphoria, only a sense of anticlimax.

As Shwetha pulled into Nilima's lane, Poorna woke up and yawned loudly. 'Thanks, boss,' Nilima said before walking into the building, Poorna's cheery 'Goodnight!' ringing after her. It was only after she had mounted all three flights of stairs and unlocked the door to her apartment that Nilima realised she hadn't heard Shwetha's noisy old car drive away. She latched the door behind her and switched on the light before climbing on the bed to push the window open. The car's engine sputtered and rumbled, and Poorna's arm waved in the glow from the streetlight as they drove away.

Nilima got off the bed to take her half-finished bottle of whiskey out of the cupboard. She filled the rest of the small bottle with water and took it back to bed and placed it next to the *Necklace of Skulls* on the windowsill. Then she lit a cigarette.

CHAPTER 16

Final Chapter

Nilima and Poorna spent most of the morning helping Anjali mop the office floor. When Shwetha came from the Sunday tour, she found the two of them with their faces pressed up against the front window. They were still keeping watch when Inspector Lamani drove in with a colleague, with more policemen following in another car. They rushed to the other window to see the cops heading for the bookshop, though Sharmila nodded at them as she passed. Nilima and Poorna waited impatiently, while Shwetha worked like it was any other day.

There was a knock on the door, and Poorna ran to open it. Sharmila had come alone, leaving her colleagues to search the bookshop again.

The inspector told them about the events of last night. Dipen had let the police in and allowed them to search the apartment. He was polite and cooperative—until they confiscated the darts. 'That's when he lost it and started swearing at us, and said some choice things about Shwetha also—he didn't remember the rest of your names,' the inspector commented. 'He was so angry he didn't realise he was confessing.'

'Why did he kill Jagat?' said Shwetha. 'I mean, why now?'

Sharmila's eyes held more kindness than Nilima had yet seen in them.

'I think it had something to do with the land deal,' said Nilima. 'He was probably upset at being kept out of it.'

'That's correct. Dipen found out Jagat was meeting Mohan that night. He asked to stay for the meeting. Jagat brushed him off—"You go home, what do you know about this? Don't I take care of you?"'

'That must have made Dipen angry,' Nilima observed. 'He probably stewed over it at home.'

'Hmm.' Sharmila tried to take over the story. 'He seemed to have a lot of resentment against Jagat, said his parents always favoured him. And he said Jagat cheated him out of the bookshop, paid him less than his share was worth.'

'Or he regretted letting Jagat buy him out,' Nilima suggested, 'especially once he spent the money.'

Sharmila nodded. 'So that night, he was at home drinking and watching football, and getting himself riled up. Then he came back to confront Jagat. It was after midnight.'

'He must have forgotten to pick up his phone,' Nilima said.

'Forgot—or he knew what he was doing,' the inspector countered. 'He didn't forget his keys, so he didn't have to wake up his wife when he got back. And he may have waited till midnight so the bar would have closed and no one would see him.'

'How would he know Jagat would still be there?' Poorna asked. 'He might have left when Mohan and the others did.'

'He bragged that he knew his brother's habits,' said Sharmila. 'He liked being in the shop after everyone had left. He'd look around to make sure everything was in order, go through the drawers ...'

'See if his employees had done anything he could upbraid them for,' Nilima guessed.

'What about the dart?' Poorna asked. 'He took it from home?'

'He said he picked it up from the office—he took a new box because one of his old ones had broken. The box of darts did seem new, and there was an older set in the house.'

'Where?' Nilima asked indignantly.

'On a shelf behind some books.'

'I was searching some shelves when he found me,' Nilima said and then bit her lip.

'No doubt that's why he got so angry,' Sharmila said calmly, not reacting to this confession of an illegal search.

'Wait, you kept searching *after* you found the weapon?' demanded Shwetha.

'I thought we had time,' said Nilima. 'If there was more evidence in the flat, I wanted to find it.'

'He could have killed us, Nilima!'

'The actual murder weapon was the one Nilima found in the drawer with the records?' Poorna changed the subject.

'I think so. His story is that he picked up the box in the shop that night when he went to meet his brother. But the darts would be on the floor below ...'

'With the gifts and stationery,' Nilima finished.

'Correct. He said he got the darts and then met his brother.'

'You don't believe him,' said Shwetha.

'Indeed, miss. I think what happened is he had taken the box of darts home earlier—maybe that evening, maybe a few days before. We're questioning the employees in the store if they saw him leave with them.'

'You could also check the inventory records,' Nilima suggested. 'Though from what we hear the records might not be impeccable.'

'But why is he lying about this?' Poorna asked.

'Culpable homicide versus murder,' said Nilima.

'Correct. He must have come to his senses and realised he was in trouble, so he tried to mitigate the damage. If the dart was on the premises, a lawyer might argue it was a fight gone wrong, or even an accident. But I think he had them nearby as he was watching TV and he carefully picked one up and put it in his pocket when he went to confront his brother.'

'He may not even have entered the store,' said Shwetha. 'Maybe he got there just as Jagat was locking up.'

'And then Jagat turned around,' said Nilima, 'and maybe said something, asked him why he had come back. And in answer Dipen drove the dart into his neck ...'

Shwetha shuddered, and Poorna inched protectively towards her.

'We're getting the darts analysed to find out which one was the weapon. And we've got a forensics team up at the flat right now. I'm hoping we'll find some blood in the bathroom, or in the washing machine. Ronita has also admitted now that she was asleep most of the night, and Dipen might have gone out without her knowledge. I think we'll get him.'

Nilima realised that she didn't care whether Dipen Desai went to jail. The mystery was solved, and hopefully Ronita would leave him. And Shwetha knew who he really was. She still looked a little shaken, but she had been so brave last night and seemed to be taking the revelation of her lover being a murderer better than Nilima had expected.

And then Sharmila asked for their side of the story.

Shwetha said they had gone to Dipen's flat to ask about the darts and warn Ronita when she came home. When they had got there the door was ajar, so they had gone in. Dipen had found them when he came home, and he had attacked Nilima, which was when Nilima had called the inspector.

Sharmila looked sceptical, but heard her through. At the end, she said simply, 'You all have been of great help to us—I must say we were far from suspecting Dipen—so I won't ask too many questions. Dipen may have a different story; it remains to be seen if he can prove it. You three come down to the station this afternoon and give your official statements.'

After she walked out, Shwetha carefully shut the door, and they waited for the sound of the inspector's car to fade before they burst into whoops.

✍

It was around four in the afternoon a week later when Nilima ambled towards the office. She had had a croissant and coffee at a nearby café and was smoking her third cigarette of the day, feeling at peace with the world. The sultry afternoon was melting into a fine drizzle that evaporated as soon as it touched her skin.

She turned her face up to feel the droplets on her skin and almost bumped into a man standing in the lane.

'Nilima madam!' It was Sampath, of course.

'Sampath sir! How are you doing?'

'I'm fine, madam. A-one! Absolutely well!'

'I'm glad,' she said sincerely.

'I was just visiting you all,' he pointed at the ground floor window. 'To thank you. So nice of you, madam, and Shwetha madam and Poorna madam.'

'Not at all, Sampath sir. You shouldn't have been arrested at all.'

'And that Dipen! I always knew he was a rascal, but to kill his own brother! What would my Desai sir have said ...'

'I'm sorry. It must have been a shock.'

'Very shocking, yes-yes. And now this shop ...' He looked up at the building.

'What's happening to it?' Nilima asked. The shop had been closed ever since Dipen's arrest. 'Is Veena staying in town after all?'

'No no, Veena madam is determined to move to Surat. But the shop ... She is very kind, and even though I didn't have enough in my savings ...'

'You mean to say you've bought it? That's brilliant!'

'Thank you, thank you, madam. I couldn't let the shop go to strangers, and Veena madam gave me a price much below the market rate and is helping me get a bank loan. It's not all done, of course, but hopefully it'll come through. I can't imagine going to work somewhere else.'

'Best of luck, Mr Sampath,' Nilima said. 'I'm sure you're the right person to take care of Jagdip Book House.'

'Thank you, thank you, that is so nice of you to say! Except, of course, it won't be called Jagdip anymore. Maybe I'll call it Doddappa.' He laughed uproariously at his joke. Nilima waved at him and walked on.

Inside, everything was quiet again, except for Poorna talking loudly on the phone, which made it better than quiet—it was normal. Nilima wandered aimlessly around the room, trailing her fingers affectionately over desks and walls. She couldn't remember when she had last been this happy.

'Sampath was here,' Poorna said when she was done with her call.

'I know, I met him outside.'

'Stop sashaying about and work, Deka,' Shwetha said as she came out of the inner room, a quirk of her eyebrow taking the sting out of her words. 'We have been inundated with calls since that article came out yesterday. A bunch of Facebook notifications too. You need to get to it.'

Nilima grinned and sat down to unlock her computer. The article stared at her from the open browser window. A photo of the three of them covered the width of the screen. They were on the terrace of this very building: Poorna perched on the low wall, looking oh so cool in her denim jacket and sunglasses; Nilima slouched beside her with one hand in her pocket (her right arm carefully snaked behind Poorna's back, for fear Poorna would lose her balance and fall three storeys down); and Shwetha, standing straight and a little apart in a yellow cotton dress, smiling her mysterious smile.

The headline above read:

The Three Heroines of Jayanagar

Just below, in smaller bold letters:

> Shwetha, Poorna and Nilima are the trinity that form Chikkamma Tours, a boutique company that provides offbeat tours of the city. The young women have another hidden talent: solving crimes. They assisted the police with the identity of the Jagdip Book House killer, the other half of the shop's name, Dipen Desai himself.

Nilima didn't really need to read this or the interview that followed; she had read it three times already. Poorna came over and stood by her shoulder.

'Mahadeva wrote us up pretty good, didn't he? I've been getting texts from all my friends.'

Nilima had received texts of congratulations too—from Hafeeza and Pallav—and an excited call from Preeti, who'd seen the link shared on a queer group with the line: 'Local lesbian solves Bengaluru bookshop murder'. Her sister didn't seem to have seen the article; maybe Nilima would send it to her later.

Poorna skipped back to her own desk, and Nilima opened the Chikkamma page on Facebook. She typed responses to messages with her right hand; her left arm was healing nicely, but typing still made the pain flare up.

'Hey, boss! Come see this. You too, Poorna.'

'What's wrong?' Shwetha rushed over.

'Nothing's wrong.' Nilima wheeled her chair aside to give them a better view of the screen.

Poorna read aloud.

> I read about you guys solving the murder. Can you help me? The police haven't done anything. I'm willing to pay.

'What should I do, boss?' Nilima asked lightly, as if she didn't care about the answer. 'Do I say yes?'

Poorna looked at Shwetha with shining eyes.

'I suppose,' Shwetha conceded, 'there's no harm in finding out more.'

Nilima leaned over and typed slowly:

> Hello! How can we help? Please tell us more.

Shwetha turned to go back to her office, but Poorna gasped. Tiny dots were appearing; someone was typing back.

> Can I meet you? Too complicated to explain here.

Nilima and Poorna's heads swivelled towards Shwetha's. Shwetha said slowly, 'We could meet here. Tomorrow? We don't have any tours except that early morning one.'

Nilima obediently typed in the suggestion. Shwetha, affecting unconcern, turned on her laptop on her desk. Poorna's eyes were glued to Nilima's computer.

'She will come at three tomorrow,' Poorna announced. Shwetha nodded briskly, but Poorna wasn't done. 'I'm going out now, to meet that group of Japanese tourists. Hopefully we'll book them for Friday.'

'Good luck.' Shwetha waved with her eyes on her screen.

'Hey, boss.' Nilima said again a few minutes later.

'Hmm.' Shwetha didn't look up.

Nilima tried for a nonchalant tone, though her heart was beating wildly. 'There's nothing urgent today—how about we go for an early dinner?'

'That's sweet, but I still have a lot to do.'

'Okay.' Nilima picked up her cigarettes and lighter and got up. She paused with her hand on the door. 'Just to be clear, I was asking you out. On a date. It's okay if you don't want to, I just wanted you to know.'

Nilima heard the desk being pushed aside and looked around to Shwetha throwing herself into her arms.

'Ow! Ow ow ow ow ow!'

'Oh no, your poor shoulder! I'm so sorry, I forgot!'

'It's okay,' Nilima panted. 'To be clear ...'

'Yes! I'm saying yes!'

'You're sure?'

'I thought you'd never ask!'

'Why didn't you ask then?'

'I'm your boss! You're my employee! I didn't want to put you on the spot!'

'But you said no the first time!'

'Pro tip, Deka: next time you ask someone out, maybe don't call them boss first. They might get the wrong message.'

'Can I call you boss once we're on the date? Or later, if it goes really well?'

'Shut up, Deka!' And Nilima did, because Shwetha kissed her. Nilima wanted to rank the kiss in comparison to all her fantasies, but she seemed to have lost the ability to think.

Acknowledgements

This book would not exist without Zac O'Yeah. The initial scene that was the first appearance of Chikkamma Tours (Pvt.) Ltd and its three women was written for an assignment in his class at Bangalore's World-Famous Semi-Deluxe Writing Programme. Since then, Zac has been a champion of *Chikkamma*, suggesting I make that one page into a novel, giving feedback on multiple drafts, introducing me to editors and agents, and through all the five years till I finally got a publisher, encouraging me to keep going. I would have given up a dozen times without him.

I am also immensely grateful to Zac's co-founders at the Bengaluru workshop, Anjum Hasan and Eshwar Sundaresan, for their feedback and encouragement.

Many books influenced this one—books set in Bengaluru, a few of which are mentioned in the first chapter, crime novels (especially those by Agatha Christie, to whom this entire novel is a homage, as well as by Raymond Chandler, Ngaio Marsh, Georgette Heyer, Erle Stanley Gardner, David Dodge, Arthur Conan Doyle, Mary Stewart, Stieg Larsson, Dorothy L. Sayers and Alexander McCall Smith, whose book titles I've borrowed from for chapter titles) and romance books by writers like KJ Charles, whose works showed me that queer characters are allowed to be heroes in otherwise formulaic genre fiction. I owe much to Ana Mardoll as a teacher too, for his many reconstructions and critiques of fiction on his blog. And I borrowed from Bhanu Sridharan's report about the infection affecting pelicans in Bengaluru.

Nilesh, apart from being the best of husbands, read over twenty versions, coached and coaxed me through my many anxious moments, and contributed a couple of jokes to the book. Manish pored over two drafts and annotated one very carefully with his lawyer's eye, and saved me from many little inconsistencies and errors. Other friends also provided helpful feedback: Srinidhi, Aditya, Koni, Amrita, Chicu, Caraway, Bishakha and Niyati. Aishwarya and Nilesh typed up handwritten pages when pain left me struggling to type. Bhuvi provided constant love and encouragement.

Friends in Bengaluru—Nadika, Pavithra, Udupendra, Babita, Sneha—showed me around and talked to me about their city. Two sets of friends—Babita and Lakshindra, and Rashi and Paras—welcomed me into their homes for a few months in 2017 when I started writing what would eventually become this novel. And Bengaluru introduced me to Padma, whose kindness and integrity I am grateful for having been a witness to.

Sushmita Chatterjee and Mita Kapur's generous feedback helped transform my amateurish drafts into a proper book. As did the advice of my agent, Jayapriya of Jacaranda Literary Agency, whose astute critique and staunch support I treasure.

I'm grateful to Karthika and Sanghamitra for taking a chance on a cold submission from an unknown writer, and Peter Griffin for his Caferati Listings where he shared Westland's open call. Sangha also for her rigorous edits, Saurabh for the gorgeous cover, Christina for the beautiful social media graphics, Jojy for typesetting the book and painstakingingly carrying out many rounds of changes and Shivani, Divya and Amrita for helping get the book to its readers: I couldn't be in better hands.

Bookstores and libraries have always been a refuge for me. It felt natural, therefore, to set my novel in a bookstore. I'm afraid that meant staging a murder there, but at least the rule of a murder mystery is that everything is all right in the end.

And to queer people who are vocal about their identities in a hostile world: thank you for showing the way.